KOSA

JOHN DURGIN

The characters and events in this book are fictitious. Any similarities to real persons, living or dead, is coincidental and not intended by the author.

Copyright © 2024 by John Durgin

Cover Art © 2024 by TruBorn Design

Interior Formatting by LM Kaplin

First published in 2024 by DarkLit Press

Second published in 2024 by John Durgin.

No part of this book may be reproduced, redistributed, or resold without the author's permission.

All rights reserved.

PRAISE FOR KOSA

"A delightfully dark, shockingly brutal novel. John Durgin is a writer worth keeping an eye on."
-**Philip Fracassi**, author of *Boys In The Valley*

"KOSA truly earns the term 'hair-raising.'"
-**Clay McLeod Chapman**, author of *What Kind Of Mother* and *Ghost Eaters*

"Creepy, magical, twisty, and twisted, KOSA put a spell on me. John Durgin is a writer to watch."
-**Jonathan Janz**, author of *Marla* and *Children Of The Dark*

"Vicious, gory, and expertly woven into a contemporary tapestry, KOSA is chock full of horrific surprises."
-**Laurel Hightower**, author of *Crossroads* and *Below*

"Shocking, sinister, equally elegant and brutal."
-**Felix Blackwell**, author of *The Church Beneath The Roots* and *Stolen Tongues*

JOHN DURGIN

"...the best kind of horror: empowerment in the face of great evil."
-Andrew Van Wey, author of *Head Like A Hole*

"Durgin's best work yet. Original, nightmarish, and utterly satisfying—a true tour de force of terror."
-Nick Roberts, author of *The Exorcist's House* and *Mean Spirited*

"Kosa is brilliantly written and gives an old classic a horrifying new twist."
-Candace Nola, Author of *Desperate Wishes* and *Bishop*

OTHER WORKS BY JOHN DURGIN

The Cursed Among Us

Inside The Devil's Nest

Sleeping in the Fire: A Collection of 9 Horrifying Tales

Blank Space

Kosa

Coming soon from John

Consumed By Evil
(*the sequel to The Cursed Among Us*)- **late 2024**

Suffocating Skies
(An alien horror novella in the *Dark Tides* series)- **late 2024**

To Sammy Scott,
An amazing writer, and an even better person.

Everybody's damaged by something.

—**Emma Donoghue,** *Room*

The cat got her, and will scratch your eyes out as well.

—**Jacob and Wilhelm Grimm,** *Rapunzel*

PART I
DESPERATE TIMES

CHAPTER 1

Alan Brock hid in the darkness, peering through the window of the old Victorian home at the elderly woman. She shuffled along in her black nightgown, her bony feet sliding along the floor, a coffee cup in hand while her cats weaved between her legs. Stealing from her wasn't something he was proud of, but he had no choice. He was desperate.

Over the last week, his life had gone to shit. His pregnant wife was currently resting in their two-bedroom apartment, oblivious to the fact that he was let go from his job only a few weeks before the due date of their baby. *Oblivious* to his newfound drug problem that had eaten away at not only their savings but the rent money and the very last of their grocery money. In other words, he was fucked. *They* were fucked. Poor Bridgett. She deserved so much more.

Alan made a point to snatch up the eviction notice before she saw it taped to their front door. It might as well have been a giant sign that said "FAILURE OF A HUSBAND" with flashing neon lights. If he didn't find a way to get money soon, they'd lose their apartment and end up living on the streets with a baby on the way. He couldn't let that happen. Which is why he now stood on the old lady's porch, in the middle of the night, staring through her window like some kind of monster about to murder a group of helpless teens.

The day his boss called him into the office to fire him, Alan knew he couldn't go straight home, or Bridgett would know something was up. So, he went for a drive to clear his head, attempting to come up with a plan to save their crumbling lives. He took the scenic route through the winding roads into the woods of Sunapee. On a normal day, the ride would have been a beautiful cruise into the mountains, the lake glistening below with the sun heating its surface. But for Alan, it was just a reminder of his failures. Driving by the massive lake houses with their floor-to-ceiling glass waterfront properties, their fancy pontoon boats floating at their personal docks, he couldn't help but feel that half the people here didn't even earn the money to buy such luxury, that they were handed their fortune by snooty rich parents.

He was driving on autopilot, lost in thoughts on how to break the news to Bridgett, when he realized he'd continued his ascent into the mountains and left the mansions behind. There wasn't even a place to turn around, forcing him to drive deeper until he came to a gravel driveway that led to a residence he couldn't see from the road. The driveway had heavily wooded terrain on each side, but somehow the trees appeared less vibrant, as if the life had been sapped from them. When a large Victorian house came into view, Alan planned to pull a quick U-turn and get out of there before anyone saw him. Then he noticed an old lady walking in the house all by herself, unaware of his car at the end of her driveway.

Alan hated himself for immediately thinking of robbing the poor woman. The worst thing he'd ever done was steal a piece of candy from the grocery store as a child, and his mom embarrassed him by forcing him to go back in the store and admit his wrongdoing. But these were desperate times. He felt as if accidentally discovering the house was meant to be. A sign.

He'd spent the last few days watching from a distance, telling Bridgett he was going to work like any other day. He was no expert in staking out a location, but he felt good enough to move forward with the job. For one, Alan had worked out there was nobody living at the house besides the lady. On a few occasions he'd seen a much younger, beautiful woman, but he assumed it was her daughter just checking in on her.

The house was immense, more resembling an old museum than a residence, with large arching windows that stared out at the mountains like enormous eyes.

As he stood on the porch, watching her from the darkness, he began to second guess his plan. What if the lady discovered him once he entered? Would he harm her to get away if forced to? He wasn't exactly the physical type, and he had no desire to change that for someone old enough to be his grandmother. Yet here he was, waiting for the right moment to break in, hoping to find anything of value to get them out of debt. He preferred cash, something easy enough to cover his tracks. If he didn't find money, he'd move onto valued goods that he could try to pawn off at some antique shops out of town.

The lady walked into another room, disappearing from Alan's line of sight. He doubted she was going to bed yet, as she'd left lights on in a couple of rooms downstairs. She appeared to have a standard routine. Feed her cats, read from an enormous book she kept sitting next to her rocking chair by the fireplace, drink some hot tea or coffee, then turn off all the lights and go to bed. At any moment now, she *should* be going upstairs.

Come on lady, let's get a move on, he thought.

Something seemed off, though. Too much time had passed without her coming back to tidy up the downstairs before going to bed. Maybe she'd left the lights on by accident, her old age possibly leading her to forget? He couldn't risk breaking in yet, he had to be sure. Alan moved a few feet, trying to see from a different angle and locate her in another room, but the rest of the first floor was pitch black. He placed his face against the glass and squinted, forcing his eyes to adjust to the darkness within the house.

Movement in the room to his right jolted him back, and he crouched down low out of sight. He didn't know if she'd seen him, but while he was busy looking around downstairs for her, she had apparently been in the room right next to his window the whole time. His heart pounded in his chest as he tried to regain his composure. He took deep breaths and waited. When nobody came, he slowly rose to look in—and came face to face with a black cat sitting on the inside of the windowsill. Again, he jumped back.

It's just a fucking cat, get your shit together.

Except the cat looked strange. It tilted its head to the side, more like a curious dog, watching him. The eyes carried human resemblance, staring back at him with intelligence more than feline, pupils far too large. Alan continued locking eyes with the animal, unaware of anything else around, *unaware* of the old lady who'd now entered the kitchen again with her back to him. Her movements snapped him out of his trance, and he pried his eyes from the strange cat to see what she was doing. She walked around, turning off the lights, then headed toward the stairs. Alan moved out of sight, clinging to the side of the house like he was a hundred feet high on a cliff-edge, afraid to fall to his death.

The faint thumping of her footsteps ascending the stairs informed him that the old woman was finally going to bed. Alan allowed himself to come free from the wall and stared back through the window. The cat was still there, its mouth was now open wide, sharp fangs flashing in the moonlight at him with predatory intent. A chill shot down his spine.

I fucking hate cats, he thought.

He quietly climbed down the porch and looked up at the second-floor windows, specifically focusing on where he knew her bedroom was located. Her silhouette appeared behind the curtain—she lifted her arms up high above her head in what looked like some type of yoga or meditation pose. She stretched her spine before going to bed, probably to ease the hunch in her back. Once she was done with her odd routine, the lights went out, sending the entire house into darkness.

As much as he wanted to get right inside and get it over with, Alan waited a little while longer to make sure the old bag had fallen asleep. He really had no intention of harming an elderly person on top of breaking and entering. After he thought enough time had passed, he approached the porch steps again. Alan turned, making one last scan of the driveway to make sure he was in fact alone—the feeling of being watched was far too real. But for someone who didn't do this regularly, he figured it was normal to be a bit on edge. The driveway was empty. The forest towering over each side of the driveway painted in black.

Maybe I shouldn't do this... Maybe I should just go home and admit to Bridgett how much of a failure I am...

Alan's self-doubt was always one of his biggest flaws, holding him back most of his life from chasing his dreams. Now wasn't the time to keep that trend going. Too much time and effort had been put into this plan, and if this didn't work out, *then* he would sit his wife down and admit everything—besides the fact that he'd broken into a senior citizen's house to take her valuables. He hated himself more every time he thought about what he was about to do, but what was new? He had the confidence of the weakest kid in gym class, dreading all the other bullies about to pepper him with dodgeballs.

His plan all along was to try to enter through a window around the side of the house instead of straight through next to the front door. As nice as her house was, Alan noticed that she didn't have any sort of alarm system in place—another reason he convinced himself to move forward with his plan. He climbed the steps and made his way around the large, wrap-around farmer's porch, approaching one of the side windows. The window leading into the dining room had the most open space to climb through, so he approached it, prepared to work his magic. As he looked around the interior now, he noticed the room was empty. Only a small table and chair sat in the middle of the room—no wall décor, pictures, or fancy Oriental rugs as one might expect in a house of this size and value.

Alan grabbed the window frame and pulled, hoping it would open with ease, that the old woman was so forgetful she'd left it unlocked for him to enter undisturbed. Unfortunately, it didn't budge. Of course, it couldn't be that easy. Nothing had *ever* been easy for him. People like him had to grind from the bottom and work their way to the top the hard way. Which is why he came prepared to break in. He pulled a thin blade from his backpack, careful not to cut himself when reaching into the sack to grab it. He'd thought to wrap it in cloth, avoiding the possibility of getting sliced up when he retrieved it. He zipped the bag up and threw it back over his shoulder.

Carefully, he unwrapped the blade and held it up to get a closer look. He wedged the blade between the glass and frame, sliding it along until he reached the lock mechanism. The window was weathered and old, so he hoped that would make the process a bit easier.

He pressed the blade up against the latch. Alan yanked it a few inches left to right, and to his surprise, the lock flipped unlocked easier than expected. The sudden lack of resistance caused the blade to slide much faster than he was prepared for, slicing into his other hand resting on the window frame.

"Shit!"

He clenched his mouth shut and looked at his hand. A two-inch gash appeared at the center of his palm. Before he could cover the wound, blood flowed down the inside of his hand in a steady stream, reaching the bottom of his palm and dripping down onto the window frame and porch. Everything was going to shit, and he hadn't even made it inside the damn house yet. Maybe this was a sign to just get the hell out of there.

No, you stupid pussy! Do what you set out to do!

Alan took the cloth previously protecting the blade, and wrapped it around his cut, tying a tight knot on the top of his hand to keep the gash covered. He wiped away the blood as best he could, trying to dispose of any evidence on the off chance the lady discovered him. Which, considering how the evening had started out, seemed far more likely an outcome than he wanted to admit.

With adrenaline coursing through him, he took a deep breath to calm himself and delicately pushed up on the window, doing everything he could to reduce the sound of it sliding up the warped frame. He leaned in and listened to see if he had been detected. Only silence and the lingering smell of old soup greeted him, so he climbed through the opening. Now, standing in the dark room, he was instantly struck by the sudden drop in temperature. The night air had been chilly, but it was somehow even colder in the house. He'd heard that rich people, specifically *old*, rich people, remained cheap and frugal with their spending. Maybe she refused to turn on her heat until the calendar flipped to November, just like his stubborn grandparents used to do. Just like he would have no choice to do if he didn't get enough money to pay the bills before the weather got colder. But that thought still didn't sit right with him. Why the hell was it *colder* in here than outside? It's not like she would turn the air conditioner on this time of year.

Alan shook his head and walked deeper into the room, not sure where to start. He assumed most families kept their extremely valuable possessions close to them, but he had no intention of entering the woman's bedroom and searching through her closet while she slept next to him. It was evident the dining room was a lost cause, so he moved on to the next room. The deeper into the house he got, the harder it was to see anything with the sparse light from the windows now left behind. Alan grabbed a small flashlight from his chest pocket and flicked it on. Tiny dust particles floated through the beam as he scanned left to right, looking for any sign of valuables.

Next up was the living room, at least what a boring old lady would consider a living room. No television set, no stereo system—only the rocking chair and small table next to it with the large book he'd watched her read before bed. Curiosity got the better of him, so he opened the book to check out its contents. The weight of it surprised him. It was a wonder the lady could even lift the damn thing. He aimed the flashlight at the cover, revealing a brown, leather hardcover that looked like it had spent the last hundred years buried in a grave and had just recently been uncovered. A strange design traveled across the cover, prompting him to slide his finger across the surface. Alan opened the book, and a musty smell blasted his nostrils, the paper wrinkled and ancient. He flipped through a few pages, realizing much of it was written in a foreign language he didn't recognize. But there were pictures sporadically scattered throughout, and he got the sinking feeling that he was looking at some sort of spell book.

"What the actual fuck..." he whispered.

He flipped to a page containing an image of a man transforming into some sort of creature. No, it looked more like a cat, but one that had suffered severe malnutrition. He leaned in to get a closer look, aiming the light at the image.

Something brushed against his leg.

"Fuck!" he yelled, involuntarily dropping the book back on the table with a loud smack.

Alan looked down and spotted a cat staring at him, the same cat from the window. Its human-like eyes judged him in a way he wouldn't have thought possible from an animal. He leaned down to pet it, hoping to prevent it from making any noise. As if that mattered. Between yelling and dropping the book, it was a miracle the lady wasn't already working her way back downstairs to check on the commotion. The feline bastard hissed at him, and before he could pull back his hand, the cat swiped, slicing a new gash across his good hand.

"Little shit..." he whispered, attempting to kick the animal, but it was too fast for him. Before he connected, the cat was gone, back to hiding somewhere in the darkness.

Alan glanced at his hands, both cut up in the span of the last ten minutes. He couldn't help but laugh at his feeble attempt to pull this off. Only *he* could get attacked by a window and a cat in a house that had no security system and an old lady sleeping upstairs. The woman must have had trouble hearing—there was no way in hell he would have gone undetected otherwise. He turned away from the book, ready to move onto the next room, when he saw those same eyes staring back at him from beneath the rocking chair.

GRRRRR...

The cat sounded more like a rabid dog growling than a feline. Its enlarged pupils bored into Alan as he hesitantly backed away from it. The cat was starting to creep him out. Cats didn't look at people like that... or *sound* like that. Then he thought back to the book, and the page he glanced at illustrating a man transforming into an animal resembling a cat. *No fucking way...* He shook off the thought, embarrassed that his mind even went there. This wasn't some stupid-ass fairy tale. It was a lonely old lady who had a ton of cats and nobody else in her life.

"Stop spooking yourself..." he whispered.

With one last look at the cat, Alan continued down a hallway that wrapped around the stairs to the second floor. He had no intention of going up those stairs, unsure of where their hidden creeks and groans lay in wait. Around the corner, the hallway expanded into a much bigger room—one that he hadn't seen from the woods with his binoculars. This room was also very bare, with only minimal furniture.

Does this lady even own anything worth stealing?

He searched, room after room, coming up empty-handed, all while struggling to shake the feeling of being watched. There had to be something, *anything*, worth taking. He needed to leave the house with something that could get his family back on their feet, something that would help turn his life around. Sure, he'd made a few mistakes along the way. But what mattered most right now was that he was trying to fix those mistakes, even if it meant doing something horribly wrong to accomplish that.

He opened every door, checked every closet. It was becoming abundantly clear he would need to go upstairs. What if he needed to escape up there? He couldn't exactly jump out of a window on the second story of a house this big. The fall would either kill or cripple him, neither of which he was willing to risk.

An unsettling creek drew his attention. Alan spun around, aiming the flashlight in the direction of the sound, expecting to see the cat. Instead, a hidden door blending in with the wall presented itself. It was easy to miss walking by, especially in the dark. But how the hell did it just crack open? Was it one of the stupid fucking cats? If it was, he might not be able to stop himself from killing an innocent animal if the thing decided to spook him again. He'd always hated them, and this particular one was going out of its way to play some twisted game with his mind. He approached the secret door and pushed in, the hinges releasing another loud shriek of rusted metal. Alan cringed, then held his breath in silence for a few seconds, as if that would somehow influence the old lady to stay in bed.

The beam of light exposed a room on the same level—no stairs heading down into the basement, much to Alan's delight. He was spooked enough, no need to enter some dark dungeon below the house. This was just some hidden room of the house the lady must have wanted protected for some reason, reasons he hoped would help get him a large sum of money. He smiled as he walked into the darkness, the frigid air circulating through the house starting to chill his nose and ears. He completed a sweeping motion with the light, taking in what the room had to offer. The walls were cluttered with shelf after shelf of books. A large, round table sat in the middle of the floor, an unlit candle and pile of crinkled papers lying on top of it. Now that he thought of it, the room smelled of recently vaporized candle wax. She must have come in here before bed.

The light revealed a stack of boxes in the corner, looking more like faux treasure chests than storage containers. They reminded Alan of the boxes he used to store his toys in growing up, along with his comics and sports cards, hell, even his nudie magazines. In other words, his most valuable possessions. He briskly walked to the boxes and opened the top box, revealing more leatherbound books.

Jesus, lady. How much can you read with your remaining years?

Annoyed, he pulled the box off the top of the stack, almost dropping it when the weight caught him off-guard. He set it on the floor and instead of opening the next box, he moved down the wall, spotting a desk in the corner littered with more papers and books.

The drawers had gold handles, and for a second, Alan considered taking the handles off and shoving them in his pockets. Then he was hit with the embarrassment of putting himself in this much danger only to be arrested for stealing drawer handles—not exactly the most spectacular of crimes. Instead, he opened one of the drawers. A small box sat inside. He picked it up and turned it, discovering a large green orb fused into its center. A faint glow illuminated his hand, reminding him of his failures up to this point as he got a glimpse of the cuts on his palm. This thing had to be worth money; he'd never seen anything like it in his life. He took off his backpack and shoved it inside. Now that he had something in his possession, his already skittish nerves cranked into overdrive. He was officially a thief. A criminal. His parents would be rolling over in their grave if they saw what he was doing.

Alan opened the other drawers, looking for money. Cash. Coins. Something he *knew* the value of. He was about to open the final drawer when he heard the familiar growl of the cat behind him. He turned around, prepared to kick it out of the room and be done with it—and noticed not just one cat, but at least five sets of eyes staring back at him from the darkness. *Seriously? I thought cats didn't move in packs? What the fuck?* He stared at them, unsure of his next move. The eyes began to spread out, as if they were working to form a circle around him. A strange mix of hissing and growling smothered him in the tight space.

He flashed the light in their direction...

...and let out a scream, dropping the light.

They weren't normal looking cats. Much of their fur was matted with some type of grime, and he wouldn't put money on it—he didn't have any even if he'd wanted to—but he could've sworn they had blood caked around their mouths. The cats began pacing around him—predators preparing to attack their prey. Alan wasn't worried about making too much noise anymore; the old lady was the least of his worries with these... *things* about to attack. He grabbed a book off the table and heaved it in the direction of the one blocking the door. The cat was too quick, gliding to the side with ease as the book smacked off the floor and slid into the hall. As they closed in, Alan ran.

One of them jumped at him, clinging to his shirt with Velcro-like determination, its claws sinking into his arm and digging their way down. He screamed, then struck the animal with his free hand, sending it toppling to the floor. The others apparently didn't appreciate this intruder harming one of their own, as they all charged toward him. Alan sprinted into the hall, slamming against the wall on the way out. He turned, trying to force the secret door shut and trap the cats inside. He pulled the door as one of the cats tried to run through the opening, the door snapping its neck and dropping it to the floor. Alan froze, staring at the dead animal, its eyes impossibly changing right in front of him. The once human-looking irises turned milky white before transforming back to a normal cat eye. *What the fuck?*

His hesitation allowed one of the others to sink its teeth into his calf, the sound of first denim tearing, followed by his muscle being punctured, sent waves of nausea through his stomach. The cat wasn't letting go, its teeth latched on trying to tear apart his muscle. Alan swung his leg toward the wall, smashing the cat's body against the sheetrock. Instead of releasing its grip, the thing bit down *harder*, forcing Alan to tears. He did it again, and this time the sound of bone crunching inside the animal was met with its teeth retracting from his muscle, but still not enough to dislodge it. A third kick into the wall dropped the cat to the floor, though it wasn't dead. The animal looked into his eyes and started to drag itself toward him. Its claws scraped along the wooden floor, its body leaving behind a trail of blood as it inched closer. He had no desire to wait around and see if the little bastard survived.

A floorboard creaked above him, followed by the lady's footsteps traveling across the upper floor. *Shit, shit, shit!*

He sprinted down the hall, pain shooting through his wounded leg with every step. The remaining cats were on his trail, stalking toward him like a horde of angry wasps whose nest had just been disturbed. Alan rounded the corner and was back in the dining room, closing in on the window he came into the house through. This entire plan was a complete failure. So many thoughts were swirling through his head that it felt like his brain might explode from an aneurism. *What will I tell Bridgett? Will she leave me? Am I going to get arrested for killing this lady's pets?* He reached the window, preparing to climb out, when he was hit with a realization. The window was now closed. He hadn't shut it after coming into the house.

He reached for the lock, preparing to unlatch it.

"What are you doing in my house, you *pest?*" the woman said in a thick accent.

Alan whipped around, coming face to face with the old lady. She stood by the stairs, hidden in shadow, only the glare of her green necklace showing. He hadn't heard her come down; it was as if she glided down without making a sound. She didn't look like a normal old lady. Eyes that had almost no white to them, just giant, black pupils like two ocular eclipses. Her top lip lifted in a snarl, exposing crooked teeth browned with age. White hair trailed down her head in thin strands, desperate to cling to her scalp. When he'd observed the house from the woods, he hadn't seen what she really looked like, and right now his eyes begged him to look away from the ugliness in front of him. He stared at the floor to avoid showing his disgust with her appearance.

"I... I'm so sorry, Ma'am..." It was all he could think of saying as he backed closer to the window, trying to remember exactly where the lock was so he could quickly unlatch it and make a run for it.

"Don't apologize to me, boy. You've done me a favor tonight, you see?" She actually grinned.

Alan was confused. This lady was off her fucking rocker, and he needed to get the hell out of the house. He felt around blindly with his hand and landed on the lock, hit with a momentary relief.

"My familiars haven't eaten in some time, and they're hungry... they don't much like when someone tries to steal from their master..."

As if on cue, the three remaining cats appeared behind her, baring their razor-like teeth at him, staring at him with those god damn eyes.

"Lady, it's just a misunderstanding, okay? I'll just be on my way, and you can go back to bed..."

She stared at him without saying anything. Only the growling animals broke the complete silence. He gripped the lock and snapped it open. The woman's eyes narrowed to angry slits.

"You aren't going anywhere with my orb... As a matter of fact, you aren't *going* anywhere at all..." she said, spitting the words out in disgust.

She nodded toward Alan, and the cats did as their master instructed, charging at him as he fumbled with the window. They were halfway across the room when he finally got the window open, taking one last glance back at the woman and her cats. She started screaming in a different language—one he'd never heard before. He dove out the window and landed on the porch at an awkward angle, bending his wrist back as he tried to break his fall.

He jumped to his feet, his calf throbbing, and his hands both pushing blood from their open wounds. From inside the house, the lady continued to yell—no it was more like a chant—she was *chanting* something toward him. Alan stared at her as she hid in shadow, her black eyes darker than the night itself. The hair on the back of his neck stood as her voice dropped to a deeper octave than it had any right reaching.

The cats were now close to the window. Alan took off in a sprint down the porch and into the woods. When he risked a look back, the lady was standing at the open window watching him. She slid her finger across the windowpane he'd just climbed through and then brought it to her nose and sniffed. Her mouth slowly opened, and Alan couldn't believe what he was watching. A long, serpent-like tongue slithered out of her mouth, licking the finger. He realized that she was *licking* his blood. She started cackling and then pointed at him—and that was all he needed to turn and run. As he sprinted through the woods back toward the main road, her laughter echoed through the forest.

CHAPTER 2

B ridgett rolled over in bed and looked at her alarm clock. It was 2 A.M. when she heard Alan in the living room taking his shoes off, breathing heavily like he'd just done sprints up and down the stairs before coming in. She knew she should probably be worried, her husband coming in at strange hours of the night while she tossed and turned, attempting to get what little sleep she could in her uncomfortable state.

The idea of bringing a child into the world, raising him or her—they did *not* want to know the gender until birth—sounded incredible. What she wasn't prepared for were all the aches and pains that came with it, *especially* the last few weeks of her pregnancy. Was he out drinking with friends to blow off steam before the baby? Maybe having an affair with someone from work? Any time thoughts like that came to her, she forced them from her mind. He wasn't the type of man to do that stuff, but the seriousness of raising a kid made life all too real. There were no more nights of partying, getting into trouble with one another before they stumbled into bed and made passionate love until the sun came up. No, now it was sitting on the floor while Alan massaged her back, grabbing her whatever abnormal mix of food her body craved. She knew it probably wasn't enjoyable for him, but she hoped he was excited and ready for the next stage of their life together.

She wasn't the type who liked confrontation, so as much as she wanted to question Alan, Bridgett told herself to let it go. If he wanted to tell her where he was, he would do it on his own terms. He had enough on his plate with the baby coming, she didn't need to add to the stress if he was just out blowing off steam. One of her closest friends had told her how when she was pregnant, her husband suffered a massive panic attack for the first time in his life and got rushed to the hospital thinking he was dying. Having a child was supposed to be a beautiful thing, yet in the real world it brought just as much anxiety as it did joy for a lot of people.

The sink turned on in their bathroom, and she heard Alan cleaning himself up before coming into the room. A flash of him cleaning off some other girl's scent before climbing in bed and lying next to her now heavyset figure, turned off by what she'd become, forced its way into her mind.

Stop it! He loves you; he'd never do such a thing!

When the sink turned off, Bridgett rolled over and faced away from the door, not wanting Alan to see she was awake and worrying while he was gone. The door opened slowly, and she heard him walk in and sigh. He sat something heavy on his nightstand and slid off his pants before carefully pulling their comforter down and sliding into bed. He didn't make any effort to get close to her, she assumed it was because he didn't want to wake her. But could he be afraid to admit something he did? She needed to stop with the insecurity bullshit, it wasn't like her.

Normally, she walked around with a sense of confidence that all her friends were jealous of. Alan and Bridgett didn't have much money, lived in a tiny apartment, and shared a vehicle. Yet, nobody would have known that seeing the way she presented herself. The pregnancy had taken that from her. In the early months, she was glowing. You couldn't slap the smile off her face. The last few weeks, however, were messing with her entire psyche.

She debated rolling over and talking with him, wanting to make sure everything was okay. Instead, she continued facing the wall, hoping sleep would find her. After almost an hour passed, she decided she needed to let him know what was on her mind. She tossed the pregnancy pillow to the floor and pushed herself up in bed, turning to face him.

He was sound asleep, mouth agape and breathing heavily.

Bridgett didn't smell booze, but with how deep he was into his dreams, it was obvious he was sloshed. Anger swept over her. Before she shook him awake, something caught her eye on his dresser. A small box with some type of green glowing ball in its center illuminated the surface of his nightstand. It was beautiful. All of a sudden, she felt like the biggest asshole in the world. *Was he out shopping for the baby and picked up this night light as a surprise?*

She massaged her swollen ankles for a moment, then swung her feet over the side and pushed herself up with a grunt. The doctor told her the baby was normal size. She couldn't even imagine carrying a large baby, or twins for that matter. It felt like a backpack full of cinderblocks hanging from her stomach.

Bridgett walked quietly around to Alan's side of the bed and picked up the box. Its weight surprised her; the sphere inside it looked hollow, with green light swimming around inside, but it was actually solid glass. The illusion was messing with her eyes. She knew Alan had been working extra hard lately, working overtime to make sure he could provide for them. It often led to him being overtired, cranky, and sometimes even a bit strange. But knowing he was doing it for them made her smile again. She loved him so much.

Her brow furrowed as she looked down at him and noticed his hands were bandaged. Instead of waking him, she walked back to her side with the box in hand and got back in bed. Many thoughts streamed through her head about what could have happened to Alan, but she soon found herself staring into the sphere's glow, resting it on her belly and getting lost in its green haze. She rubbed the glass with her finger and the light brightened at the point of contact.

"You're gonna love this thing, kiddo..." she whispered, rubbing her belly with her free hand. The baby kicked, startling Bridgett. She chuckled at herself for letting something growing inside her own body scare her. The baby kicked again, and this time Bridgett noticed the green light gravitating to the bottom of the orb, like it was moving toward the baby. A sharp pain rocketed through her stomach out of nowhere, forcing a scream out of her.

Alan jumped up, instantly waking from his deep sleep. They had practiced many times while prepping for the possibility of a late-night trip to the hospital should she go into labor.

"What is it? Are you okay?" he asked.

"The baby was kicking... and then a sharp pain..." she trailed off.

He looked to her stomach, and she witnessed his shock of being awoken mid-sleep turn to straight up fear.

"Why are you holding that?"

"It was glowing on your nightstand, I thought it was a night light you got for the baby. Is it—"

The sharp pain rippled through her insides—this time somehow more painful than the last. Bridgett grunted, taking short, heavy breaths to try and calm the baby. With all the videos, research, books read, none of them explained labor feeling quite like this. But she was due in only a few weeks, could she be having the baby early?

"I think I'm having contractions, Alan. I need you to time these. We might need to go to the hospital tonight..."

He was out of bed before she finished her sentence, running out into the living room and grabbing his watch. A few seconds later, he burst back through the door and sat on the bed.

"Okay, let me know when the next pain comes."

"I don't think I'll need to tell you..."

She thought she was prepared for the feeling to return after experiencing it twice now, but the third time felt like an animal trying to claw its way out of her stomach.

"Ahhh! It fucking hurts so bad!"

"Okay, we need to go to the hospital right now," Alan said.

Bridgett couldn't say anything, but she knew he was right. She was either in labor, or something was extremely wrong. She attempted to sit up, but the pain was unbearable. She placed the nightlight on her nightstand and got up. When she looked at the sphere, she noticed the circle was now clear, the light had completely vanished. The thought of some poison gas somehow getting to her child set her in a panic. Bridgett moved much faster than her body had any right to, tossing on her travel slippers they'd bought specifically for this moment. Alan grabbed the hospital bag they kept packed under the bed and helped her out into the living room.

"Is this really happening? Are we having our baby?" A smile chipped through the fear as he said it.

"I don't know, Alan. I think something might be wrong."

She didn't want to say anything about the light, afraid it would sound completely ridiculous. His smile disappeared with her statement, replaced once again by panic. No matter how many times they'd prepared for this—talked through step by step what they would do—it was completely different in the moment. They had their bag, the apartment was tidy in case anyone had to drop by to grab something for them, everything was as good as it could be. She looked at him and forced a smile.

"Okay, let's go have our baby."

CHAPTER 3

Alan stared out the window into the hospital's parking lot, waiting for the doctor to come back with news. They'd spent the last few hours running tests on Bridgett, determining that she *was* in the early stages of labor but not far enough along to keep her overnight. When Bridgett explained to the nurses the pain she was feeling, Alan noticed concerned looks exchanged between the medical staff. They said there was nothing to worry about, that the baby was healthy, but he wasn't buying it.

A rollercoaster of emotions surged through him. Embarrassment for losing his job. Fear for what he went through in the old woman's house. Excitement for the possibility of his firstborn child being welcomed into the world at any time. He also felt *pain*. His hands were killing him, and his calf felt like someone had just taken a cheese grater to it. The fact that he'd slept for maybe an hour before being awoken didn't help the situation. He needed to be strong though. For Bridgett. For the baby.

He glanced over at Bridgett, watching her zone in on the television, likely trying to take her mind off awaiting the doctor to come back. He could only imagine the thoughts running through her mind, wondering what he'd gotten himself into. Anything she thought of likely wouldn't be half as bad as what he'd really done tonight. He had to tell her; he just wasn't sure how to do it. A soft knock at the door was followed by their OB doctor poking his head in. Before the doctor could get a word out, Alan was up on his feet.

"Dr. McCloud, please give us some good news..."

The doctor forced a smile. Whether it was because he was about to deliver bad news instead of a baby, Alan couldn't tell. McCloud was an older man, one who typically made Alan and Bridgett feel they were in good hands. He'd been doing his job for many years, but not so many they were worried about him slipping up. He came highly recommended. But right now, Alan couldn't read him, and the silence carried on longer than it needed to.

"Well... I'll start by saying the baby's fine. Healthy as can be. And so is Bridgett. You guys can take a deep breath and relax."

Bridgett slouched with relief, but Alan couldn't allow himself the same luxury. Dr. McCloud's tone sounded like a good news-bad news situation. Alan was just waiting for the "but" to come.

"But..."

There it is.

"There were some things we saw in the blood work that were... *abnormal—*"

"What do you mean, *abnormal?* Is she going to be okay?" Alan asked.

"As I said, she should be fine. There are just things we want to keep an eye on is all. We think it's best if you guys stay here until the baby's delivered. Normally we'd send you home until the cervix is more dilated, but I want to err on the side of caution. With these lab results, I feel at this point it would be safest to deliver your baby here. I'm going to have a chat with the nurses, and one of them will be in shortly with our plan."

Bridgett squeezed Alan's hand, the concern rushing back after a short stint on the sidelines. Alan didn't know what any of this meant. McCloud was being so vague, yet Alan didn't know the right questions to ask—not that the doctor would necessarily have answered them if he did. Instead, he reminded himself they were in good hands, that if anything *was* to go wrong, this is where they wanted to be. He should be thankful they were able to stay instead of going home and being left to wonder what the hell was happening with the baby. Bridgett was normally outspoken, but she remained silent, taking it all in.

"I'm sorry I don't have more answers for you two right now, but I promise we're going to keep checking to make sure everything's fine. In the meantime, you should both get some rest, it could be a long night." Dr. McCloud offered another smile, then walked out of the room.

Bridgett rubbed her stomach, soothing the baby as it kicked around, like it was finishing a round of Tae Bo against her uterus. She wanted to ask the doctors so many questions, but she was too scared. They'd told her things were okay so many times, she couldn't stop thinking that was far from the truth. The sharp pain she'd felt earlier, the blood tests, all of it overshadowed her enjoyment of giving birth with an eerie sense of dread.

Bridgett continued having pains, but they were mild tightenings, nothing much worse than her period cramps. She ticked the minutes away, trying not to watch the clock as her anxiety about this whole process started to set in. She was about to birth a human, and she suddenly wasn't sure she was ready. All of the prenatal classes they took had helped prepare her some, but they didn't cover all the what-ifs.

She looked over to Alan and was happy to see he'd finally fallen asleep in the recliner chair. He didn't look comfortable at all, but he had to be so tired. She wanted to ask him more about the object he'd brought home. This all started when she touched that thing, and the baby went wild when she held it close to her stomach. It was hard to explain, but she knew the baby wasn't in pain, but instead going crazy because it wanted whatever was inside the glass sphere. While Alan slept, there was no chance she could do the same. She'd already flipped through every single channel the hospital had on its shitty cable package multiple times. After various infomercials and religious shows appeared over and over, she finally left it on one of the music channels and hoped the soft melody would help put her to sleep. Although the contractions were starting to get more uncomfortable, she felt her eyes start to weigh down. As yet another contraction eased, her eyes started to close but caught something darting by outside the darkened window.

Bridgett looked over to the windows, squinting to see through the reflection of the room's interior lights. She remained focused on the window—she had nothing better to do. With their room on the first floor, it could have been anything passing by. A person taking a shortcut to the main entrance, an animal trying to find its way back to the forest. Whatever it was, it apparently had moved on, giving her nothing to look at but a parking lot full of vehicles. She started to turn back toward the door of their room when movement again shot past the window. Was that a damn cat? Are strays something common around hospitals? It made sense, all the unfinished food that sick patients couldn't stomach getting tossed in the dumpsters out back. She remained focused on the window, waiting to see if the animal returned. The room was so quiet that she could hear the clock ticking above her head. The beeping of machines out in the hallway faintly present.

THUMP!

The cat jumped up, smacking off the glass and landed on the ledge outside the window. Bridgett jerked back at the jump scare, sending a shot of pain through her abdomen. She yelped in surprise, waking Alan, who jolted out of his chair to run to her side. His body blocked the window, and Bridgett attempted to look past him when the pain returned, pulsing.

"Are you okay? Should I get the doctor?" Alan asked, doing a poor job of hiding his panic.

"Yes, go get him, *please*! Something's happening..."

Alan ran out of the room, leaving Bridgett alone. She took one last look at the window, but the cat was gone. All the commotion apparently scared off the stray. She couldn't help being spooked by the strange animal, but her baby wasn't going to give her time to worry about that. Again, the intense pain ravaged her insides. She squeezed hold of the sheets to try and ease the discomfort. Forced, heavy breaths escaped her clenched jaws. *Please be okay... Please be okay...*

A group of nurses walked through the door, Alan trailing right behind. Even with the pain she was dealing with, she couldn't help but feel bad for him. His eyes were wide in fear. Dr. McCloud rattled off instructions to the nurses as he checked the monitors hooked up to her. He might as well have been speaking a different language, reading off numbers and data that made no sense to her. The doctor gave her a quick glance and his mouth curved upward in a smile. His eyes, however, told a different story. He was worried.

"Please don't let anything happen to my baby!" Bridgett yelled.

"We won't, you have my word. Things are still okay. We need to check your cervix so we can assess how far your labor has progressed. Typically, it wouldn't progress this quickly, but it's not impossible."

Dr. McCloud went through the uncomfortable process of checking Bridgett's cervix. It was almost impossible to relax.

"Well, Bridgett, you're ten centimeters dilated! I'm going to have the nurses get set up so you can start pushing and we'll meet this sweet baby," Dr. McCloud announced to everybody.

She wasn't sure why that concerned him, but she heard concern in his voice. If everything was okay, why did they all seem agitated, like they were about to deliver the spawn of Satan? The pain was unbearable. All Bridgett could envision was the baby trying to claw its way out of her, thrashing around as it got closer to its escape.

Alan stood behind the doctors, his heart jumping further into his throat with every beep a machine made, every concerned look the doctors gave one another. All he could do was stand around like an imbecile and pray everything turned out okay. What had he done to deserve any goodwill though? Rob a crazy old lady? Blast through their savings by popping Oxy on his breaks every day until that wasn't enough, and he needed it regularly? Hell, with everything going on right now, with all the pain he'd been feeling due to the overtime, getting fired, his run-in with the old lady, he wouldn't mind a fix. That made him feel even worse about himself. His child, and his wife for that matter, were possibly fighting for their lives, yet all he could think about was getting high.

"What's happening? Tell me what's happening to my wife!"

The staff ignored him, going about their business and focusing on getting the child out safely. Bridgett hadn't stopped screaming since he came back in the room with them, roaring so loud he thought she might burn the room down with her rage. They were telling her to take deep breaths, to try and calm down. Dr. McCloud was seated at the end of the broken-down bed, ready to deliver their baby when Bridgett finally pushed it out. What followed was a flash of snapshots, all blurred around the edges like an unfocused set of photos, while Alan tried to stop himself from fainting.

Blood dripping to the floor. Was that normal? Was Bridgett bleeding out?

Nurses rushed around the table, handing each other medical tools he didn't know the name of. Silence. There should have been so much noise for all of their activity, but it was eerily quiet. And then, as if the blood wasn't bad enough, a bright green fluid pumped out of Bridgett, splashing on the floor and covering Dr. McCloud's shoes. Was that amniotic fluid? It didn't look right. Monitors beeped. Bridgett continued to scream. Alan struggled to stay upright, his legs beginning to wobble. Before he could catch himself, he was falling, and then everything went black.

When Alan opened his eyes, a calmness had overtaken the room. Instead of Bridgett screaming and yelling, or the awful silence of that final push, he heard laughter. He sat up, noticing that he'd either fallen onto the recliner, or someone had moved him to it. Based on the sharp pain throbbing in his face, it was safe to assume he'd hit the hard floor and not the cushioned chair upon impact. He blinked away the pain and looked over to Bridgett. Nurses still surrounded her, but there were less of them, and they were talking calmly with her. Panic clutched at his throat when he realized there was no baby in the room. Alan jumped to his feet, again feeling dizzy, when one of the nurses turned and realized he was awake.

"Woah, woah. Take it easy, Mr. Brock. You had quite the fall," one nurse said.

"Where's the baby? Is it okay?"

Bridgett made eye contact with him and smiled. *That was a good sign, right?*

"The baby's fine. They had to take her down to run some tests, but she is perfectly healthy, Mr. Brock."

"*She?* We have a daughter?"

"Yes... Congratulations!" the nurse said, putting her hand on his shoulder.

Alan had no words. Tears flooded his eyes, pouring down his face. After everything he'd gone through over the last few days, he finally had a reason to be happy. He ran to Bridgett's side, grabbing hold of her and kissing the top of her head.

"We did it, Bridge, we have a baby girl..."

For a moment, they hugged in silence as the remaining nurses busied themselves. After the warm embrace, the realization hit him that he hadn't seen his baby girl yet. Alan stood and looked to their doctor.

"Can I see her please?"

Dr. McCloud nodded. "Of course. Let's give Bridgett some time to rest, she's been through a lot these last few hours."

Alan wanted them to all be together for the first time, but it would have to wait. He looked at Bridgett who beamed with happiness.

"She's beautiful, Alan. So much red hair, no wonder I had crazy heartburn," she joked.

"I'll be right back, honey. A name! We need a name!" His mind was all over the place, the lack of sleep, the added excitement, the overwhelming sense of love—it was all ricocheting inside his head like a game of Pong.

"Let's wait until we're all together later, okay?" Bridgett asked.

Alan nodded, then leaned back down and kissed her on the cheek one last time before following Dr. McCloud out of the room. They walked down the hall, weaving in and out of nurses going to check on other patients. The sight of the room up ahead with its sliding glass doors shut, machines and incubators scattered throughout the room, made Alan feel uneasy. This didn't seem like a place where a healthy baby would be placed, away from her family and hooked up to a bunch of machines. The nurses insisted she was healthy though, he had to remind himself that and not let his thoughts go to the dark corners of his mind. On the way through the doors, Alan bumped shoulders with a woman exiting the NICU.

"I'm sorry—" he started, and then looked at her.

She was gorgeous. He wasn't checking her out in the sense that he wanted to pursue anything, but he couldn't stop staring at her. She gave a smile back without responding and continued down the hall. Alan watched her walk away and round a corner out of sight. It wasn't just her beauty that pried his attention off meeting his baby. She looked *familiar*.

"Mr. Brock? Are you coming?"

Alan snapped back to Dr. McCloud.

"Yes ... sorry. Let's go see my daughter."

The room was dark, he assumed to help the babies try and sleep in the moments between being hooked up to breathing tubes, getting blood drawn, or having a continuous wave of medical staff coming in to check on them. Alan had his eyes locked on one specific bed in the nursery, instinct telling him it was his child as they walked toward the end of the room.

"And here she is, your beautiful baby girl... I'll give you a moment with her. I'll send Dr. Grey, the NICU neonatologist, over in a few minutes to give you an update. Congratulations again, Mr. Brock."

"Thank you so much," Alan said, as McCloud walked to the desk and began chatting with the nurse on call.

Alan stared down at his daughter, tears once again filling his eyes. She was perfect. He'd never seen so much hair on a baby, not that he was an expert on the matter. He knew some babies were born with more hair and lost it until they got a little older. But she had thick, red locks hiding part of her face. She slept peacefully, wrapped in her swaddle, and sucking on a pacifier. All he wanted to do was pick her up and hug her.

"Hi, little lady. You put your mom through quite a night..."

She let out the softest moan in her sleep, and Alan's heart melted into a warm ball of love. He couldn't believe after months of planning she was finally here. His eyes remained glued on her when an object in his peripheral vision caught his attention. Something was covered by the blanket she lay on top of, obviously out of place. Alan carefully reached under her body, pulling out what appeared to be a wooden symbol. He had no idea what the symbol meant, but just its presence disturbed him. This wasn't something a doctor would leave with a baby. It almost looked like some makeshift pentagram, but the design was slightly different. He glanced back at McCloud, still talking with the nurse. Alan stormed over to them.

"What the hell is this?" he asked, holding up the object for them to see.

The nurse, Grey, and McCloud exchanged concerned glances. It was obvious none of them knew what he was holding. The nurse squinted and looked closer at the wooden design.

"It looks like some sort of dreamcatcher, or decoration. Where'd you get that?"

"It was in with my fucking baby, that's where I got it! One of your nurses must have put it in with her; don't you guys have access to see who comes and goes?"

"Please, Mr. Brock. Stay calm. We don't want to wake the babies. I can check the log to see who's been in here if you will just give me a moment—"

"Check it!"

Alan's mind flashed back to the woman bumping shoulders with him. Everything clicked at once. The reason she looked familiar. It was the woman who he'd seen visiting the old lady he robbed. Why the hell would she be here? How would she even know who he is? And why would she put this thing with his daughter? The nurse looked through the log, but Alan knew what her answer would be before she spoke.

"I don't see any other names here, sir. Just nurses and doctors—"

"Who was that woman that we just walked by when we came in? She wasn't a doctor!" Alan interrupted.

"What woman? Nobody else has been in here since your daughter arrived..." The nurse said, uncertainly.

Alan looked to McCloud, who apparently was more confused than he was. "Doc, you saw that woman when we came in, right? She fucking bumped right into me!"

"Please, Mr. Brock. Let's keep our composure. I don't recall seeing any woman, but then again, I was glancing at my paperwork as we walked in. And Dr. Grey says your daughter's okay. Whatever this thing is... it's meaningless." He took hold of the wooden circle.

"I'm telling you something was wrong with that lady. I've seen her before..."

Alan snatched the symbol back out of the doctor's hand and rushed out of the room. As he marched down the corridor to the hallway where their room was located, he studied the circle. *Dreamcatcher...* The nurse said it looked like a dreamcatcher. In a way it did, but it sent gooseflesh spreading across his arms just holding the thing. He flipped it in his hand once more, and almost choked on his breath. The symbol... It was the same one he'd spotted on the old lady's necklace. He knew, at that moment, the old lady had something to do with this.

CHAPTER 4

Bridgett knew something was on Alan's mind. He'd been acting strange ever since he came home late carrying that weird ornament, and now that the excitement of their baby arriving had calmed a bit—as much as it *could* calm after bringing a living thing into the world—he was acting skittish again. Maybe even more so than he had been earlier. She wanted to talk with him, but the baby now lay nuzzled up on her bare chest, soaking in the skin-to-skin contact while releasing cute, infant snores. Alan sat in his recliner chair, looking out of the window into darkness. He looked hypervigilant, searching the parking lot for a threat.

They still hadn't named the baby. Bridgett planned on doing it when they all finally got together with no doctors around, but that moment hadn't arrived until the baby was sound asleep, and now she didn't want to start a long conversation for fear of waking her up. In the months leading up to the birth, they'd talked at length about names, specifically boy names. If it was a boy, they planned to name him after both grandfathers. For some reason, when it came to girl names, they couldn't agree on one that fit. A few were mentioned here and there, but neither of them fell in love with any in particular. For now, Bridgett was content just having a daughter. The name could wait until the time was right.

A strong gust of wind blew outside, causing the bushes alongside the window to rattle. Alan jumped back, startled. Had it not been for his strange behavior throughout the night, Bridgett would have found the moment hilarious. But something was scaring him, and she needed to know what it was. His quick movement forced the chair back slightly, scraping it along the tile floor. The sound woke the baby, who began crying.

"Ah, shit. I'm sorry Bridge..." Alan got to his feet and picked up the baby, shushing her quietly.

"Alan, what's going on? You've seemed on edge ever since you got home tonight."

He looked at her, and his eyes told a story of their own. Yet he forced a smile.

"I'm sorry. I just didn't get enough sleep. I'm going crazy seeing things over here." He bounced their daughter gently up and down, bringing the baby's cries to a low moan. She was quickly falling back asleep.

"You better get used to no sleep, honey. This is just the start," she said, feeling it was best to keep it light-hearted for now.

He smiled, drawing close to the hospital bed.

"My little angel is going to be a great sleeper, isn't that right? You're going to let Mommy and Daddy sleep *all* night."

The baby cooed, bringing pure joy to the new parents.

"So... how 'bout that name?" Bridgett asked.

"I know I seemed iffy about it when you mentioned it before, but I think we should go with Elizabeth. It was your top choice, and it's really growing on me. Ellie Brock. Has a nice ring to it, right?"

"Yes, it's perfect. Elizabeth Grace Brock. Look at your beautiful hair..."

"I've never seen anything like it. You think she'll lose it like babies tend to?" Alan asked.

"No... These locks aren't going anywhere. She's got her mama's hair," Bridgett said with an ear-to-ear grin.

"Sure as hell doesn't have mine!" Alan said, rubbing his receding hairline.

For the first time since arriving at the hospital earlier, they got their first taste of being a family of three. But Bridgett's smile hardened, the memory of her husband's abnormal behavior coming back.

"Al, what's going on with you today? I know we've got a lot of pressure on us, but it's more than that, isn't it?"

He wouldn't even make eye contact with her. His lips trembled slightly; something was scaring him, more than she'd ever seen him scared. As much as she wanted to pry, she waited for him to gather his thoughts. Finally, he looked her in the eye. At this point, Elizabeth had passed out in his arms again.

"There's a lot I need to tell you. What's most important right now is what I need to *show* you. I promise I'll give answers. I'm just trying to figure out what the fuck is going on..." He lay the sleeping baby back on Bridgett's chest and tummy. "When I went down to see her, I bumped into a lady on the way in the room... I'd seen her before."

A sinking feeling hit Bridgett in the gut. He was about to confess to an affair. Why else would he care about seeing some lady he'd run into before?

"Then when she was out of sight, I walked into the nursery with Dr. McCloud. He brought me to Elizabeth, and I completely forgot about the lady. Until I noticed something under Ellie's body..."

He pulled something out of his pocket and held it up for her to see. She almost laughed. In Alan's hand sat a small, wooden circle with some strange design in its center. It reminded her of a shitty Christmas decoration she would have made during arts and craft time as a child. Alan didn't share the same humor when staring at it. This is what had been scaring him? A damn tree branch?

"Alan, honey... what the *hell?* Please tell me you're messing with me?" she asked, but as the words came from her mouth, she caught his hand shaking slightly while he held the thing. "What is it?"

"That's the problem... I don't know what the hell it is. But I know that lady put it with her. I can't help but think it's some sort of hex, or curse, something to harm the baby..." He trailed off; she hoped he realized how ridiculous he sounded.

"You need sleep, my love. Why would some lady 'curse' our child?" She used one-handed air quotes.

"It's not fucking funny, Bridgett. I could feel the evil, just being in her presence. She put it there to—"

"Alan, you're not making any sense. Even if she did place it there—which you have no reason to think that—since when have you believed in all that crap? How do you know one of the nurses didn't make her something and just put it with her?"

"Bridge ... I'm telling you. No nurse left that there. They didn't even know what the hell it was. And I wouldn't believe in any of that stuff, not until tonight. There's so much I need to tell you. I just don't want to ruin this moment—"

"What'd you do? Did you sleep with this lady? Is that why you were getting home so late the last few nights, acting strange the last few months? Just spit it out," she snapped.

Alan narrowed his eyes into two confused slits. "Huh? No... Of course not, Bridgett. I'd never cheat on you." He seemed genuinely taken aback by her accusation.

"Then what's the problem? I've held it in, trying to just tell myself you were out trying to adjust to the fact you would have a child soon, but I can't sit here and just play the ignorant housewife anymore..."

He swallowed guiltily, his eyes glistening with early-stage tears. She was losing her patience waiting for him to respond. If he didn't cheat, and he was *this* worried, what the hell did he *actually* do?

"I lost my job last week... And I couldn't bring myself to tell you with a baby on the way..." He paused.

Somehow, it was relief Bridgett felt, and not fear or anger. A job could be replaced. But she still didn't see the connection with this woman.

"Al, we can get through this together. It's okay. Just take some deep breaths. Why would they let you go? Weren't you one of the top performers in your role?"

"Yeah... A few months back, Timmy called me over during our lunch break. I was in so much fucking pain; it was after one of those doubles I worked, my back and elbow hurt so bad. But I knew I needed to keep those hours; we needed the extra money. He offered me some Oxy—"

"Fucking pills? *What?* You've never done drugs in your life!" She realized she was getting louder and glanced down at their daughter, who thankfully could have slept through a rock concert at that moment. It was easy to forget that birth was hard work for the baby, too.

"I know, but it's not like that's why I got fired. I wouldn't be the only one at a factory to pop pills. It's what the stuff did to me, Bridge. I liked it. I got addicted to it. It progressively got worse over the last few months—hell, I didn't even realize how bad I'd got at my job without the stuff cranking through my system until I was called to the office. They fired me because they really had no choice. *I* would have fired me. Even right now, I crave that feeling... I'm in so much damn pain without it."

Bridgett was in shock. Of all the things he could have confessed to, this was the last thing she would have guessed. Still, she was determined not to let this ruin their moment. They would make it work. He could get a new job or stay at home with Elizabeth, and she would go back to work as soon as she was able to do so. They could use their savings to get by for now until they figured it out.

"I... I don't know what to say. But we're a team, Alan. You shouldn't be scared to come to me with stuff, you know that. Especially if you're needing to get help."

"With the baby coming, the last thing I wanted to do was stress you out, Bridge. Please understand where I'm coming from. I wouldn't hide anything from you in any other situation..." He looked a little relieved, though tears still streamed down his face.

"So, we get you help. We search for a new job. Everything will be okay... But what does that lady and this symbol have to do with any of this?"

He closed his eyes before looking down at the floor. After taking a deep breath, he said "After I lost my job, I was depressed. I couldn't bring myself to come home, so I went for a ride through the mountains to calm my nerves before confessing to you. Before I knew it, I was further up in the woods than I'd ever been—past all the lake houses and mansions. I was turning around in someone's driveway when I saw some frail old lady walking into her home. I'm ashamed... But I had this idea to take something from her, to help get some money to tie me over until I got a job..."

"You *what*? You tried to rob an old lady? What the *fuck*, Alan? We could have just used our savings to hold us over until you got a job; don't you think that would be a bit more reasonable than stealing?" Her shock now turned to complete anger.

"Bridge... The savings are gone. I blew through it the last few months..." He couldn't finish his sentence, choking on tears.

Bridgett wanted to scream. They'd had almost five thousand dollars sitting in their savings, something they'd worked very hard to build up. Worse than the lost money was how differently she now viewed her husband. At the moment, she wished he *had* cheated on her. Her heart pounded furiously in her chest while she thought of what to say next. He spoke before she said something she might regret later.

"That thing you found on my nightstand, that's what I grabbed from her house. It wasn't even intentional; her cats attacked me and chased me away. But when I looked back and saw the old lady watching me, I knew something was wrong. She was pure evil, Bridgett. And that girl I bumped into in the hallway had visited the old woman's house a few times. I think it's her daughter—"

"A few times? How many times did you go there, Alan? This doesn't sound like some spur-of-the-moment bad decision. You actually *planned* this?" She found it impossible to hide her disgust.

"Please... I know I fucked up bad. Whatever I gotta do to make it up to you, to prove I can get clean, I'll do it. Right now, I'm more concerned with this lady and whatever this thing is she put with our baby. I don't know if we're safe..."

Bridgett bit down on her lip, unable to say anything. As angry as she was, she didn't want to admit how she was also frightened by what he was saying. If all this was true, why would the woman have come here? And why would she have been leaving the room their baby was in? It couldn't be coincidence. Not that she believed in any of the curse stuff, her fears were more practical. *Did she do something to our child? Is she a danger to us?* Bridgett shifted her focus back to Alan, not quite ready to let him off the hook for his mistakes.

"I don't even know what to say... Not only have you been lying to me, but you've put us in a financial crisis that we can't come out of easily. What do you expect me to do with all this information, Alan?"

"I... don't know. All I can do is try to fix it moving forward. But none of that will matter if this lady keeps stalking us."

"So, we call the police. Let them know some creep is messing with us—" Bridgett started.

"We can't. What if they ask how I know her? I can't exactly tell them I broke into her mother's house. I'll figure something out, I promise…"

"Yeah, look where that got you," Bridgett snapped. She knew she was being mean, but he was lucky that's as far as she was taking it. He recoiled, her words doing their job.

"Listen… I don't expect you to be happy right now. Hell, there's a reason I didn't want to say anything while we were here enjoying our baby. But this friggin symbol changes everything. I don't know what it means, but it feels like some kind of warning. And I *know* she bumped into me on purpose. She wanted me to see her leaving that room…"

"So, we can't call the police… What do you suggest we do? Stand guard with a baseball bat?" she asked sarcastically.

"I think for now we do nothing. I'll try and find out what this symbol means. She could just be scaring us. Then I'll bring back the box I took from her and leave it on her porch, an act of goodwill… I don't know. Christ, I'm so sorry I got us in this situation."

"I just want to spend time with my baby, Alan. I'm done talking about this. I'm done talking to you. What I need is time to think about what you did and how I should handle it."

He didn't say anything in response. Instead, he got up and walked to the window once again. Bridgett stared at him while he scanned the parking lot, wondering just what he'd gotten them into. She wasn't about to let it ruin the best moment of her life.

CHAPTER 5

After two days at the hospital, Dr. McCloud said they were okay with letting the family go home. All the tests run on Elizabeth passed with flying colors—she was as healthy as could be. Alan was relieved the rest of their time at the hospital went by without any further incidents. At least, incidents involving the lady. As far as he and Bridgett were concerned, that was a different story. He knew she was holding in her rage, and because he wasn't the type to confront his issues head on, he instead allowed the remaining time to go by without bringing the incident back up again. When they were together with Elizabeth, strangers were easily fooled into thinking everything was still warm and fuzzy in the Brock family. Any time the infant was sleeping—which was most of the time—Bridgett rarely spoke to him.

By the time they were packed up and ready to go—an oversized manilla folder full of papers to remind them of appointments, vaccines, and even how to install a damn car seat in their vehicle crammed under his armpit while carrying said car seat in his other hand—the last hint of daylight had sunk below the horizon. A fog warning had blasted across the weather app on Alan's phone, bringing another layer of stress to their first time in the world with a child depending on them for protection.

The sliding doors opened as they walked into the haze suffocating the parked vehicles. It was difficult to see a few feet in front of them, and that was just walking. Alan couldn't imagine how the driving would be. They walked in silence toward their car, Elizabeth sound asleep in her car seat. Alan glanced at Bridgett, who continued to stare straight ahead, jaw clenched. He knew she saw him looking toward her, but he got the hint. She wasn't ready to talk yet. He carefully set the car seat on the ground and unlocked the car. The base for the seat was already installed, one of the many things the hospital staff helped with during their stay. Alan grabbed the car seat and clicked it into the base, the sound causing Elizabath's eyes to flutter before she quickly passed back out. Bridgett sighed and got into the passenger seat. With a deep breath, Alan got in the driver's seat and quietly shut his door. Without a word he started the car, triple-checking everything to make sure he didn't mess up. When he considered the vehicle safe enough to travel with their precious cargo, he pulled out of the parking lot with white knuckles wrapped around the steering wheel, driving at a speed he'd normally laugh at if he'd seen someone else behind the wheel.

"I'm sorry, Bridge... about everything. That stuff doesn't make you think straight, I—"

"Alan, I don't want to hear it right now. Let's just get home and get Ellie situated. My mom's coming tomorrow to help out. Do you think you can make it through tonight without selling off baby toys to buy drugs?" Her voice was cold as she stared out the window into the foggy landscape.

Alan didn't respond. Instead, he focused on holding back tears. He swallowed what felt like a pound of rocks, the guilt overshadowing any hint of happiness he'd been feeling over the last few days. How could he let it get to this point? Every day he'd got out of bed, ready to go to work and turn his drug use into a thing of the past. Then he'd hit that afternoon crash, his body resisting even simple movements until he fueled his bloodstream with opioids. He wanted to scream, but held it down, keeping his attention on the horrible driving conditions.

He kept the vehicle at a steady thirty miles-per-hour, squinting to find the lines on each side of his lane. At the very least, the treacherous driving helped keep his mind off his wife currently hating his guts. *Small victories*, he thought. The headlights fought for clarity, ultimately just expanding the haze instead of lighting up the road ahead. Alan wanted to pull over, reach across the car, and hug his wife. He wanted to tell her it would be okay, and that he would take care of everything. He continued driving, hoping that by the time they got home to their familiar space his wife would forgive him. The possibility seemed highly unlikely, considering it had already been a few days of almost complete silence between them.

Elizabeth awoke crying. It was the first time this had happened with no nurses to help or guide them, where they needed to do everything on their own. Bridgett unbuckled her seatbelt and leaned over the center console, stretching until her hand was in the car seat soothing their daughter. It only helped momentarily; the cries intensified to the point where Alan thought something might be wrong.

"Do you want me to pull over?" Alan asked over the squealing cries.

"No, we have to get used to this, I'll get her calm... Shhh, little girl, it's okay..."

With Bridgett leaning over the seat, Alan reached across to open the diaper bag below her feet while keeping his eyes on the road. He imagined this is what driving on a highway through the clouds would look like: just thick, white masses sliding off the car while it plowed through. Elizabeth continued screaming. Bridgett continued whispering calming phrases to her. Alan's head felt like it was going to explode. He risked a look over at the diaper bag, making sure he was reaching into the right pouch. His hand landed on the familiar squishiness of the pacifier tip, and he pulled it out, bringing his attention back to the road—and slammed on the brakes.

"Shit!"

A reflective set of eyes peered into his headlights from out of the fog, dead center in the road.

Bridgett flew back into her seat, smacking the glove box in the process. Elizabeth continued to scream. Alan looked quickly in the rearview mirror, bracing for impact, but was relieved to see no other vehicles on the road at the moment. *Of course, why would anyone drive in this shit?* he thought.

"Are you okay?" he asked over Elizabeth's cries.

Rubbing her back, Bridgett cringed. "What the hell, Alan?"

He looked back to the road, the eyes were still there—along with multiple other sets, all burning a hole through the wall of fog, staring directly at their car, which now sat parked in the middle of the road. Bridgett turned and followed his stare.

"What are those things? Drive around them!" She was getting worked up herself, which really brought out the cries in their daughter.

They couldn't see as much as an outline, but Alan knew what they were, and it twisted his insides with dread. The lady called them her "familiars", and they were sending a message. Bridgett climbed over the center console into the back seat, putting her focus on calming the baby. Alan pulled his foot off the brake and punched the gas, heading right towards the cats. As he got closer, they fled to the sides of the road, off into the blanket of darkness the fog provided. Elizabeth's screams eased; Alan wished he could say the same for his stress. He continued to speed up, the fog no longer scaring him the way it previously had. It was easy to look past things like that when real life monsters were stalking you. He glanced in the rearview at his wife and daughter, a tear sliding down his cheek. An unsettling feeling wouldn't go away—those creatures weren't done.

CHAPTER 6

The drive home would have normally taken less than twenty minutes, but when Alan looked at the clock, he couldn't believe over an hour had already passed. They pulled into the parking lot of their complex, parking in their assigned spot. Alan leaned back in the seat and closed his eyes, steadying his nerves the best he could. *We made it home—that has to be a successful moment in parenting, right?* But everything else that'd occurred from the moment they left the hospital was an utter failure. Alan's eyes were still closed when the click of the car seat coming unlatched from the base brought his focus back to the car. Bridgett opened the door and climbed out of the backseat without a word, softly shutting the door and walking through the haze toward the building. Alan watched her round the corner and go out of sight. He couldn't help but wonder if she planned to leave him after they had settled in. He wouldn't blame her.

He grabbed the diaper bag and got out of the car, telling himself to just take whatever verbal beatings were going to come his way when Bridgett snapped out of her angry silence.

The thought of those eyes staring at them from the dense mist came back to him, instantly chilling him to his core. Were they here somewhere, watching from the woods? They clearly knew when and where Alan would be, always a few steps ahead. That brought his focus back to his family, who were likely heading up the stairs to their apartment. Alan's stomach clenched at his guts; he couldn't let anything happen to them.

Throwing the diaper bag strap over his shoulder, he quickly shut the car door and walked toward the apartment complex at a brisk pace—fast enough to shorten the normal time it would take, but not so fast that neighbors would start to question what he was doing. Not that he cared. If his family was in danger like he thought they were, his neighbor's opinions could get fucked. The fog wasn't as dense in their parking lot, but it was still enough to hide the features of the surrounding woods. Alan opened the main door, taking one last look back to the woods, expecting to spot the eyes watching him once again. To his relief, he didn't see them. The relief was short-lived, broken by a scream coming from the second floor.

Bridgett!

When Bridgett opened the apartment door, she was expecting to feel relief. Instead, she was hit with a shock that would have dropped her to the floor had she not been carrying Elizabeth in the car seat. The apartment was trashed. Furniture turned over, drawers open, plates and glasses shattered on the floor. She didn't even realize she'd screamed until Alan came barreling around the corner toward their apartment. Elizabeth began to cry again, so Bridgett took her out of the seat and attempted to calm her as Alan approached the door.

"What's wrong? Are you okay?"

"I'm fine, but look at our place, Alan... Someone broke in and trashed it."

Just saying those words made her want to vomit. They were supposed to come home, get acquainted with their new lifestyle, and get some rest. As she bobbed up and down, shushing her daughter, the destruction surrounding them told her the night would be far from relaxing. Alan walked in and his shocked gasp said it all. He scanned the apartment, the gulp in his throat full of guilt.

"Stay in the hallway, I need to make sure nobody's here..."

He walked in, leaving them in the hallway. Bridgett wasn't sure she was much safer out here, as the apartment directly next to them was currently vacant, and the one across the hall belonged to an elderly couple who couldn't help her in a struggle if they tried. She heard belongings being tossed aside in their apartment, along with Alan's hurried footsteps through each room. Bridgett debated going in to check on him but decided against it. She waited for what felt like minutes, when in reality it was likely thirty seconds. The door opened and Alan wiped his forehead, nervous sweat dripping down his face.

"It's fine, nobody's here..." He turned and walked back in, motioning for her to follow.

She walked in and shut the door, instinctively locking the deadbolt as soon as the door clicked shut. They walked through each room together, taking in the destruction, and all Bridgett wanted to do was cry. Not only had Alan put them in a place financially they hadn't been since they first got out of college, but now she had to worry about the few remaining possessions they actually cared about being stolen. It all felt like karma, something Alan did coming back to bite them in the ass. Or worse, revenge. With everything that happened at the hospital and then on the drive home, it was becoming more of a possibility in her mind that Alan's fears of the woman messing with them could be true. But what the fuck would cats have to do with it? Why trash their apartment and not take anything? There was also the chance this was some random break-in, maybe somebody that knew they would be gone a few days and wanted to find something valuable. Boy, must they have been disappointed when the most valuable thing they found was a gift card to Applebee's.

They made it to their bedroom, which actually appeared mostly unscathed. What the hell was the point of this break-in if they didn't take anything? Bridgett sat on the bed, staring down at her daughter, who had finally calmed down to a low whimper. She'd held babies before, but nothing compared to holding your own child—she could stare at her for hours. Alan muttered something behind her, dragging her out of her joy... again.

"I think I know what they came for... The box, it's gone. I knew it was her, I fucking *knew* it."

"Alan, we need to call the damn cops. I don't care what you said. You can come up with a story as to why you were at her house, you're clearly good at lying to people..."

As she said it, Bridgett knew she needed to stop with the hateful comments. It was just so hard to feel anything but anger toward him right now—but she needed to try. She'd read in the baby books how children, even infants, could detect stress in the household. That it could help morph their personalities at a young age. The last thing she wanted was her daughter to grow up having been dealt early-life struggles.

"I'm sorry... I can't just pretend all these things didn't happen, but I know right now that sarcasm's the last thing we need," she said, then walked over and hugged him.

The change of attitude brought Alan to tears, and Bridgett immediately felt awful for the things she'd said to him. He took a deep breath and nodded his head.

"Thank you... And I think they got what they came for. Let me pick this place up, it's my fault it happened. I'll start with the living room and bedroom: that way we can get as comfortable as possible tonight. Then I'll work my way through the rest of the apartment. I really think they got their point across and will leave us alone now."

Bridgett thought about it, then nodded in agreement. She didn't have the heart to tell him what happened with the sphere, how it emptied out and apparently entered her bloodstream. The more she'd thought about it, the more she realized the sphere had sent her into labor, crazy as it sounded. But there hadn't been even a remote sign of contractions until she set it on her belly. She didn't know what that meant, but as more weird things happened to them, the more she was starting to believe there was something abnormal about all of it. She wasn't one to believe in the supernatural, or magic of any kind, and for all she knew she might have been half asleep and seeing things when the glow transferred from the glass to her body. But it couldn't be a coincidence that all these horrific things had happened ever since. She wanted to believe Alan; it just wasn't that easy to let her guard down. Still, the desire to have a normal night on their first evening back in their apartment allowed her to agree with the idea that they were now safe. Alan kissed her on the forehead and headed down the hall to begin cleaning up the mess.

CHAPTER 7

For the first time since before he lost his job, Alan felt relaxed. The apartment was now tidied up, the woman had taken what she came for, and the weight of losing his job and their savings was now off his chest. There was still the issue of needing to find a job—and find one soon—but he would make sure that happened. While he cleaned, he came up with a list of things he needed to do in order to make sure this was the end of his problems. He knew the craving would become an issue soon. Right now, he was trying his hardest to not think about oxy. His body was calling for it, and the stress of everything wasn't helping that need. Alan planned to get out in front of that craving, to go and find help before it was too late. When he was out job searching, he'd make a small detour in town to the clinic and see what they could do to support him.

Bridgett finished nursing the baby and carried her to the bedroom, setting her in the pack-and-play in the corner. Alan watched from the bed, a smile forcing its way to his face as he observed her natural ability to be a mom. Anyone watching would have thought she'd been doing this for years. After making sure the swaddle was firmly wrapped around Elizabeth, she turned and joined Alan on the edge of the bed, both of them watching their baby sleep peacefully in the corner of the room. Bridgett leaned her head on Alan's shoulder, boosting his confidence that *maybe* this marriage wasn't ruined just yet.

"We've got a lot to work on, huh babe?" he asked.

After a moment of silence, Bridgett said "Yeah... Through the good times and bad times, right? I just wish you'd told me sooner. But what's done is done. The only way to fix the problem is to move forward with our lives."

"I love you so much... I can't believe I fucked up this bad. You know how I bottle everything up inside instead of talking about my issues. From now on, that won't happen. No matter how bad things get—I'll always come to you first... I promise," he said with glossy eyes.

Bridgett said nothing back, but her expression told him she believed him. That was all he could ask for right now. They sat in silence, and Alan loved every second of it. This was everything they'd dreamed of. A nice home-cooked meal and Netflix binging sounded like a great way to end the night.

It sounded amazing—until they both crashed from a few days' worth of adrenaline.

They crawled into bed and turned the light out, not even having enough energy to brush their teeth. Sleeping in their comfortable king size mattress instead of the damn fake leather recliner in the hospital was a blessing to Alan. He spooned with his wife and hugged her tight, intent on making things right and being the dad he'd always dreamed of being.

Bridgett was asleep within minutes, her soft snores breaking the silence of the room. Alan's eyelids weighed down like a pair of cinderblocks, and he soon followed his wife and daughter into dreamland, certain things were finally looking up for the Brock family.

Alan awoke to Elizabeth's cries—not the first time during the night, and likely not the last—signaling she wanted to eat again. Their first night home had been far worse than he expected after a relatively calm few nights of sleep at the hospital. The nurses and lactation consultant warned them of this happening. They said the baby would more than likely wake frequently the first few nights until Bridgett's milk came in, and Alan had just shaken it off, thinking their red-headed angel was simply going to prove them wrong. He stretched, his eyes still closed, hoping that Bridgett would offer to get up and feed her this time.

"It's your turn…" she mumbled into her pillow.

He sighed, turning to face the corner where the pack-and-play sat—and shouted.

A dark figure stood over the baby, reaching toward her. Alan couldn't make much out clearly in the dark, save the long, bony fingers he'd seen in the old woman's house.

"What is it?' Bridgett yelled.

She jumped out of bed and when she spotted the old woman's back to them, she let out her own scream.

"Get away from my baby!" she yelled.

The old woman turned to face them, exposing her crooked, rotting teeth. The black eyes that had haunted Alan the last few days burrowed into his own. The old woman started shouting in a different language, and then raised one of her hands, pointing toward the distraught couple. Alan didn't think, he reached down to grab the baseball bat under the bed, when something brushed against his hand. He pulled back and looked down, but there was nothing there. Bridgett screamed again and Alan shot around. Three sickly looking cats had her cornered against her nightstand, baring their fangs. The animals closed in, providing no room for escape.

A ripping sound tore through their fur, and Alan noticed their bodies were expanding. He looked back to the lady who momentarily had taken her attention off the baby while she chanted in her strange tongue. Alan realized she was enacting some kind of spell, transforming the cats into something far worse. They shrieked as their skin tore apart, revealing raw muscle below the bloodied fur. Elizabeth continued to scream from her pack-and-play, and all Alan wanted was to comfort her. But he was frozen in place, unsure of what his next move should be. He looked back to his wife, watching as she grabbed the lamp from her nightstand and ripped the cord from the wall. She heaved it toward the animals, who hardly reacted as their bodies continued to transform into larger monsters. It reminded Alan of watching a werewolf movie, the bodies painfully stretching beyond normal capacity as limbs extended with loud cracks and pops. He realized they were growing into human-like forms, yet their heads were still those of the feline variety. He had to stop the spell before they got bigger.

Alan grabbed the bat and charged at the old lady, ready to strike her. She stopped her chant and stared into his eyes, fear locking his feet in place. His body began to shake as he got closer, her true features finally revealed with the moonlight shining in through the window. She laughed at the terror displayed in his eyes, briefly looking down at the bat in his hand and shook her head.

"You have no idea what you've done, you scum. You took something very important to me, something I needed to survive... Now it's my turn to return the favor!" Her thick accent made it hard to understand her words, but he knew what she was getting at. She looked back down to Elizabeth—who had turned a dark red from her strenuous cries—and cackled in delight.

"Don't fucking touch her, you bitch!" Alan screamed, and then continued his charge toward her.

The woman kept her eyes on the baby but lifted her hand in Alan's direction, and once again began to chant something.

He raised the bat prepared to strike...

...And felt his throat begin to tighten, an invisible hand clenching tight around his windpipe. There was nothing there, but he could feel the grip locked around his throat, squeezing tighter by the second. He forced himself to continue, swinging the bat toward her face. But she was prepared, and his weakened strength softly brought the bat down as she caught the end of it, snapping it in two. He dropped to his knees, clutching his throat. He wanted to pry the hand away, but there was nothing to grasp. Alan's vision began to darken when Bridgett's screams brought another sense of urgency to him. He reached up and clawed at the old woman's face, her skin peeling off like withered wallpaper and caking under his fingernails.

"*Osjetit ćete bol*!" she screeched.

Alan had no idea what it meant. He looked up at her shredded face. A black liquid slid down her cheek like the thick sludge of old motor oil. Her breath was rancid, burning his nostrils as he attempted to take deep breaths and free the suffocating tightness pressing against his Adam's apple. The woman backhanded him in the face, and to Alan's shock, sent him flying back across the bed and tumbling to the floor next to his wife in the corner. Bridgett screamed again, leaning over to make sure he was okay.

He shook out of his confusion, pulling himself back up by grabbing hold of the bed sheets. When he got to his feet, he put his arm around his wife and came face to face with the cat creatures. They were almost eye level with him, patches of slick fur sporadically located across their otherwise nude bodies. Their skin was drenched in a slimy substance that made the woman's breath smell minty fresh in comparison. In a week full of terrifying moments, it was the scariest thing Alan had ever seen. Their hands and feet still displayed sets of life-threatening claws, designed to rip apart their prey.

"Leave us alone! You got your fucking box back, I'm sorry I took it!" Alan yelled.

The cat things hissed, and one of them expelled its claws and swiped him across the face, forcing him back into Bridgett as they both fell into the nightstand.

"No... No, you did far more than steal my precious sphere. You transferred its power..."

Alan had no idea what the old woman was talking about, but Bridgett tensed up when she said it, and Alan looked to his wife.

"What's she talking about, Bridgett?"

"I... I wasn't sure what happened, but the night I went into labor, that thing did something to me. Whatever was inside it, it came into my body—" She couldn't continue. As Elizabeth's cries intensified, they looked at the old woman in horror. She'd lifted Elizabeth from her mattress, pulling her close to her face. Alan had a horrifying image of her biting the infant's head clean off. Instead, the old hag removed the child's night cap and dropped it to the floor, revealing the unnatural red locks that didn't belong to an infant.

"It didn't travel to you, my dear... It travelled to Kosa."

"Don't touch her! She has nothing to do with this. Kill me if you want, but don't you dare fucking harm her!" Alan screamed.

The old woman let out her hoarse laugh once again.

"Kosa... Mmm. My precious Kosa." She inhaled deeply, then twirled a strand of the baby's hair around her bony finger. Alan thought she was toying with the child, but then the woman yanked the hair free from her scalp, bringing on another bout of blood-curdling cries from Elizabeth.

Alan had seen enough. He jumped towards the bed, ready to lunge at the evil bitch and save his baby. His plan never advanced to the next step. One of the creatures grabbed hold of his ankle with its clawed fingers, pushing pinpoint nails into his heel and tearing out the Achilles tendon in one fluid swipe. He dropped to the bed, screaming in agony, and clutched his heel. Bridgett came to his side, forgetting all about the monsters surrounding them.

"Alan! No!"

One of the other creatures pounced on her back, forcing its weight down on her and holding her in place. The third jumped on Alan's back as he tried to stop the blood from pumping out of his wound.

"Make them watch..." The woman spit the words out like they were drenched in venom.

Alan felt more claws puncture the back of his head, then yank back, forcing him to face the woman holding his baby. He looked in the corner of his eye and saw the other monster was doing the same with Bridgett. Their cat-like heads with human eyes remained emotionless, awaiting their master's next set of instructions. It felt like some horrific terrorist execution, something they appeared to have done before.

The old lady lifted the strands of hair to her mouth and opened wide. The disgusting tongue that Alan had seen a few nights ago slid its way out of her mouth, wrapping up the hair and pulling it back into her throat. Her eyes rolled in her head as she moaned in ecstasy. Alan watched in horror as the lady's face began to shift, her decaying, wrinkled skin rippling like a computer glitch as movements beneath the skin's surface escalated. Her thin, white hair started whipping around with a life of its own, pulling at the liver-spotted skin of her scalp. Elizabeth continued to cry at a deafening level in the woman's grasp. Alan made an attempt to escape, only to have the claws dig deeper into the back of his skull to hold him in place. They had no choice but to watch whatever this woman was doing to their child.

The woman's face was changing. Not just her face, but her entire body. Her hair suddenly filled her head—long, black strands forcing up through the previously dead hair follicles. The skin on her face stretched, eliminating the wrinkles that had formed after years of aging. With her mouth still open wide, Alan watched her rotten teeth crack and bend back into place, all while clearing to a healthy white color fit for a dental commercial. He now realized who he was looking at: the young woman from the hospital, the one he'd assumed was the daughter of the old lady. They were the same person. He felt sick to his stomach.

"You see... I have no intention of harming this little one. In fact, I have far too much use for her to do such a thing. Kosa now carries what I need to get my strength. You, however... you very much can get your wish, Mr. Brock."

He realized that she was referring to him demanding she kill him instead of his daughter. But the realization came too late. The creatures perched on their backs pulled their scalps back, forcing Alan and Bridgett to expose their throats. They both struggled to break free, but it was of no use.

"I will take good care of this one... As for you two, my familiars are hungry. I've made them wait long enough..." She nodded, a silent instruction.

Alan forced his head to the side, looking at Bridgett who remained focused on her newborn child. Tears flowed down her face, but she couldn't talk. Alan knew all of this was his fault.

"I love you, Bridge..." he mumbled.

Before she could respond, the creatures ripped out both of their throats with their teeth, fountains of blood shooting out of their shredded necks. The baby continued to cry, drowning out the remaining sounds gurgling out of her parents' torn throats. Alan, still alive, pulled himself along the bed sheet, trying to get to his baby. His body felt numb, his fingers losing the strength to grip. The warmth of his own blood pooling underneath him brought on a sense of relaxation. With one last effort to save Elizabeth, he tried to push himself up on the bed, staring at his child one last time. The last image he would ever see was his baby screaming as the Croatian witch ate strands of her hair before his eyes stopped working.

PART II
MOTHER'S RULES
6 YEARS LATER

CHAPTER 8

Kosa sat on the floor of the dark room, playing with her toys. Mother often spent long parts of the night out in the woods, leaving Kosa home alone. Kosa didn't like that. While Mother was gone, she was to follow the rules. Stay in the attic. Clean up her mess. Most of all, do not let anyone see her. At six years old, Kosa knew it was dangerous to be home alone, but Mother insisted the kitties would protect her if anyone came, and that if she didn't come out of the attic, nobody would see her.

On occasion, Mother would bring a friend over for her to play with, but that only lasted a few hours before the kids had to leave. Usually, she kept to herself during the day, playing with the dolls Mother made her and the other items she had designated as toys. She looked around at the toys she'd lined up: a mix of dolls, sticks, and some of the smooth bones Mother let her keep. Her favorite toy was a large, white bone that she'd colored a face on. She liked it most because of the smile she made all by herself. Every time she looked at Lennie—named after her favorite character from *Of Mice and Men*—she couldn't help but smile back at him. He was always happy.

"Lennie, do you want some tea? You've already had four cups!"

He smiled back at her. She knew that meant he did in fact want another cup of tea. She poured the water into the small cup and set it back in front of him. Next, she shifted her attention to her favorite doll, who she named Mary after her favorite song "Mary Had a Little Lamb." Lennie and Mary went everywhere with her. Kosa realized Mary wasn't paying attention though, her head was facing off to the side.

"Mary! Mother says it's rude to get distracted at the dinner table. What are you looking at?" Kosa looked in the direction her doll faced, spotting one of the cats sitting in the dark corner of the room, watching them play teatime.

They were *always* watching.

As much as she loved the kitties, sometimes they spooked her when it started to get dark. Their eyes always shined back at her from the shadows. If she attempted to leave the attic, the one she'd named Tom would sit in front of the door to prevent her from leaving. Mother had them trained well.

"That's just Tom, Mary. He's a nice kitty. Tom? You're scaring Mary... Please stop looking at her like that..."

The cat didn't move.

Kosa badly wanted to turn the light on, but another of the rules was to *never* do that. She couldn't risk allowing the outside world to see she was up in the attic. So, she had to sit in darkness, hoping to keep herself occupied enough to avoid thinking of what lurked in the corners. Mother was always telling her how awful things were outside the house, and why it was so important she never stepped foot outside.

When Kosa was younger, she'd asked why it was okay for Mother to go out, and for the friends she brought over for Kosa to play with to live in the world if it was so dangerous. Mother hated being questioned, and that particular question got Kosa locked in the attic for three whole days. Now, if she didn't understand one of the rules, Kosa just kept it to herself.

A squeak in the corner of the room brought the cat alert. Kosa turned to spot a tiny set of eyes peering out from a hole in the wall.

"Stop it, Tom... That's just Jerry! He's a nice little mouse."

Tom ignored her, the black fur on his back standing straight up like finely pointed needles as he waited for the mouse to make a mistake so he could pounce. Kosa named the cat and mouse after the *Tom and Jerry* book that Mother had given her. Kosa loved the book because it had a golden spine that made it feel fancy. Mother told Kosa the characters were from a television show, but Mother wouldn't get a TV. She said it ruined the mind, and that reading and playing was far better for a child than watching the awful things going on in the world. Kosa couldn't believe there was more to the universe than just the house. She'd spent her entire life inside, only on occasion getting the chance to go on the balcony or backyard when Mother felt it was safe enough.

Jerry squeaked again, then backed farther into the hole out of sight. Kosa left crumbs for her friend any chance she got—which was often—as Mother left food for her to eat during the day to hold her over until dinner. Poor Jerry just wanted to come out and snack, but Tom scared him away. Kosa wondered if they would fight like in the book. Or maybe Tom would become friends with Jerry like she had.

"Tom, stop being mean to him! He just wants to come say hi to us..."

Kosa got to her feet and walked to the attic window, looking out at the backyard for any sign of Mother. While it was unlike her to come home this late, it had happened before. Each of the previous occurrences were moments in her young life that she'd like to forget. Mother needed her rest and needed to perform their nightly rituals to—as she put it—heal fully. Any time she was gone this long, she came home in a bad mood and would have little patience for Kosa. Sometimes, she wouldn't even read her a bedtime story or feed her dinner.

While nightfall had not yet arrived in full, it was getting close. Mother would transition to her older self when the sun started setting, and she hated being away from home when that happened. Kosa was about to pull away from the window when a flash of movement in the forest caught her attention. A figure, too far away to make any real details out, approached through the trails leading to the house. *Mother*. Her face might not have been distinguishable yet, but her movement and cloak were. Whenever she was out, she always wore her black cloak to stay protected. She was moving much slower than normal, which likely meant she wasn't feeling well.

Kosa continued to watch her approach, but then Mother stopped as she came into the clearing leading to the backyard. She glanced up at the attic window, and Kosa immediately dropped to the floor out of sight. If Mother saw her looking out the window, she'd be furious. Another of the rules, of course. Do not look out of the window. Kosa's heart was slamming against her chest; if Mother had seen her, while also arriving home this late, that would mean a much more severe punishment than normal. *Please don't let her see me...*

She sat against the wall, taking deep breaths to calm herself. Her toys remained in position, ready for the tea party to resume, but they would have to wait. Tom, who had sat back down after Jerry scurried back into his hole, got back to his feet and began purring. The cat rubbed against the door, awaiting his master to arrive home. Kosa didn't know if the animal could smell Mother this far away, or if it was her reaction that alerted the cat to Mother's presence, but he sensed it was feeding time.

Quietly, Kosa crawled back across the floor to get near her toys, hoping if she pretended to play when Mother came upstairs that she would get away with looking out the window. She picked up her doll and absently went through the motions of the tea party, all while keeping her eyes locked on the door. Waiting.

CHAPTER 9

Heather Ann Larson slammed the hatchback of the van shut and looked down at the very last suitcase. She was exhausted. A four-hour drive with two children, an empty passenger seat where her husband was *supposed* to be sitting—until he came down with the flu and left Heather with the decision to either cancel their family vacation or suck it up and take the kids by herself. God forbid the kids help her unpack. They were already running through the vacation house, exploring the emptiness the lakefront home provided them.

But the fact that her kids were getting along was worth the extra work she had to put into bringing the luggage in herself. Mike was her oldest, a teen who thought he knew every damn thing the world had to offer, even when he was proven wrong. He was going through the awkward stage of becoming a man while his voice hadn't caught up yet. At thirteen, he was on the older side to start puberty, but Heather wasn't complaining. It seemed like just yesterday he was born. He wanted nothing to do with the family vacation until they pulled into the driveway of the rental home, and he saw the lake behind it with the private beach and firepit.

The Larsons could not normally afford a house so massive, even for a three-day weekend getaway. But her boss told her she needed to get away and clear her head before coming back to work, ready to rock in the new quarter. He'd offered her the house before, but she always felt awkward at the thought of staying at her boss's beach house. She'd finally caved and hearing the happiness of her children made it all worth it.

Her youngest son, Bryce, came bursting out the front door into the driveway, startling Heather from her thoughts. He flicked his shaggy hair out of his eyes, revealing his freckled face.

"Mom! There's this cool hiking trail out back in the woods around the lake. Can we go check it out?" he asked, with pure glee.

"It's getting pretty late tonight, sweetie. How about we unpack, play some games, and relax. After breakfast tomorrow we can go for a fun little hike, sound good?"

She saw the disappointment on his face and considered changing her mind. But then she looked up and saw the sky fading to darkness and decided it was the right call. The last thing she needed was to get lost in the woods in the middle of the night. She leaned over and grabbed one of the bags.

"Okay... Can we play Uno? Mike hates it when I beat him," Bryce said with a grin.

"Sounds good, buddy. Can you grab the last bag for me?"

Bryce came closer and picked up the smaller bag. Heather rubbed the top of his shaggy head. "Thanks, kiddo. It's a bummer Dad couldn't come to check this out, but I'm glad we still decided to do this, how 'bout you?"

"Yeah! This place is awesome."

They walked through the front door and set the bags down on the beautiful hardwood floor. Mike was standing on the side porch, looking down at the water. Heather imagined him staring at the water, picturing some teen girl in a bikini as she bathed on the sand. She tried to give him privacy, but teenage boys weren't exactly the most adept at hiding their desires. On multiple occasions she'd found old Playboy magazines in his room and decided not to say anything. Her husband gave her the generic dad answer of "boys will be boys."

She walked out and stood by his side.

"Beautiful, isn't it?"

"I guess so... Think that water's warm?" he asked.

"You can find out for us tomorrow... I plan to lounge and read my romance novel after we go for a hike," she said.

"You and those stupid books... Aren't they all the same?"

"I wouldn't expect you to get them, but no. There's a reason they're so popular."

He'd already lost interest in the conversation, walking toward the other side of the deck and gazing off into the forest that Bryce must have been referring to. While the opening to the lake was clear of any trees, dense forest sat on both sides of the clearing, swallowing up any possible light. It was impossible to see much of the trail leading into the woods.

"You think you'll be up for a hike with us tomorrow?" she asked.

Mike turned to her and rolled his eyes. "Maybe. I might just hang back here, though."

"I'd really like it if we got to spend time as a family. When we're home, we all get tied up in the day-to-day grind. This is the first chance we've had to just relax in years."

"I said maybe, Mom. Can we eat? I'm starving..."

"Sure, I brought some of those frozen pizzas you guys like. I'll cook one up."

Mike nodded his approval and walked back into the house without another word. Heather was about to follow him but took one last glance back at the woods. An unsettling feeling came over her, and she didn't know why. She stared into the darkness, half wanting something to show itself, so she didn't feel crazy, and half wanting the feeling to just go away.

Movement behind a batch of trees let her know she wasn't crazy after all. She swallowed down the fear, prepared to yell at whoever was out there, when she spotted a set of sparkling eyes staring back at her from the shadows. Before she could scream, a black cat sprinted off through the woods.

Jesus... It's just a damn cat, she said to herself.

Seeing the animal only made her feel slightly better, however. Something seemed off about the cat, something wrong with it. It watched her like she was its next meal. Heather shook the feeling and headed back inside.

CHAPTER 10

"Kosa! You can come downstairs now, dear..."

Kosa closed her eyes and sighed in relief. Mother sounded in good spirits. Maybe the night wouldn't go as badly as she thought. Maybe she would get that bedtime story after all. She was also grateful that it hadn't yet gone completely dark outside, otherwise she would have been tempted to leave the room before Mother granted her permission. Kosa stood and approached the door as Tom paced back and forth, waiting for her to open it. She turned back to Lennie and Mary, giving an enthusiastic wave goodbye.

"I'll see you guys soon!"

She opened the door and Tom darted out of the room. The hall was dimly lit. Mother liked to keep the house mostly dark, even when she was home. She told Kosa she had sensitive eyes and that bright lights really hurt. Kosa walked down the stairs and into the dining room. Mother had her back to Kosa, prepping dinner over the stove. Her cloak was still on, giving her the resemblance of a shadow standing in place.

"Hi, Mother..." she said, quietly. Mother didn't like it when she was loud.

Mother continued to stir the soup as steam wafted up from the pot. Kosa's stomach growled loudly at the smell of food. While Mother did provide her with snacks to eat during the day, she was forced to ration the small amounts she ate, unsure of when she would be allowed to leave the room.

"Hello, darling... Have you been a good girl today?" Mother asked without turning around to face her.

"Yes... I followed all the rules, just like I'm supposed to," Kosa said, thinking back to when she almost got caught looking out the window. Did Mother know? Was she testing Kosa's honesty? The hunger in her stomach turned to a ball of panic. She'd already lied, at this point she had to continue with the lie.

Mother turned off the burner of the stove, then grabbed two bowls from the cabinet above her. She slowly poured the soup into each bowl, her boney hands shaking as she did. Kosa knew from looking at the hands that Mother wasn't well. She was in the middle of transition, and they needed to hurry and do the nightly ritual, or it would get worse. Mother insisted they eat before doing so though, saying that Kosa had to be strong for the ritual to work to its fullest.

"Can I help, Mother?"

The old lady dropped a spoon into each bowl of soup and picked them up, turning for the first time to face Kosa. It was hard to hide her fear when Mother looked her in the eyes. She was far into transition, her skin wrinkled and cheeks sagging. Dark circles sat below her pitch-black eyes. She blew a strand of thin white hair from her face and smiled, revealing her rotten teeth. Kosa knew her teeth only got this bad when she went too long without what she needed, what Kosa provided her.

"No need, dear. Let's eat. We must get on with the night, yes?"

Kosa nodded and sat at the table.

The dim light did little to hide Mother's deteriorating state. If anything, it made it *worse*. Every shadow and wrinkle stood out, making the old lady appear more like a rotting corpse. Kosa tried not to look at Mother's face, afraid that if she showed her disgust, there would be consequences. Instead, she kept her hands folded in her lap—something that wasn't normally easy for her—and willed her eyes to remain focused on the table. Mother sat the bowl of soup down in front of her and walked around to the other side of the table.

As many of their nights went, they ate dinner in uncomfortable silence. The slurping of soup, and the purring of cats rubbing against Mother's legs, sporadically interrupted the dead air. Kosa knew one of the other rules. *Don't speak unless spoken to*. She wanted to ask Mother where she went today, what took her so long to get home? She wanted to tell her about her day in the attic, how she held her potty in all day like a big girl. With no bathroom in the cramped space upstairs, she either had to hold it all day, or have an accident. When the latter happened, Kosa was forced to scrub the floors and handwash her soiled clothes as punishment.

With hardly any meat in her soup, Kosa finished her meal quickly. Mother ate much slower, leaning over her soup to shorten the distance from spoon to mouth. Kosa sat quietly while Mother finished her meal. When she was done, she lifted her head and looked at Kosa.

"You may be excused from the table. Wash the dishes while I set up."

Kosa gathered the dirty dishes and carried them to the sink, careful not to drop them and cause a loud bang that would surely upset Mother. As she scrubbed the bowls clean, she heard Mother get up from the table and go to the sitting area by the fireplace where they read books and helped heal Mother every night. Kosa dreaded the ritual, but also knew it needed to be done. She didn't want to lose Mother and be left to take care of herself. The thought of that made her chest feel funny. She dried the dishes with a towel and put them in their proper places. With one final look at the kitchen to make sure she didn't miss anything, she took a deep breath and headed toward the sitting area.

The room was dark, just the way Mother liked it. Kosa sat in her designated chair, facing the fireplace so Mother had easy access behind her. Not that she wanted to watch this part anyways. The pain was bad enough: watching it transpire would make it even worse. The fireplace was more for aesthetic than function, as the house was always freezing. Mother insisted on this because it was important for her body. Kosa had woken up every day in icy shivers until she became used to it. At least the attic trapped what little heat rose through the home.

Mother's shadow appeared on the wall in front of Kosa.

It was time for the pain.

"My dear... Mother needs more tonight, I am weak."

Kosa closed her eyes, fighting back tears. She wished she'd brought Mary downstairs with her to hold until it was over. Instead, she just hummed "Mary Had a Little Lamb," hoping the distraction would take away some of the suffering. Mother placed her bony hands on the top of Kosa's head, as if she was about to massage her skull. That was far from the truth. She knew Mother was feeling around for what would help the most tonight. It was as if the hair talked to her.

Her stick-like fingers continued to travel through the red locks until she stopped her hand, taking her index finger and twirling a strand of hair around it. Kosa held her breath as she felt her hair tighten around the finger. Mother spoke in her Croatian tongue, chanting the nightly words that Kosa knew all too well. Then, without warning, Mother yanked, tearing the hair from Kosa's scalp. A stinging sensation throbbed at the base of her hairline as Mother pulled up the strands she needed.

Kosa found it difficult to look in the mirror after the routine, knowing there would be red patches of skin underneath her hair by the time they were done. She didn't hate Mother for it, however. She knew it was necessary for her health. She just wished there was another *way* to help. She'd once asked if she could cut the hair and do it that way, but Mother insisted the power was strongest at the root, where it broke from her scalp.

Kosa continued to hum her song and fight off crying, afraid to turn around and see this part of the act. She didn't need to see it. She could *hear* it. The soft, slurping of Mother forcing the torn hair into her mouth, her tongue wrapping around the strands of hair like a vine sapping the life from a plant, sucking the energy from it before eventually swallowing. Mother moaned in delight, and then began breathing heavily. Kosa heard the transition taking place—Mother's body shifting and cracking as the hair did its job.

Why my hair? Why does it have to be what makes her better? Kosa asked herself those questions every night.

She knew it wasn't over, that she'd have to endure the process a few more times before they could do story time. That was all she wanted.

To sit with Mother and read "Tom and Jerry," or "Goodnight Moon." She loved looking for the mouse on each page because it reminded her of the real Jerry who lived in the attic wall. Did Jerry have a mother? Was she like this? Did he get punished—

RIPPP

Mary had a little lamb... little lamb... little lamb...

Kosa did whatever she could to keep her mind off the pain.

More moaning behind her.

A moment of silence passed, leading Kosa to think it was over. Mother coughed, startling Kosa from her daze. She turned to make sure everything was okay, that her mother wasn't dying. Turning was a mistake. She watched the slithering tongue retracting back into Mother's mouth, pulling the last strand of hair in with it. The old lady's features had grown drastically younger compared to her appearance at dinner, but she was still far from her best. As cold as the house was, Mother was sweating, pulling in deep breaths while her body struggled to adjust.

"Is everything okay, Mother?"

The piercing black eyes of the witch shifted to meet Kosa's, and she immediately knew the question was a bad idea.

"I'll... be *fine*. The energy is doing its job... Don't question me, little girl."

"I'm sorry Mother... I just want to help."

"You've helped enough for tonight. Off to bed with you. Mother's tired..."

"But... Can we read a story first?" Kosa asked.

The obsidian eyes narrowed. "Not tonight. I said go to bed, girl. I need my sleep to let this do its job properly. Brush your teeth and go to the bathroom. Tomorrow may be another long day for you my dear."

Kosa's heart sank into her stomach. The thought of another full day in the attic was awful. So was the thought of no bedtime story. But she knew there was nothing she could do about it. Mother had spoken, and that was that. She nodded at the old lady—who now looked twenty years younger—and headed back upstairs to her bedroom. Her room wasn't anything special, but it beat the grimy attic. At least she had a mattress in the bedroom, something she didn't have the privilege of when she got punished and had to sleep up there.

She went through her nightly routine of brushing her teeth, going to the bathroom, and brushing her hair. She was careful to avoid the sore spots on her head as she brushed. Kosa couldn't help looking at her scalp in the mirror, and the sight made her nauseous. The areas where hair had been ripped out weren't only red but leaking blood from the pores. She dabbed the sore patches with a facecloth, wincing at the touch. At least when she woke up, most of the hair would already have grown back. Whatever gift she had that helped Mother heal also helped her body heal quickly as well.

With one last glance at the mirror, Kosa turned off the bathroom light and went to bed. She could only hope that Mother found whatever she needed tomorrow to get back to normal. Whatever it took.

CHAPTER 11

Bryce Larson jumped out of his oversized bed and ran to the window. He pulled the curtain back and eagerly observed the sun rising behind the trees. His mother wouldn't appreciate him waking her too early to go on their hike, but he was too excited to wait much longer. From his vantage point, he could see the trail disappearing into the woods; he had to know where it went. The lake glistened in the background as sunshine burned through the early morning haze lifting off the water. He shut the curtain and walked over to his suitcase—still packed from the night before—and pulled out his clothes for the day. Before bed, his mom said they would need to dress in layers for the hike. For one, it would be cooler out at the start of the day, though the temperature was supposed to get warm enough to wear a short-sleeved shirt later on. She was also concerned about ticks, something they usually didn't have to worry about much, living closer to the city. But out here in the woods they were everywhere, or so his mother said, and Bryce could tell ticks spooked her from the way she talked about them.

Once he was dressed, he walked into the hallway, again taking in the massive size of the house. The ceiling was higher than any he'd ever seen. It was an open concept house, allowing him to see down to the living room from the second level as he stood at the banister and looked around. Some day he hoped to have enough money to buy a home like this. His dad worked hard, but the closet in Bryce's vacation room was bigger than his entire bedroom back home. He was really bummed his dad got sick before the trip; they had talked about going fishing in the lake, using the kayak, and so much more. Thank goodness his mom didn't get sick too and still offered to take them.

Bryce approached her bedroom door and nudged it open a crack. She was sound asleep, but he had to wake her. Excitement overtook him and he ran into the room and jumped on the bed.

"Mom! Time for the hike..."

"Bryce... Please let me sleep a little longer. Can't you go explore downstairs some more? Mom will be down in a few..." Heather said, then buried her head in the pillow.

"Mom, *please*! I've already looked around, and I'm all dressed, just the way you told me to!"

She let out a muffled sigh, then turned over to face him. He saw a smile cracking through the morning grogginess and knew he had her right where he wanted.

"Okay, okay... Let's go."

Heather sat up in bed and yawned. Bryce smelled her morning breath and scrunched up his face; the stinky yet familiar smell brought him comfort.

"Yeah, I know. I need to brush my teeth. In my defense, *you* woke *me* up; it's not my fault."

"It's okay. Do you think Mike will come with us?"

She laughed. "You never know with that one. Let's go ask him. I doubt he'll be thrilled to be woken up this early though. You know your brother. Stays up all hours of the night when he doesn't have a bedtime."

They walked down the hall to the room Mike occupied, and before Bryce could burst through the door, his mom put a hand on his chest to stop him.

"It's best if you let me wake him. He's a grump in the morning; don't need him taking it out on you, kiddo."

Bryce nodded and stood back.

His mom opened the door quietly and, even though it had only been one night, the scent of teenage boy wafted out, a mix of body odor and junk food. Bryce moved back and forth on the balls of his feet, anxious to get the day moving. From the hallway, all he could hear were muffled voices, but at least his brother wasn't snapping at their mom. Mike was usually nice enough to him, but Bryce wanted more of a relationship. He looked up to his big brother, but felt he was always annoying Mike.

When his mom came back to the door, she was visibly concerned.

"He's getting a fever. I think he caught what your father has. We may have to go home early, bud."

Bryce dropped his eyes to the floor, unable to feel anything but disappointment. He knew she was right, but it wasn't fair that he finally got to go somewhere cool only to have it ruined early. It was as if his mom could read his mind.

"How about we get this hike in first, then we can see how he's doing? He told us to go ahead and that he didn't want to get out of bed yet anyway."

Bryce lifted his head with a huge grin. "Okay! Maybe he's just tired and will feel better so we can stay?"

"Maybe..." She sounded less than confident. "Let's go pack up a bag and get out there before it's too hot."

Bryce was on the move as soon as she finished her sentence, taking the stairs two at a time. He couldn't believe he was finally going to see what was out in those woods.

Heather watched as her son took off ahead of her toward the trail. She was ready to pack up and head home before Mike got too sick. She played it off for Bryce like it might not be too bad, but this was exactly how her husband felt when it started. The longer they waited, the worse the poor kid would feel on their four-hour drive back home. When she saw the glossy eyes of Bryce looking away from her at the first mention of leaving early, she couldn't help herself. She had to do this for him. Give the kid an hour in the woods, allow him to burn off some of the energy before the long ride back home. She assumed the trail looped back around as the lake didn't allow for the woods to get too dense—at least to their left. If the trail went right, that might take a bit longer, but she'd just tell him they had to turn around.

"Don't go out of my sight! Bryce, do you hear me?"

"Yes, Mom!"

He dashed through the woods, acting as if he knew where he was going and had a destination that he couldn't be late for. She couldn't help but smile. Here they were, in this huge mansion of a house, and it was just the good old-fashioned outdoors that made him happy. Her husband would be proud of him. Heather picked up the pace to make sure Bryce didn't get lost on his own. That would be a hell of a way to end the trip. One kid in bed with the flu, the other lost somewhere in the woods with no idea how to survive. She wouldn't be getting any "mom of the year" awards if that were to happen. Not that she'd been the best to them in the first place. With the stress of her job, the forever growing pile of bills, and the arguments at home lately, she had trouble being present—even when she was in the same room with them. She often found herself wanting to escape, to leave work early and stop at a bar just to sneak in a few drinks while her family assumed she was still working. This trip was as much for her as it was for her kids. She needed to recharge.

Heather stopped walking to listen for Bryce. She didn't hear his footsteps crunching the dead leaves ahead of her anymore, and panic wrapped around her body like a cocoon.

"Bryce? Buddy! Where are you?"

He wasn't responding. Heather took off in a jog, hoping the trail didn't have any hidden divots for her to roll her ankle in. The problem was that Bryce had gone off the trail, but she wasn't sure which side he'd run to. She looked down at the dirt path, desperate to find footprints that might help her. *Who are you kidding? You aren't some hunter who knows the first fucking thing about tracking something*, she thought.

"Bryce!" she yelled, desperation in her voice echoing through the woods.

Shuffling in the trees to her right pulled her attention to that side of the forest. Heather urged herself to move, praying it was her son playing a trick on her. As she got closer, the scattering of leaves got louder.

"Bryce! Stop messing with me, this isn't funny!"

A squirrel darted up the side of a tree in front of her and she jumped back with a start. The momentary embarrassment of being spooked by a rodent quickly evaporated. Bryce was still missing. She struggled to maintain enough composure to continue searching, but she had no choice. Heather trekked deeper into the woods.

Bryce turned around, realizing he'd gone so far in that he couldn't see his mother anymore. She was going to be so mad at him. He didn't know why, but something pulled him to these woods, luring him deeper into the mass of trees, a voice in his head telling him to come see what was out here. It was an odd feeling, like someone tickling the inside of his brain. He shook it off, trying to focus on which direction he'd come from. It couldn't be that far out, could it? His legs were throbbing like he'd just run for miles, but had he? He tried to remember how long it had been, but his memory was clouded. *What the heck? Why can't I remember anything?* He wanted his mother.

"Mom? Mom!"

His heart rammed into his ribcage, threatening to break through. Sweat began to trickle down his forehead, whether it was from running or the fear sweeping over him, he had no idea. He turned and saw a figure off in the distance, under the shade of a large canopy. That had to be where he came from, his mom finally catching up. Bryce took off in a sprint, ignoring the burning muscles pulsating in his quads.

"Mom! I'm sorry! I didn't mean to go too far—"

He stopped. As he got closer, the figure became much clearer. It didn't look like his mom at all, but it was *definitely* a lady. A much older lady who was moving with a hunch. Most of her body was covered with a black blanket or jacket, but he could make out the outline of her face. From this distance, it reminded him of a melting candle, the wax slowly sliding down the side, except it was her facial features drooping down her skin. She looked sick. Bryce was raised to help the elderly; he spent a good amount of time every winter shoveling their neighbor's driveway because they were too old to take part in strenuous work. But he was also taught to avoid strangers, and this lady was sending off red flags, even from fifty yards out.

Instinct told him to turn in the opposite direction and run. Run as fast as he could and get away from whoever he was staring at. He was about to do just that—and then she spoke.

"Young man... Come help an old lady, would you? I'm afraid I've got myself lost out here and I may need help getting back to the trail..."

Her voice carried through the woods, thickly accented. She sounded nice. But whatever was wrong with her face, Bryce wasn't sure he wanted to get any closer to see more detail. What would Mike do right now? Would he help her? Or would he worry about getting himself to safety first? The lady slowly limped along, not leaving the shade. It was as if she knew her appearance would frighten him and wanted to stay hidden to avoid scaring him.

"I'm not supposed to talk with strangers. I can tell my mom you need help though..."

Her heavy breathing was getting louder, and he assumed she was getting closer to him... Then he looked down at his feet and realized *he* was the one getting closer. He was walking toward her without even realizing it. The woman was whispering to herself, though he couldn't quite hear what, but it sounded like a different language. Was she doing this to him? He tried to will himself to stop moving, planting his feet in the undisturbed soil.

"We can't be strangers if I introduce myself, right? My name is Marta. I live somewhere in the woods and my little girl is home alone. I need to get back to her..."

"You live in these woods and don't know where you are? That doesn't make sense... And aren't you too old to have a kid?" He immediately felt bad for asking it, but it was too late.

To his surprise, the old lady laughed.

"You're a smart one, young man. What's your name?"

After a moment of awkward silence, he responded, "Bryce."

"See? We aren't strangers anymore, *Bryce*. If you take me to your mother, we can all have lunch together and you can meet my little Kosa. She's about the same age as you."

"Kosa? That's a weird name." Again, he felt bad for saying something he shouldn't have. "I'm sorry, I just mean I haven't heard a name like that before."

Although he didn't feel like he was moving, the distance between them was shrinking. He was struck by a bout of dizziness and attempted to steady himself.

"It means *hair*..." she said.

Bryce furrowed his brow, confused. "What does?"

"Kosa... my Kosa has the most beautiful hair you'll ever see. And it's magic, can you believe that?"

Bryce's eyes lit up at the thought. Was this lady serious? Mike told him magic was fake, that the magic shows he watched on YouTube were all just an act. How could *hair* be magic? As if she could read his mind, the old lady—Marta—spoke.

"Would you like to see it?"

The way she said it... Her voice sent goosebumps scurrying across his body. He looked over his shoulder in the direction he'd come from, hoping his mom would be close behind by now. All he saw was an empty forest. He turned back to face the old lady—and screamed at the top of his lungs.

The woman was only a few feet away from him, now out of the shadow for the first time. Her eyes were completely black, fighting to hold themselves in her droopy sockets. She had the mouth of someone that looked like they chewed on rocks, and Bryce had a fleeting thought her mouth had to be in pain. Her foul breath would have made Bryce's eyes water had he not already been crying. But it wasn't just age. Marta's face had the appearance of roadkill after it had festered on the side of the highway for days.

Bryce attempted to scream once again, but before he could, the old lady wrapped her brittle hand over his mouth, her bony fingers clinging to his cheeks.

"Shhhh... No need to alarm the forest, isn't that right Bryce?"

She began chanting in a different language as Bryce tried to break free. His vision began to blur, her words taking hold of his body. He was terrified. But nothing showed on the outside, his body going limp, his eyes fighting to focus. Even listening was becoming a struggle as his ears began to clog, as though he'd quickly ascended a few hundred feet in the air. All he wanted was for his ears to pop to relieve the pressure. His entire body began to shut down. And then, as he fought to stay conscious, she spoke one last time.

"Let's go find your mother…"

CHAPTER 12

Kosa stared at the glass of water sitting on the floor next to her days' worth of food that Mother left her. Her throat was so dry, all she wanted was to take a large gulp and save the rest for later. The constant fear of having to go to the bathroom and having nowhere to go kept her from drinking most days. But today, she was beginning to think she wouldn't be able to help herself. She swallowed a dry mouthful of air, remaining focused on the water. It looked so quenching. She needed to do something to take her mind off the drink, so she got to her feet and walked toward the window.

After almost getting caught looking out the previous night, Kosa was extra careful to cling to the edges of the frame, peering out toward the woods. She had spent enough hours and days in this attic that it was becoming second nature to tell time based on where the sun was located. Right now, it remained high in the sky, letting her know there was still a long way to go before this day was over. Maybe it would be worth the gamble, take a sip and hope that Mother came home earlier today. Based on how Mother looked when she left the house this morning, that seemed highly unlikely. The improvement she'd shown the night before was almost completely reversed. Mother needed to get better soon, or Kosa worried she might fall ill. The aging process seemed to be much more unpredictable these days. What if the ritual was starting to have less of an effect? Then what? What would she do without Mother? As mean as she could be, she took care of Kosa. Fed her. Read to her. Taught her everything she knew about the awful world outside. If Kosa was forced to go outside and fend for herself, she worried she wouldn't make it a day.

Still, if she didn't drink soon, she thought she would pass out. The day might still have a way to go, but the heat rising in the house was already in full effect. While the house below remained cool to Mother's liking, the attic could become unbearably hot on summer days. When Mother was thinking more clearly, she would sometimes bring a fan up for Kosa to keep her as cool as possible. But she insisted that the window always remain closed. Not that Kosa could open it if she wanted to—it had been nailed shut. She closed her eyes and cried. After a minute, Kosa turned around to face the room again. The one good thing about the sun shining bright this time of day was that the attic was well lit, eliminating all the creepy shadows that seemed to watch her in the evening. She looked at Lennie and Mary on the floor and wiped a tear away with the back of her hand.

"Guys... I'm really thirsty. What should I do?"

Kosa couldn't handle it anymore. She marched over to the glass of water and swooped it up, almost dropping it as some of the early morning perspiration still slid down the glass surface. She didn't allow herself to think it over anymore, taking a big gulp of water and swallowing it down. She didn't care about the possible consequences. The cold liquid was the best thing she'd ever felt in her life. Tears of stress turned to joy as the icy sensation slid down into her tummy. She forced herself to stop drinking when half the glass remained—she wanted to make sure there was enough to go with her snack later.

Tom purred by the door, as if he wanted to let her know he was happy for her. As mean as the cat could be, Kosa still felt he cared for her. It was the other cats that stayed with Mother who were *really* mean to her. Kosa hadn't even cared to give them names and avoided being in the same room as them. They would hiss at her just for walking near them. And if she got close enough, they would even swipe at her. One time, when she was four, she ran toward one thinking it was Tom, and it clawed her across the face, leaving three long gashes down the side of her cheek. Instead of punishing the cat, Mother told Kosa she should have known better than to get the cat worked up.

Kosa held the glass to her forehead, pressing the slightly chilled drink to her face in hopes it would cool her off. She wiped away the strands of coppery hair that stuck to her face. Now that the water was working its way through her system, she felt a sudden resurgence in energy and decided she would look at one of the books she kept up in the attic to keep her busy on the long days. She grabbed a stack of books, prepared to narrow down to her final choice.

A muffled voice carried through the window from outside. Kosa jumped to her feet and again approached the window. If it was just Mother, she wouldn't be talking to herself. Tom got to his feet behind her and arched his back in a long stretch. He, too, was curious about who was disturbing their normal routine. Leaning against the wall, Kosa peered out, and sure enough, Mother was exiting the woods. Except, she wasn't alone. A little boy, close to Kosa's age, followed her. A funny sensation fluttered through Kosa's stomach at the sight of the kid. It had been so long since Mother brought a friend over to play with her. Suddenly, she couldn't help feeling self-conscious. What would she do with the boy? Would he like Lennie and Mary? Would Mother let him stay for dinner?

With them getting closer to the house, Kosa ran to her friends to warn them.

"Okay, guys. Mother brought a friend for us to play with! Be good, okay?"

She picked Lennie up, followed by Mary, and quickly went back to the window, holding her toys up to the glass.

"See? He's going to love you guys!"

Kosa was so excited; it was hard to contain it. She needed to try, though. Mother didn't like it when she got too hyper. She squeezed her toys tight and stood in place, waiting for Mother to call her downstairs to introduce herself. After months of only playing in solitude, Kosa was ready to make a new friend.

CHAPTER 13

Mike rolled over in bed with the unfortunate feeling of a fever consuming his body. He thought he noticed something in the back of his throat on the ride to the vacation home, but he didn't want to tell his mom and ruin the trip. While she thought he wanted nothing to do with her, the truth was he was looking forward to getting away from his friends for a bit. Everyone always warned him about the teenage years and how some kids moved on to new friends and lifestyles. He just never expected it to happen with his closest friend. He and Curtis had been inseparable during their elementary and middle school years, but now that they were entering high school, Curtis was a different kid. He even embarrassed Mike in front of others to look cool, spilling some of his biggest secrets—such as who he had a crush on, or the fact that he still played with action figures when nobody was looking. So, to say he was happy to get away for the weekend was an understatement.

Now, as he lay in bed, sweating through the clothes clinging to his clammy skin, he thought maybe he'd made a mistake telling his mom to go on the hike to make Bryce happy. He'd figured it would take longer to get to this stage of the illness, but ever since his mom woke him up, things had gone downhill in a hurry. His body throbbed with every movement. The inside of his head thumped like a stereo with the bass cranked up to full blast. Mike wasn't a little kid anymore, but right now all he wanted was his mom to get back and take care of him. His plan was to lie in bed until they were back, but his bladder had other plans. If he didn't get up to take a piss soon, he feared his bladder might explode. Every little movement exerted too much energy, getting to the bathroom might as well have been across town. He had no choice though.

Mike pumped himself up, taking a few deep breaths. Then, he rocked slightly in bed until he had enough momentum to sit up. Being upright brought on a whole new sensation, one of lightheadedness and nausea. His eyes began to water, tears trickling down his face and falling onto the already damp bed sheet. Mike wiped away the tears, blinking to try and clear his vision.

His mom had been kind enough to shut the curtains before she left the room, allowing him to remain shrouded in darkness to sleep away the morning. The digital clock on the nightstand was the only light, giving off a few feet of dull illumination. He looked at the clock and again wiped his eyes, thinking maybe his blurred vision was messing with him. But no, it really was almost dinner time. Bryce and his mom had left right after breakfast, before the sun had even risen fully. Maybe they were already back and letting him rest? Or it was possible his mom had already checked on him and he was so out of it from the fever that he didn't even realize it? That had to be it. There was no chance they went on a day-long hike. Bryce could barely walk to the bus stop without complaining, let alone go miles into the woods.

He got out of bed, grabbing hold of the nightstand to steady his balance. The throbbing in his skull intensified now that it wasn't permanently buried in a pillow. The bathroom was right down the hall, he just needed to make it there. There was no shame in sitting like a girl while he pissed. Curtis would've told all the popular kids if he knew, but he wasn't here to make Mike feel ashamed right now. *One step at a time. You can do it...* Mike moved toward the door with his body shaking from a wave of chills coming over him. He opened the door, relieved to see the bathroom was closer than he remembered. He moved as quickly as he could, pushing the bathroom door open and dropping his shorts before the door shut behind him.

The coolness of the toilet seat relaxed him as he let his bladder release. He'd held it so long that even once he finished, the internal pain only subsided slightly. He flushed the toilet and walked to the sink, turning the water ice cold before splashing it up on his face. The cold water provided a momentary relief to the heat burning through his core. Mike turned the sink off, prepared to exit and plop back into his bed. He wiped his hands on the towel next to the sink.

A shuffling noise came from the living room area. *They're finally home*, Mike thought.

"Mom? Can you come here? I'm not feeling so hot."

Hot is exactly what you're feeling, genius...

More movement from somewhere else in the house. It didn't sound like anyone was coming his way, though; it sounded like they were in the kitchen taking care of dishes. The clinking of silverware all but confirmed it.

"Mom!"

The house returned to silence, leading Mike to think maybe he was hearing things. Regardless, he'd used too much energy yelling for her. He needed to get back to bed, whether she was here or not. He walked out into the hallway, taking a quick glance toward the kitchen before he headed back to the bedroom. It was empty, but things looked out of place. Odds were that's just how his mom left it as they scrambled out of the house on their morning hike. Mike shook his head—immediately regretted it—and started walking down the hall, but then felt a cool draft sweeping down the narrow passage he stood in.

What the hell?

He turned back to look in the kitchen again, and that's when he noticed all the curtains drawn. His mother could have done that last night and just left them shut. But he knew his mom. The first thing she did in the morning was walk around and open curtains to allow the natural light to bring some energy into the house. And where the hell was that draft coming from?

Shadows sprawled across the walls like blotches of ink, shifting with the breeze. All except one shadow. It remained in place, the shape of a person standing still. Mike's heart began to pump so hard he could hear it thumping through his eardrums. He swallowed a mouthful of dry air.

"Mu...*Mom?*"

The shape didn't move.

Mike wiped his eyes, which had glossed over thanks to the fever. He blinked a few times, trying to adjust his vision once again, looking in the direction of the kitchen. The shadows were gone. The more he thought about it, the less sense it made that he'd even *seen* shadows to begin with. The curtains were closed, there was nothing to shine in and create them. This fever was messing with his damn head.

He ignored the constant breeze, assuming it was just the chills. It took every shred of energy he had left, but he made it back to the bedroom. He fell onto the bed, allowing the mattress to absorb him, and pulled the comforter over his body. Sleep immediately tried to force itself on him, but something about what had just happened in the hall bothered him. He knew he was being crazy, but the feeling was impossible to shake.

His throat hurt. His head was pounding. His body would have felt less pain had it been run over by a dump truck. Yet, he forced himself to stay awake, listening for anything else stirring in the house. Even though he didn't see anyone, he *sensed* them. *Where are you, Mom?* Had his mom truly been here, Bryce would be with her, and there was no way in hell Bryce could stay this quiet—even if his mother told him to keep it down to let Mike sleep.

It must have been someone else...

...sleep forced itself on Mike.

He awoke to another noise coming from the house. How long had he been out? With the curtains closed, he couldn't tell how much time had passed. He glanced at the clock... but it was blinking 12:00, over and over. *It's a sunny day, why would the damn power go out?* He thought.

The door was cracked open, but he didn't remember leaving it that way when he came back from the bathroom. Mike widened his eyes, and he focused his attention on the narrow slit looking into the hall. It remained mostly dark out there, but he let his eyes adjust and continued watching. He heard breathing on the other side of the door. This time, he didn't dare yell out to his mom. He remained as still as possible, holding his breath. Hoping it was just this bout of the flu kicking his ass. Movement slid by the small opening and Mike flinched. He swallowed a bolus of spit. The fever had constricted his throat, so swallowing caused a sharp, needle-like pain to stab there.

The door creaked open slightly, but there was still nothing visible in the hall. Mike wanted to scream; his sore throat be damned. He was about to do just that when a voice spoke from the other side of the door.

"Mikey? How you doing in there?"

It was his mom. She sounded different though, like she was reading from a teleprompter. He wanted to respond, but his voice was trapped in his chest, unwilling to come out.

"I'm going to come in now..."

The door opened wider; his mother's silhouette now visible with the little light the hallway provided. He let out a sigh of relief. After all this, it really had just been him losing his damn mind. The sight of her familiar shape instantly made him feel at ease. But where was Bryce? And why was she acting so strange?

"Mom? Is everything okay? Where's Bryce?"

She took another step forward, still too dark to see her clearly. "He's with a friend we met. Everything's fine. How are you feeling?"

"*Awful*... I definitely have what Dad has. Wait... You met a friend in the woods and let Bryce go with them by himself?"

Things didn't add up. She would never do something that stupid. She rarely even left Bryce at home with Mike while she ran to the store.

She took another step closer. And this time, she brought the chill with her. The temperature in the room dropped to an uncomfortable level. Mike pulled the blanket tighter, trying to stop his body trembling. His teeth chattered, sending rapid-fire shots of pain through his head. He squinted, trying to get a better look at his mom. Her hands were behind her back, her face staring down toward the floor, her hair hanging in front of her eyes to block her features.

"Mom... are you okay? You're acting weird..."

She lifted her head, finally revealing her face, and Mike was thankful he'd just released his bladder, or he would have done it right there in the bed. It was his mom all right, but her eyes were as black as the darkest corners of the world, two empty holes sucking him in. Mike whimpered, and squeezed the comforter even tighter, as if that would somehow protect him from the evil stalking toward him.

"She said... no loose ends... she said, we could all be together again," she whispered.

Her breath smelled of decay, like a sick animal had crawled into her mouth and died. She continued to whisper, saying things that didn't make any sense.

"What are you talking about, Mom?"

"Oh, Mikey... I'm so sorry. We had no choice..."

Heather Ann Larson took a final step closer to her son, now only a few inches from his bedside. She brought her hands where he could see them, and this time Mike *did* scream. She held a large steak knife in her trembling right hand. Blood poured from her left palm—apparently from squeezing the knife so tightly behind her back. He tried to move, but the bed was positioned against the wall, and he had nowhere else to go.

She wouldn't really do anything to him, would she? She was his mom; any second now she'd snap out of this trance. She stared at him with two dark shadows where her lovely brown eyes used to be. There was no life in them.

Heather raised the knife eye level, and then drove it down. Mike rolled out of the way just in time as the blade punctured the mattress and continued to penetrate until the handle met springs. Mike sat up and kicked at her, but the comforter was wrapped around his feet, and his body was sluggish and weak. The kick hardly fazed her. She grunted and pulled the blade free.

"Mom! Stop it! You're going to kill me!" Mike screamed, his early-stage puberty causing his voice to crack.

"No... No. Honey, I'm *saving* you."

She jumped on top of him, pinning him in place. He slapped at her arms, trying to break free, but it was no use. She again lifted the knife, this time not missing her target as she brought it down. Over and over, she stabbed into his midsection. Each time Heather ripped the blade out, blood sprayed across her face. Mike felt his body going numb. His mother stopped stabbing, but remained mounted on top of him, panting like a crazed lunatic. Mike was fading, unable to say anything. He wanted to ask her why. He wanted to ask if Bryce would be okay.

Instead, he let out muted choking sounds, and then watched as his mom lifted the blade to her own throat. He closed his eyes, urging his body to die before she did it, and the sound of the knife sliding across her jugular was the last thing Mike ever heard.

CHAPTER 14

"**M**y name's Kosa, what's yours?"

The boy stared at her without speaking, his mind wandering in his imagination. All the friends Mother brought home behaved like this at first. Mother said this was because they were shy. He was taking it all in, looking from the high ceilings all the way down to the wooden floors before moving to the window and staring out into the yard.

Mother had called Kosa downstairs when she got home, and Kosa was relieved to find the two mean cats absent. Tom was currently rubbing up against Mother's leg as she knelt to scratch under the cat's neck.

Marta pulled back her hood, and Kosa held in a gasp. Mother *hated* it when Kosa showed fear at her appearance. The ritual seemed to be helping less and less each night. She feared if they didn't figure something out soon, Mother would fall to pieces in front of her one of these days. The skin—if that's what she could call it—sagged on her cheeks, displaying the raw area usually covered by a bottom eyelid. Her breathing was labored from crouching too long, so she got to her feet and smiled at Kosa. Just looking at her diseased mouth made Kosa's teeth hurt. Mother was in a real bad way.

"Kosa... This is Bryce. He's a nice young man who wants to play with you for a while... What do you say?"

Kosa had nodded excitedly but now she was losing some of the joy. Bryce was still staring out the window, lost in his thoughts. Why did they all act like this? When she was shy that's not how *she* was around people. Not that she got to see many people. There was so much to show him in such little time. She knew that before dinner time, Mother would take Bryce back to his family and she'd be alone again.

"Wanna come see my toys?" she asked.

The boy blinked, snapping out of his fog and looked at her. "Yeah... that sounds fun."

He said it *sounded* fun, but he didn't look like he was having fun. Did she say something wrong?

Their eyes were always black like Mother's. She needed to try and make him happy; she didn't want to lose a new friend.

"My favorite toys are Lennie and Mary. I'll share them with you! Usually, I have to stay in the attic, but when I have a friend over, Mother lets me play in the Big Room..."

"Kosa! Don't talk the boy's ear off. Go play. I'll call you when it's time for him to leave," Mother said.

"Okay! Let's go. You can use Lennie first..."

She sped down the hall, briefly looking back over her shoulder to make sure he was following. The start of a smile was forming on the boy's mouth, and it sent butterflies fluttering inside Kosa's stomach. It had been so long since she had a friend over, she couldn't believe it was really happening. They rounded a corner and came to a large room with an open floor plan. She'd thought ahead and brought the toys down from the attic when Mother called her. The toys still sat in the middle of the spacious floor, waiting to be played with.

Kosa picked up Lennie and handed him to Bryce. She waited for his reaction, hoping he would find Lennie as cool as she did. He looked confused. As he investigated the toy, she could have sworn his black eyes changed color slightly, the black fading around the edges to reveal some of the white like she had in her own eyes.

"Is this a... *bone*?" he asked, holding it out away from his body like it was about to infect him.

"Yes! It came from an animal Mother found in the woods. She cleaned it and let me have it..."

The silence that followed killed her. Did he think she was weird? Had he even seen Lennie's face? She worked so hard on it during arts and craft time.

Bryce smiled, this time it wasn't just the start of one, but a full-blown smile that spread across his entire face. "So cool! Did you put the face on it?"

"Yeah! He's named Lennie after my favorite book, *Of Mice And Men*. Have you read it?"

He shook his head. "No... But I've heard of it. My brother had to read it for school."

School. Mother told her about it when another one of her friends mentioned it before. She said that Kosa would learn everything she needed to know about the world from her, and that would be better than any school could ever teach her. Mother said they liked to fill kids' minds with filth and false truths, leading them to a future where they'd serve no real purpose. Kosa didn't know what she meant by it, but she was so grateful she had Mother to teach her the real ways of living.

"You have a brother? What's his name?"

Bryce lifted his gaze from the bone and met her eyes. He looked confused. She noticed his eyes were completely black again.

"Brother? Oh... His name's Ma... Mike."

He was being shy again, like all the other friends. They always seemed to forget stuff when they were talking. Tom pranced into the room, his black fur giving off a shimmer as the sunlight hit it, the thin beam of light poking through the curtain. He sat in the corner, watching them.

"Is he nice? Can I pet him?" Bryce asked.

"Don't do that. He can be nice, but he claws me sometimes and it hurts. Not as much as the other kitties, but they usually stay with Mother. If you leave Tom alone, he'll leave you alone."

"Okay. So... What do you want to do? Play a game?"

The thought of a game excited her. She hadn't played a board game in so long. It was always her favorite, but Mother said children's games wouldn't make her any smarter, so she never played them with Kosa. The only time she got the chance to play was with friends.

"Wanna play Candy Land? I love it!" she said.

"Sure. My brother won't play games like that with me anymore, not since he got a PlayStation."

"What's a PlayStation? Like a room where you play all day?"

Bryce laughed, and Kosa felt her cheeks burn with embarrassment.

"No... it's video games, you play it on TV," he said.

"Oh. Mother doesn't own a television. She says they're bad for the brain."

Bryce scrunched his face up, but didn't say anything else about it, and Kosa was thankful to change the subject. She didn't want to come across as different or weird. She took advantage of the silence and walked over to a shelf with books and the few board games Mother got her. Candy Land had seen better days, but it still worked. She carefully unfolded the board and set it up on the floor, mindful not to accidentally rip the duct tape holding the four sections together. She set up four game pieces and smiled.

"Who are the other two for?" Bryce asked.

"Lennie and Mary! I always play against them."

If he found it unusual, he didn't say anything. Instead, Bryce sat down, ready to play. His obsidian eyes were glued to the board, and for the first time since his arrival, Kosa thought maybe he was coming out of his shell. The room was too dark for her to see the board clearly, so she got up and headed to the closest window. Bryce looked over to see what she was doing. She pulled back the curtain, letting a ray of sunshine blast into the dimly lit room.

Bryce screamed, immediately burying his face into his hands. Kosa looked back at him confused, thinking Tom must have swiped at him or something. He was kicking his feet in obvious pain.

"The light! Shut the curtain, please!"

Kosa did as he asked, pulling it shut quickly. The room returned to darkness, but Bryce was in a fetal position, panting like an out-of-shape dog. She felt awful, knowing she caused that much pain to someone.

"Sorry! I didn't know..."

He hesitantly lifted his face from his hands, and she noticed he'd been hurt enough to start crying. When he spotted her watching him, he wiped the tears away. She didn't know what to say. Her first day with a new friend in a long time and she was ruining it.

"It's okay, I don't know why that hurt so much. It was like being poked in the eyes over and over," he said, rubbing his eyes while he spoke.

"Do you still want to play with me?" she asked desperately.

"Sure. I really want to go back to my mom soon, though. I don't remember why she didn't come with us. I brought your mom back through the woods to meet my mom, and then I remember walking here. But why can't I remember saying bye to my mom?"

Kosa didn't know the answer, but before she could respond, a floorboard groaned behind them in the doorway.

"Your mom asked me to look after you while she went to check on your brother, Bryce. We'll head back to them soon, okay?" Mother said from the doorway.

Her voice startled Kosa, but she thought Bryce looked far more scared than he should have. Was he afraid of Mother? That didn't make sense. She could be mean to Kosa, but that was what Mother called "life lessons." Tough love. When she punished Kosa, it was to make her a stronger person. But Bryce had never seen that side of Mother. *Maybe he's just not used to being away from his family for so long*, Kosa thought. After a moment of silence, he nodded without a word and Mother left the doorway to let them be.

Over the next few hours, Kosa and Bryce played board games, cards, and colored in Kosa's coloring books. She noticed that after Mother spoke to them, he wasn't quite the same. He talked with Kosa, but his answers were short. His mind wandered again, off somewhere else. Kosa's internal clock was telling her their time was coming to an end soon, and it made her sad. Who knew the next time she would have a friend to play with besides Lennie and Mary? Part of her knew her toys didn't *really* talk back to her, but she liked to pretend they played games with her, read books with her, and kept her company all day when Mother was off tending to her chores.

As if on cue, the door opened slightly, and Kosa turned to see Mother's face peering through the small opening, watching them. She whispered something as she watched, like she always did at the end of playtime, and then Bryce stood up, his eyes going impossibly darker than they already were.

"I have to go home now..." he said, robotically.

Kosa knew better than to beg for more time, that Mother would punish her with a night in the attic if she didn't do as she was told. Without a word, she picked up the coloring books and walked them over to the shelf, putting them away. She turned back and Bryce was still standing in place, his posture stiff and awkward. His head slowly turned toward the door while his body remained rigid. Kosa wanted to cower in the corner at the sight of his soulless eyes. She followed his gaze, spotting the door now open fully, Mother standing in the opening. Her mother continued to whisper, raising her brittle finger like a rotting twig, and gestured for Bryce to come to her. He nodded and departed the play area without saying goodbye to Kosa.

"Kosa, go to the attic until I'm back, understand?" Mother demanded.

"Yes, Mother."

Kosa watched as Mother and Bryce walked out of sight. She wanted to cry. While Bryce wasn't the nicest of her friends, they still had fun for a few hours. She knew not to disobey Mother, however, so she grabbed Lennie and Mary and exited the Big Room. By the time she rounded the corner, Mother and Bryce were already gone. Kosa stopped at the foot of the stairs and looked up into the dark hallway above. Her heart sank as she ascended the stairs, mentally preparing herself for another day of isolation.

CHAPTER 15

The attic was getting darker by the minute, and Kosa knew nightfall was approaching. She hoped that Mother would be back soon, that Bryce made it back to his family safe and sound. Maybe someday she would even get to play with him again? Every time she said goodbye to a friend, she never saw them again. Mother said it was because the families in the area were always on vacation and didn't live there. That made sense, but she wished that for once one of the families would come back. She was so shy around new friends, and they around her, and half the time she could spend playing with them was wasted just trying to get the kids to open up.

The sky was extra dark as a storm approached. Kosa hated being stuck in the attic when it was raining, especially if thunder and lightning came with it. Mother insisted she was safe, but the sky sounded so loud, so *angry* when it stormed. As usual, Tom sat guard by the door, observing Kosa's every move. She still couldn't tell if he was watching out of pure curiosity, or if he was in fact keeping an eye on her. She knew it was silly, but she couldn't help thinking Mother communicated with the cats. The one time she questioned it, Mother said that was a ridiculous statement.

"Tom, why do we have to stay up here? I know you share secrets with Mother... Can't you persuade her to let us go downstairs? It's scary up here in the dark."

The cat didn't respond, instead licking his paw and plopping his head down upon it like a pillow, still watching her. Maybe he'd fall asleep, and she could sneak out? It's not like she would do anything bad. She would be extra careful to keep an eye out for Mother returning and run back upstairs before she came inside. The not-so-stupid cat would never give her that chance though, she knew it.

Kosa decided that would be her mission tonight, to watch Tom until he closed his eyes and try to sneak by him. Why couldn't she at least spend the days in her bedroom? Strangers wouldn't see her in there. Again, she knew not to question Mother's rules, but it didn't make any sense to her.

She sat below the window, leaning with her back against the wall. Lennie and Mary sat next to her, somehow making her feel safe. If Tom knew she was watching him, he'd stay extra alert, so she pretended she was tired and closed her eyes, hoping he thought she was taking a nap. It wouldn't be the first time; she often took naps in the attic to pass the hours.

She tried to see through her squinted eyes. Tom stood and arched his back, stretching his spine, then did a few circles in place and laid down, burying his face between his paws. Kosa knew better than to act right away, but she was so tempted. When she heard the soft purring snores coming from the cat, she slowly got to her feet, careful to avoid the floorboards that made the most noise. That was nearly impossible in the old attic. But luckily for her, her small body lacked the weight to really make them creak.

Kosa tiptoed around Tom, and right as she was about to pass him, the cat stopped purring. She looked down, but his eyes remained closed, no longer hidden in his paws. Instead, he continued to sleep with his head facing the door. She swallowed, realizing she'd been holding her breath the entire time. Carefully, Kosa grabbed the doorknob and turned it, hearing it click as it gradually opened a few inches. She glanced back down at Tom, only this time his eyes were open—and he was *watching* her. He bared his fangs and hissed, jumping to his feet. Kosa backed off, afraid of getting clawed.

"I'm sorry, Tom. I just... I just wanted to get out of the dark for a few minutes, I promise..."

Even her soft tone did nothing to defuse the cat's anger; his teeth were so white they almost gave off a glow in the dark room. She backed further from the door, then sat down in the middle of the floor and started crying. Why did she just do that? Every other time she'd tried to leave the room before Mother got home, it always ended badly. Not only did she risk getting a set of sharp claws swiped at her face, but Mother would find out and she would probably face punishment now. She buried her face in her knees and wept, hoping she was wrong about her likely punishment. A scuffling sound behind her pulled her out of her funk.

Kosa turned to see what the commotion was and noticed Jerry peeking his tiny little mouse head out of his hole. She imagined him coming out to check on her, to see if she was okay. What was more likely was that he wanted food. She wiped away the tears and smiled.

"Hi, Jerry. I don't have much for you today. Maybe tomorrow... Sorry."

The mouse came all the way out of the hole—the first time Kosa remembered him doing that in a long time—and began sniffing around for crumbs. She had been so focused on the mouse that she forgot about Tom. He darted by her, a black blur in the darkness as he attempted to pounce on the mouse. Instead, Jerry evaded the predator and skittered through the doorway out into the hall. Kosa was grateful she didn't shut the door after her failed escape, allowing the mouse to flee before Tom got him. Tom hissed and launched himself through Kosa's legs out into the hall after the mouse. She heard the thumping of his feet pattering down the stairs, his customary grace now forgotten as he sought out his nighttime snack.

The room returned to silence and the darkness of the night. With the door now open wide, the faint light of the hall tried to force its way into the tar-black shadows surrounding her.

Kosa had to stop Tom from hurting Jerry. She ran to the hall and took the stairs two at a time, reaching the second floor. Glancing around, she didn't see the cat anywhere, nor where he could have gone as all the doors were closed. That meant he must have gone down to the first floor.

A crack of thunder almost made Kosa's heart burst through her chest. She looked to the window and saw the storm had arrived, and the rain was coming down aggressively. Maybe the only silver-lining to chasing after Tom was the fact that she wasn't in the attic when the storm decided to rip through the area. She shook her head and moved down to the first floor.

"Tom? Where are you?"

Kosa approached the hallway, the dull light making it far more difficult to see than it had any right to. She stopped to listen, hoping she would hear Tom moving through the house, or hissing at his prey. Instead, she heard what sounded like someone moaning. The noise was muffled, coming from somewhere deeper in the vast mansion. She considered running back to the attic and letting Jerry fend for himself. If she wasn't so scared, she would have laughed at the thought of going *back* to the attic for safety.

A flash of lightning momentarily lit the hallway. In that brief second, she noticed a door up ahead slightly ajar. It was the door to the basement. Mother had never allowed her down there, it was forbidden. Not that she wanted to go somewhere even *darker* than the attic anyway. The moaning returned, and it was coming from the opening. It could be Tom trying to scare the mouse. But the noise sounded like pain, not the feline trying to intimidate the smaller rodent. Kosa's breath came in short, rapid bursts as she approached the door. She looked over her shoulder, making sure Mother wasn't following—she had a habit of appearing out of nowhere. When Kosa had determined it was clear, she reached out for the basement door.

A crack of thunder echoed through the house, startling her again. Kosa stifled a scream, taking a deep breath to try and calm herself. Jerry better be grateful that she'd put herself through something like this to save him. She pushed the door open, revealing an infinite darkness in front of her. *No way...* She wasn't about to go down there with no light. She reached into the darkness, feeling around for a light switch. A sudden thought that something was waiting out of sight, ready to grab her arm and pull her in, drove her to feel around much quicker. Finally, the familiar shape of a switch met her hand, and she flicked it up. At first, nothing happened, but then a tick-tick-ticking noise sounded off, a dim light flickering on below.

The moaning got louder with the light coming on. While it helped brighten the stairs slightly, the bulb was far too weak to provide much more than the outlines of objects below. The floor was still mostly dark, but she could at least see enough to move without thinking she was walking into an empty void. She stepped down the first of the stairs.

"Tom? Is that you?"

More moaning...

Kosa moved to the next step, then the next. Each one brought on a new sense of fear, but she had to try and save Jerry. The poor mouse was only trying to look for food when Tom scared the critter to death. As she descended, more of the room came into view. She'd always wondered what was down here, what Mother did when she spent so much time underneath the house. The dark space was lined with bookshelves, the tomes far bigger than the ones she read with Mother at story time. There were glass vials and jars, full of odd colored liquids. She stopped at the bottom step, debating internally whether she wanted to go any further, or turn around and run back upstairs.

The light continued to flicker sporadically, providing the room with a strobe effect. It was a struggle to see more than a few feet. She realized it wasn't just one big room, but an entire floor plan. There were multiple doors, all of them shut, which she assumed led to more rooms.

What was this stuff? The room was huge, at least what she could see of it. There was no sign of Tom, nor the source of the noises she'd heard at the top of the stairs. The only sound was the random ticking of the light bulb flickering on and off. On the plus side, being down here helped to block out the ferocious storm outside. That didn't make her feel much better.

"Tom?" she whispered.

Somewhere in the shadows, Tom meowed. Kosa's posture stiffened. The sound of the cat scared her when she thought it would ease her concern. He meowed again, but she still couldn't get a grasp on where he was. The light flickered again, the dimness temporarily brightening. Tom's outline appeared in the corner of the room. She approached him, calling his name calmly—much calmer than she actually felt inside. He was hunched over something. Her heart sank when she realized it must be Jerry, that he had finally caught the mouse after all these years and was feasting on him.

Please don't let it be the mouse... Please...

She attempted to shoo Tom away, even though whatever sat in front of him wasn't moving. If it was in fact Jerry, she was too late. The lightbulb flickered once more, darkening. Kosa could no longer see what Tom was doing, nor what he had in front of him.

"Shoo, Tom! Get away from him!"

She swiped her hand in the air, hoping that would scare him off. Instead, he hissed at her, unwilling to budge. She saw the outline of the cat's head lower, then heard him slurping and chewing on the meat. *Poor Jerry...* Down here, the moaning sounded different to her though. Instead of pain, the cat sounded like he was full of joy while devouring his meal.

Again, the lightbulb flickered, bringing the room back to semi-visibility.

Now that she was close enough, Kosa got her first good look at the pile in front of Tom. The shape was a similar size to a mouse, but it looked like a slab of marinated meat in red paint. The copper scent she'd become familiar with as blood hit her nostrils, forcing Kosa to gag. Tom picked up the last piece of meat and pierced it with his sharp incisors, shredding it into smaller pieces.

"Oh, Tom... What is—"

A pained moan came from further in the darkness up ahead.

Kosa squinted, and once her eyes adjusted, she realized there was another door on the far wall. It was closed, but the noise was coming from behind it. She now understood the sounds coming from Tom were not what she heard upstairs.

This was.

She walked past the cat, who ignored her and continued scarfing down his meal. Now that she knew the door was there, she couldn't believe she missed it until now. Multiple locks lined the doorframe above her reach, but as she inspected them, she noticed they were all unlocked. Why would Mother keep all these locks here? What was she trying to hide? While it was hard to see in the back corner of this room, she noticed a light emanating from under the door of this secret room. It reminded her of the fireplace they sat in front of during story time.

Something thumped behind the door. She froze, too terrified to do anything. If it was Mother, Kosa would be in deep trouble. An uneasy feeling sank into the pit of her stomach, but curiosity pushed her forward. She knew if Tom hadn't been so focused on whatever he was eating that he'd try to stop her. With trepidation, she opened the door and stepped forward. There was indeed a fire, fed by large logs, a metal pot hanging above the flames. A tall, brick chimney went up through the ceiling. The pungent scent of seasoning invaded her senses. That scent was nothing new to Kosa, as Mother used it in everything she cooked.

Kosa took in the new scene. More jars lined the old, rickety shelves. They looked as if they would collapse from a simple touch. The shelves below the jars were cluttered with something she couldn't identify. She walked to the second shelf, and as she approached it, she felt sick to her stomach. Piles of bones filled the space. Some were big, some small, but the entire shelf was loaded with them. She lifted one, observing its features and thinking it looked very similar to Lennie. How many animals had Mother found in the woods? She set it back in its place and moved down the line—and stopped in her tracks. In the far back corner on the shelf of bones, a face stared back at her from the darkness. Kosa screamed and fell back, landing on her bottom. The floor's surface was made of compact dirt, giving off a stale earthy smell. She got back to her feet and stared at the face but not daring to get any closer.

It wasn't a face... it was a skull. What looked like a *human* skull.

She threw her dirty hand over her mouth, holding back more screams. Why did Mother have this stuff down here?

It was time to leave the basement before she was discovered. Kosa forced herself to walk back toward the door when she heard a babbling murmur behind her. She shot around and looked for the source.

It was coming from the fireplace.

Kosa's muscles softened to jelly. She grabbed hold of the shelf to stop herself from collapsing. She wished she'd never come down here. The murmuring didn't stop. Instead, it got louder. The thumping sound returned as well. The hope that it was just the fire throwing off some strange noises in the tight space evaporated when she spotted a shadow inside the chimney, above the flames.

Something was floating above the boiling pot.

Before she realized what she was doing, she was a few feet closer to the chimney, subconsciously preparing herself to look up through the opening and see what was producing the sounds. She leaned in, careful not to let the flames get too close, and looked up the chimney.

The charred, blackened body of Bryce swayed back and forth, hanging by the feet over the fire. His body slowly spun until his unrecognizable face stared back at her. She thought he was dead, and then he blinked, forcing sounds out of his shredded mouth. The low moans transitioned to an ear-piercing squeal. It was so loud that she didn't hear the movement behind her.

"Huncut... glupa djevojcica!" Mother screamed from the doorway.

Kosa whirled around, seeing the fragile old woman in the opening, her black cloak giving her the appearance of a floating head in the shadows. Blood painted her mouth and chin, filling her brown teeth with the shade of crimson.

"Mother... I'm sorry! I came after Tom—"

"Enough of your excuses! You know never to come down here. Come..."

Kosa knew better than to hesitate. She walked toward Mother, each step twisting the uneasy feeling inside tighter. Mother's hand shot out of the darkness and grabbed her by the hair. The snarl spread across her face was unlike any Kosa had ever seen before. The glow of the fire brought out the worst features of the old woman, and Kosa knew she'd be having nightmares tonight. She dragged Kosa through the doorway, back to the main room of the basement.

"It's time you learned what real punishment is, little girl..." She said it calmly, but that somehow made it even worse than when she yelled. The tone made Kosa feel as if thousands of invisible spiders were crawling across her skin.

As Mother dragged her toward the stairs, Kosa risked a glance back toward the hidden room they'd just left. The screams from the fireplace continued, and it was the worst thing Kosa had ever heard. Bryce was *suffering*. And in that moment, she knew that she'd probably be making similar sounds shortly.

PART III
VISITORS
10 YEARS LATER

CHAPTER 16

Ian Warner slammed his cellphone on the nightstand and sat on the edge of his bed. He couldn't believe it'd been three months since his wife died and the police still had no answers. He'd spent hours of each day obsessing over the case, telling them there was no way his Chelsea would've killed herself. They seemed content to chalk it up to suicide—even when there had been zero signs of any mental health issues or strain on their relationship. Ian knew they were just doing their job when they looked into his background, but it didn't help the accusation feel any less personal. He felt that maybe he was the only one in the world that gave a shit about her, that nobody else felt a desire to get to the bottom of it. Even her parents had resigned themselves to settling on suicide.

He thought over the conversation he had just finished with the chief of police in charge of the case. It made his blood boil. That smug prick treated Ian like just another desperate spouse trying to get answers to a phantom murder that never happened. Ian could have handled himself better, but the chat ended with him telling Chief Roberts to go eat another fucking donut.

"Fuck!" he yelled to the empty room.

His dog Scooter pranced into the doorway with his jingling dog tag, making sure his owner was okay. The beagle-terrier mix tilted his head, watching Ian for instruction. His black and white fur reminded Ian of a cow, but his nephew said he looked like Snoopy. Snoopy and Master Splinter from *Teenage Mutant Ninja Turtles*. Ian thought it was an apt comparison, especially for a nine-year-old to make. The dog had wiry fur and a face covered in a bushy white beard. Scooter sat—obedient as always—watching Ian's every move.

"Sorry, buddy. I'm just frustrated, is all. You want a treat?"

Scooter's tail whipped back and forth, fanning the area behind him and blowing old fast-food wrappers across the floor. He ran to the bedside and started licking his chops. Ian grabbed the bag of treats he kept in his nightstand and pulled one from the bag. Before he could even instruct the dog to sit, Scooter plopped his bottom on the carpet and sat erect, waiting for his next instruction. Ian couldn't help but surrender a smile, it was as if the dog knew how to cheer him up.

"Paw..."

Scooter lifted his white paw and placed it in Ian's hand.

"Good doggy. Here you go." He held the little bone-shaped treat out, and Scooter nabbed it from his hand, careful not to bite his master. He crunched it in his mouth and swallowed it down, then went back to his sitting position waiting for another.

"Easy does it, chunk. The vet says I need to watch it with your weight. No more."

Scooter whimpered, instinctively giving Ian the puppy-dog eyes that he knew would land him another snack.

Ian laughed and shook his head. "You little son of a bitch, how can I say no to you?"

Scooter's tail sped up when he saw the hand going for the treats again.

"Okay, *dooown*..."

The dog dropped low to the floor, making sure his belly was completely touching the carpet like he was taught. Ian tossed another treat to him.

"Good boy!" Ian said, then got up from the bed and scratched the top of his dog's head while walking into the bathroom.

He looked in the mirror, and even with the light off, his appearance disgusted him. Ever since Chelsea died, Ian had really let himself go. Too depressed to cook any meals, too lazy to clean the house. Personal hygiene had taken a backseat to obsessing over his wife's mysterious death. The local police had become quite acquainted with him over the last couple of months, and not in a good way. While they should've been investigating her case, they decided to take the easy path. Why waste the time and resources when an easy answer was handed to them? But he knew better. And he'd stop at nothing until he found out what happened to her.

Every single night, Ian relived the phone call he received, letting him know they had discovered Chelsea on a hiking trail with her throat slit. He'd been home, watching the Patriots game, polishing off his fourth beer when his cell rang. She always tried getting him to go on hikes, especially during the fall when the foliage of New Hampshire was booming. What most people in the neighboring states had to drive three hours in traffic to experience, all they had to do was take a quick ten-minute drive to the mountains. When she didn't come right home, he'd assumed she decided to take a longer walk along the trails and enjoy the nice weather. The phrase "you know what they say about assuming" never felt so true.

He took a piss and brushed his teeth, not bothering to shower. There was no use when he knew it would just be another day spent sitting in the dark house, trying to take his mind off the misery festering inside. Scooter followed him down the hall, curious what the day might bring—likely eager to get a walk in. Ian opened the refrigerator and was greeted with the scent of week-old Chinese food. He sighed and shut the fridge, then grabbed a glass and filled it with sink water. After swallowing two Advil, he looked to Scooter sitting by the door. The dog nudged his leash hanging from the hook where Ian kept his car keys.

"I know, I know. You wanna go for a walk?"

Again, the dog had trouble holding in his excitement, pacing in front of the door while he impatiently waited for Ian to get his boots on. As Ian went to grab the leash, his cellphone rang. He checked the ID and ground his teeth, not really in the mood to talk with his sister. Every day, she checked in on him to see how he was doing. She meant well, but if she asked him to come stay with them one more time, he'd consider tossing the phone against the wall and completely breaking off communication from the outside world.

"Hi, Kristen... How are you?" He tried not to sound annoyed but knew there was only so much he could do to hide it.

"How you holding up today?"

"Do we really gotta do this every damn day, sis? I told you, I'm fine. One day at a time, right?"

"Ian... I know you. I can hear it in your voice. You need family around you right now, yet you keep shutting us all out. Let us help you, please?"

Ian closed his eyes and sighed into the phone. "For the last time, Kris... I'm not coming to stay with you guys, okay? I'm not about to put your whole family out just to try and make me feel better. I'm a big boy."

"You're not coming here; I know that by now. Which is why we're coming to you."

"What? Hell no, that's a terrible idea. My house is one notch above a fucking frat house right now. I don't need Sammy to see his uncle living like a bum. I've built up this image I need to live up to for the kid." He hoped his attempt at a joke would deflect her from noticing the audible anger in his tone.

"Oh please... I shared a room with you half my childhood, I've seen what you can do to a room. I wouldn't feel right staying in the house, anyway. So, I talked with Jack, and we agreed to take a winter vacation up your way and rented a house on the lake. The best of both worlds. I can see my big brother, all while not needing a hazmat suit to sleep in."

"You really wanna see me that bad, huh? To spend your hard-earned vacation time hanging around these parts? You do realize renting a house on the lake in the winter kinda defeats the purpose of having a lake house, right? That's just a damn tease to the kid. Shouldn't he be spending time with his friends? Shouldn't *you* be spending time with friends? What exactly do you think being around me will accomplish?"

"It's not up for debate, Ian. We already paid for the house. The bags are already packed. And believe it or not, we all like spending time with you. We'd like you to come to the lake house to celebrate Christmas with us. And that so-called image of yours is on the line—we already told Sammy his uncle was coming to hang with us. He's already packed his laser tag guns and everything," Kristen said.

Ian didn't respond, instead looking down at Scooter, who had now stopped pacing and sat at the door impatiently with his head tilted. He whimpered as soon as they locked eyes.

"I don't know... I can't leave Scooter here by himself, and I don't wanna drive back and forth."

"Nice try. You'd almost think I don't know my brother. I made sure the house allowed pets so you could bring your pup."

Ian rolled his eyes and looked at the ceiling. "Fine... But as soon as I sense you being all over-the-top lovey-dovey with me to cheer me up, I'm out of there. Got it?"

"Thank you! You'll be happy you did this, Ian. I need to go tell the boys I got you to agree. We'll be at the house in time for dinner if you can swing it?"

He really wanted to say no. But then he looked to the fridge and decided anything would be better than the sludge that used to identify as Lo Mein.

"Okay. I can only stay for the night, though; I still have to work next week, unlike the rest of the world."

"That's completely fine. Ian... I love you. Hang in there. See you soon, brother."

"Love you too, sis."

He ended the call and shook his head. *Hang in there*. Easier said than done. He threw on his jacket and winter hat, then hooked the leash to Scooter.

"Okay, pup. Let's get that walk in."

CHAPTER 17

Over the years, Kosa learned how to trick Tom. The cat was getting older, not as spry as he once was, and she was getting smarter with age. Now at sixteen years old, she could navigate her way around the house with ease on days she knew Mother would be gone for a while. She still had no desire to see the basement again, not after the incident that traumatized her as a little girl. It took years to push those memories to the back of her mind, to try and bury, as deep as she possibly could, what Mother told her after discovering her in the cooking room. But Kosa now spent a good part of her days out on the second-floor balcony, reading books as the sunlight beamed down on her beautiful red hair, enjoying her secret freedom. Today, it was a bit too cold to stay outside for very long, but she still felt the need to get some fresh air.

She stood at the balcony's edge, looking up at the sky and admiring the gray clouds that looked like crinkled tinfoil with the sun trying to poke through. It wasn't just the clouds that helped her sense the incoming storm, but the air itself blew gusts of wind that warned of precipitation. Kosa loved snowstorms and hoped it would start before Mother got home so she could enjoy the magnificence of it for a bit. She wrapped her blanket over her shoulders as another gust of frigid air blew through her.

The first flurry swam through the air, zigzagging around until it landed on her palm. A smile spread across her face as more white dots descended upon the backyard. The lawn was already covered in snow from the previous storm, and Kosa observed the footprints heading from the house to the woods beyond.

As beautiful as the snow was, the forest lining the property chilled her to the marrow far easier than any arctic breeze could. Even though it was the middle of the day, the trees still painted patches of blackness between them. Tall, white birch trees sprouted from the ground like ancient fossils towering over the property. Mother spent much of her time in those woods, and while Kosa was never quite sure what happened out there, she knew it was something that needed to be done. Mother had never let her down. The years of punishment and tough love weren't always easy, but Kosa was taught from the time she was a little girl just how important Mother's rules were. She also knew that as tough as it could be, time and time again she'd seen how truthful those rules really were. How *important* they were.

She was just happy that Mother's younger form had come back more often over the last few years. There were times where Kosa felt useless. Her main purpose in life was to help heal Mother, yet it hadn't been working properly for a very long time. Until her friend Bryce came along. After that, she noticed the ritual they partook in each night had a longer lasting effect. Mother no longer looked like she was on the verge of death. Kosa told her she was the most beautiful woman she'd ever seen, to which Marta smiled and said she had Kosa to thank for it. Compliments were hard to come by from Mother, so when she got them, it warmed her heart.

As Kosa got older, her friends remained younger. She'd asked Mother if she could bring friends more like her instead of little kids to play with, but Mother told her to stop being ungrateful and enjoy them. The sessions turned from playing with dolls and little kids' games to Kosa reading them books and teaching them how to play checkers. The inner child in her still enjoyed playing, and the teen girl in her loved nurturing them just as much. It was always sad to see them go, but there had been so many friends over the last few years it helped ease the letdown. Even knowing what Mother did to the children afterwards.

After she discovered Bryce hanging above the fire, Mother punished her a great deal. She'd spent two weeks in the attic with minimal food. But once her punishment was up, Marta sat her down to tell her the hard facts of what was going on, that the children were there to serve a single purpose, and that was to give them the power they needed. Over the last few years, Kosa had played with many children before handing them off to Mother for what would be the end of their lives. At first, Kosa struggled with the whole concept. To kill children and leave their families without their kids felt so cruel. But Mother made her realize it was all part of life. Just like a hunter bringing a meal home for their family.

It had been a while since anyone came to play with her. The last one was a little girl who reminded Kosa of herself when she was younger. It was bittersweet to see her go, knowing her inevitable demise. Mother said very few families went on vacation in October and November, so there weren't as many kids around to invite over.

But it was now the holidays, and Kosa stood a much greater chance of having some friends to keep her company soon. She just had to hope the storm didn't stop people from coming out this way.

The snow increased in intensity, now slicing through the air and quickly covering the floor of the balcony. Kosa kneeled and scooped up a handful of snow, admiring the beauty of it until it chilled her palm. She tossed it over the balcony to the lawn and turned to go inside.

Something shuffled in the forest, and Kosa paused, praying it wasn't Mother getting home early. If she caught Kosa out here, punishment would surely follow.

There it was again, movement in the trees. The tree line was at least fifty yards from the house, which made it difficult to see with any clarity, especially with the snow now falling much faster. She crouched below the wall of the balcony, hiding herself from view. She crawled to the wall and placed her face against it, peering through one of the thin slits where two boards met. Kosa knew she should just go inside and not risk it, but if there was an intruder, she wanted to know in advance so she could prepare.

Just when she thought maybe it was a trick of the forest—possibly branches swaying in the breeze—two tiny figures exited the woods, prancing onto the back lawn. Even with minimal visibility, Kosa recognized them. It was Marta's cats. The cats that she kept locked in a separate room because they were so vicious. Tom wasn't the nicest, but he at least left Kosa alone most of the time if she followed the rules. These two monsters would swipe at her just for getting close. Mother did nothing about it. She liked them ferocious, saying they would protect the house. She took them with her into the woods to help her hunt.

Seeing the cats meant Mother would be close behind, and Kosa needed to get inside immediately. She turned, prepared to crawl into the house, and then realized the snow-covered porch would leave a trail. If Mother came out here before the snow covered it again, she would see the prints and know Kosa had broken one of her rules. It wouldn't just be punishment that came next, Mother would make sure there was no way for her to ever get back out here while she was gone. Kosa couldn't live without her few minutes of freedom each day. Leaving the house had never been an option for her—it was too dangerous, according to Mother. To leave the property would expose Kosa to the real world and the dangers that waited "out there". She was far safer following the rules, staying in the house, and doing exactly what Mother said.

She crawled toward the door on the balcony, stopping every few feet to try to spread the snow over her path in hopes it would at least cover the trail enough until more snow piled on top. The distant meows started increasing in volume, warning Kosa the cats were getting closer to the house—and more importantly—*Mother* was getting closer to the house. When she made it to the door, she didn't dare glance over the side and see how close they were, and instead reached up and slowly turned the doorknob, pushing it open just enough to crawl through and then shut it softly. Would Mother hear her? Would her familiars? Her heart danced around in her chest as she got to her feet and hurried toward the stairs, praying she would go undetected.

Downstairs, she heard the back door open, followed by Mother walking in and speaking in Croatian to the cats. Kosa always wondered what Mother was saying when she spoke Croatian, but anytime she asked for Mother to teach her the language, Mother said it was nothing she needed to know.

Kosa got to the stairs leading to the attic and climbed them quickly, knowing they creaked more than any other spot in the house. It was almost as if Mother intentionally installed old boards that would alert her if Kosa tried to escape the attic. She knew that was a ridiculous thought, but Marta always seemed to be two steps ahead. Kosa reached the top step and opened the attic door to unwelcoming darkness. As she stepped inside and shut the door behind her, she leaned against it and closed her eyes, taking a deep breath she'd been holding since the balcony. *That was way too close.*

She opened her eyes...

...and locked gazes with Tom, who sat a few feet in front of her, watching the door. His human-like eyes narrowed, and then he slowly opened his mouth to reveal his awful teeth, which still somehow appeared much brighter than they should in such a dark space. He stood and walked toward her.

"Tom... Good kitty," she said, crouching down and reaching out to pet him.

He ignored her and kept coming. The cat hissed and stood on his back feet—an odd position for a cat—and swiped his claws across her face. Kosa screamed in pain and fell back against the closed door. She put her hand to her face out of instinct, pulling it away to see it covered in blood. Tom lifted his paw, prepared to strike again when Mother yelled from downstairs. His posture immediately changed from predator to a child-like pet at the sound of her voice—a friendly meow even escaped from his throat. The shift in mood disturbed Kosa. These cats would do anything for Mother, enforce any rules she put in place.

She wiped away more blood as it trickled down her cheek. A tear slid down to dilute the blood, but she tried to hold back the crying. She didn't want Mother to see her weak; it disgusted her to see Kosa acting like a pathetic child from the outside world. She got up and exited the room, preparing herself for her hair to be ripped from her scalp. Preparing to give Mother her strength.

CHAPTER 18

Ian pulled into the driveway of the address his sister had given him and put his car in park. The snow continued to fall at a steady clip, and he was thankful he'd left before it got too bad. According to the weatherman on the radio, it was supposed to continue into the night, bringing with it that magical looking Christmas that so many desired this time of year. He grabbed his bag and glanced toward the front of the house, seeing the bright colors of Christmas lights decorating the interior through the window. It didn't surprise him in the slightest to see the house his sister had rented already fully decorated for a short vacation getaway. He loved her to death, but it had always driven him nuts how seriously she took everything. There was no simple family retreat for her. Everything had to be done in a way that made it all a big spectacle.

He glanced at Scooter, who remained curled up on the backseat. He decided to hold off on waking the dog up. Then he looked back to the front of the house. For a moment, he just stood and watched as the family moved about inside, finishing their decorating. The thought came to just get back in the car and leave, go find a local tavern and drink his sorrows away. Then he saw his little nephew, the kid who looked up to him like some sort of superhero.

Ian knew Kristen was right. Sammy would be so excited to spend the holidays with his uncle. Every time they hung out together, they almost always left with new memories that would last a lifetime. He was a sweet kid who deserved the best in life, and considering Ian didn't have kids of his own, he viewed himself almost as a second dad to his nephew. It wasn't that he never wanted kids, but after years of trying, he and

Chelsea had given up, assuming it wasn't meant to be. If it happened, it happened, as the old saying went. But then Chelsea was gone—just like that, and they'd never get to try again. It all made his relationship with Sammy feel that much more important.

He marched through the deepening snow to the front porch. Before he could even knock, the door flew open.

"Uncle Ian! Thanks for coming!" Sammy shouted and squeezed Ian in a bear hug.

Ian fought back tears; he hadn't felt this much love since before Chelsea was gone.

"Hey punk, how's it going?"

"Good! I got my laser tag set for us to play with later, and Mom is making homemade pizza for dinner tonight. Then tomorrow morning we are going to do presents since you have to leave early," Sammy said, still smiling.

"Oh… I got just the gift for you," Ian whispered. He knelt to the boy's level, wanting this to be a secret between them. "It's going to drive your parents nuts." He winked and stood back up.

"I can't wait. Hey, where's Scooter?"

"He's sleeping in the car, I didn't wanna grab him until I got my stuff inside. Why don't you go wake him up?"

"Sounds good!" Sammy said, then ran down the stairs toward the car.

"Is that my big brother I hear whispering secrets to my son?"

Kristen appeared in the doorway, a phony frown on her face. Ian wasn't sure how many of those looks he could handle this weekend. She walked out the door and gave him a big hug, similar to the one her son had given him just seconds ago.

"Hey, sis. Thanks for having me. The place looks great."

"You know me. I couldn't rest until we got this place looking festive." She looked over his shoulder at her son running to the car. "Sammy don't go too close to the lake! That ice isn't safe enough to walk on yet." She turned her attention back to Ian. "This was all done within the last hour too!"

"Poor Jack. The guy probably just wants to relax, and you got him decorating his second house of the season."

"Oh, he knows who he married. Come inside, let's get you situated in the room you'll be staying in," she said.

They both turned to the driveway as laughter cut off their conversation. Sammy couldn't help himself as he watched Scooter try to navigate through the snow toward the house. The little dog could barely see over the fresh powder, so he hopped between Ian's previously formed footsteps to ease the burden on his aging body.

"That dog really does look like a giant rat," Kristen said quietly.

"Hey! Don't insult my dog, he looks perfect," Ian said with a smirk.

Sammy and Scooter finally made it to the porch, and then the dog stopped and shook his body aggressively, sending snow flying in every direction. That got another laugh out of Sammy. In that moment, Ian was happy he'd come to join them. It had been a while since he heard laughter or felt the pure joy Sammy let out so often. This weekend might not be so bad after all.

The snow continued to fall while they all sat at the table and ate Kristen's homemade pizza. One benefit of having a sister who was obsessive about everything she did was that she was an amazing cook. Ian thought there probably wasn't a pizza place within fifty miles that could make a pie as great as she just put together.

"This is delicious, Kristen. You been stalking Pinterest too much again?" Ian asked.

"Pinterest, YouTube, you name it. Your sister can't do anything halfway, always gotta be the best, am I right?" Jack wiped away pizza sauce from his long bushy beard. He looked part mountain man, and part GQ model, the latter of which likely came from Kristen trying to groom him into something he wasn't. But Ian had to give Jack credit. His sister could be a handful, but she always meant well, and it was clear that Jack understood that.

"I don't see either of you complaining about how much planning I put into it while you sit there scarfing it down!" she joked.

"Uncle Ian, can I give Scooter my crust?" Sammy asked.

Ian noticed the dog sitting next to Sammy's chair, eyeing the crust in his hand. That look told him the boy had likely already snuck some before asking. Scooter wasn't the type of dog to beg without being provoked first.

"Sure buddy, but please don't give him too much. Not unless you wanna be smelling dog farts all night. Believe me, you don't."

Sammy laughed and then held the crust out for the dog to eat, which he grabbed quickly and then paraded out of the kitchen into the living room to eat his new treat in privacy. They all ate in silence for a few minutes, watching the snow fall outside of the large floor-to-ceiling window along the dining room wall. The sun was now setting behind the storm, adding to the beauty of the image refracted on the glass.

"Man, you guys must have paid a fortune for this place, even for just a few nights. People would kill for this view," Ian said.

"Don't worry about that, we're just happy to have you here," Jack said.

Sammy swallowed his last bit of pizza, then, like so many children tend to do, decided to take over the conversation as if the adults weren't already in the middle of talking.

"Can we go play laser tag out in the snow now, Uncle Ian?"

Before he could answer, Kristen did it for him. "Why don't you go play with Scooter for a few, let the grownups catch up a bit, okay?"

Ian spotted the letdown in Sammy immediately.

"Don't worry, I'll be out there kicking your butt in no time. Just need to let this food settle for a few minutes. Why don't you go pick which gun you'll use? I'll be right out buddy," Ian said.

"Okay! I've been practicing all the time at home, though. Dad can't even beat me anymore," Sammy said, puffing his chest out with confidence.

Jack shook his head and chuckled. "Kid's developed quite the aim with those things..."

"I'll still take him down," Ian said, egging Sammy on.

"Hurry up and come! I can't wait to show you how good I am now!"

"Okay, okay, I'll be right there."

The answer seemed to satisfy Sammy, as he ran out to the living room. Ian couldn't help but smile. The smile quickly vanished when he glanced back at his sister and saw her watching him with a scrunched brow, like she just wanted to come over and sing a lullaby to him.

"Ian, how are you *really* doing? I know you hate me asking this stuff, but it's a bit concerning that you keep going after something that isn't there with Chelsea's death," Kristen said.

"Wow... Going right for the jugular, huh? Jesus, Kris. I told you I didn't want to come here and hear this crap. And the first chance you get Sammy out of sight you dive right into it?"

"I'm sorry. It's just... you know how much I love you. The police combed through that entire area where she was found, and there's no sign of foul play. Don't you think the issues of her not being able to have kids may have had a hidden effect on her that you didn't see on the surface?"

Ian bit the inside of his gums, holding in the rage beginning to fester inside. Not only did she bring up the one thing he asked her not to, but she had the fucking nerve to mention their struggles with infertility. The worst part of it was that exact thought had crossed his mind on many occasions. But Chelsea seemed like she was in a good place before her death. They had even started discussing the possibility of adopting. He took a deep breath, forcing the anger down.

"Listen... I know you're trying to help. But I'm telling you, she'd never do this. You know damn well that isn't the type of personality she had. She was a fighter, and she would keep fighting until she figured out a way for us to be parents. I also notice you didn't have any problems booking a house close to where she was found, huh?"

"Her body was found miles from here, Ian. I booked this house because it was close enough to you but far enough to give you space. I'm sorry if this place still reminds you of her, I didn't really think of that," Kristen said.

"Are you? Are you sorry, Kristen? I think if you were, you wouldn't be bringing her up right now. Just let me grieve in my own damn way."

Jack sat in silence, watching the siblings argue about something he didn't dare get involved with. A fleeting thought of feeling sorry for Jack passed through Ian's mind, but he was too pissed off to care much about it.

"Please try to understand, Ian. It's not grieving if you're obsessing over her death and trying to figure out what happened. That's just you not letting go—it's not grieving. I want you to grieve. And I want to help the way a sister is supposed to help in these situations. What I don't want is to see you continue doing this to yourself. It's not healthy…"

Ian's teeth began to hurt from clenching them so hard behind closed lips. He knew he needed to get away from the table before he said something he'd regret. If it wasn't for Sammy, he'd just get back in his car and drive home in the storm, even if that was an awful idea.

"That's enough, Kristen. I'm done talking about it. And if it gets brought up again, you can be the one to tell your son that you forced me to leave before he got to celebrate Christmas with me."

"Just let it be, babe," Jack said quietly.

Ian pushed his chair back, and the legs screeched as they dragged across the floor, making his sister jump. He didn't care though. He didn't give her the chance to respond or make eye contact, instead just turned his back and walked out to the living room to find Sammy sitting on the couch with Scooter curled up next to him as he watched something on the television. The laser tag guns sat in his lap.

"You ready, kid? Let's get your snow gear on and go have some fun."

The Christmas lights lining the fireplace blinked, bringing a new color—this time blue—to illuminate the living room. Sammy jumped to his feet, startling Scooter. The dog leapt off the couch and started howling toward the window, as if he was trying to scare off an invisible enemy. They both laughed, and Ian scratched the top of his dog's head.

"It's okay, pup. There're no bad guys out there, just an excited kid ready to get his butt kicked."

"Oh, it's on now!" Sammy said.

The boy threw his winter gear on with precision and was ready to go outside within a minute. He looked at his uncle with pure joy filling his eyes.

"Last one to find a hiding spot is a rotten egg!" Sammy yelled, and was out the door, running into the blistering storm.

The boy's bright orange winter jacket would make it difficult for him to find a great hiding spot—even with the blankets of snow falling. Ian threw his winter hat and gloves on, then slid his boots over his feet and tucked his pants in at the ankles, tying the laces tightly. He'd not thought to bring snow pants, if he even owned any that fit anymore. The last time he recalled using them was when he took Sammy sledding a few winters ago. He'd put on some weight since then, and then more after Chelsea's death.

He zipped up his jacket and went outside—Scooter in tow—shutting the door behind them. The arctic chill immediately slapped him in the face. *These cheap ass guns probably can't even detect each other with the snow blocking their range*, he thought.

"Let's go find him, boy. Go find Sammy!" he instructed his dog. Scooter darted toward the woods, leaping through the mounds of snow toward the darkness. Somehow, Ian hadn't noticed just how dense the forest was when he pulled in the driveway earlier. Sammy was a smart kid, hopefully smart enough to not go out too far into those woods with the visibility so poor.

"Sammy! Buddy! We haven't started yet..."

It was pointless, the wind blowing through the tightly spaced trees acted as a makeshift alarm, letting off a piercing whistle that most likely blocked out Ian's pleas. He checked over his gun, noticing for the first time that there was a light on top of the fake scope. He switched it on and let out a little laugh as the beam of light shone all the way to the forest's edge. *This shit's way more advanced than when I was kid...* Large, white flakes filled his field of vision, but he squinted through, following the tunnel of light as it bounced off the trees in front of him. As much as Ian hoped Sammy wouldn't go too far out here, it was the better alternative to the lake at the front of the house.

"Sam! I'm not playing until you get your ass out here! This isn't funny..."

Something felt off. He hadn't come out that long after the kid; how could he have lost him so quickly? And where the fuck were Kristen and

Jack? They had to have heard him yelling Sammy's name. Ian picked up the pace, closing the distance on the line of trees. His eyes flitted left to right, looking for any sign of his nephew, or his dog for that matter. Instead, he was only greeted with branches swaying back and forth in the wind. His heart hammered, the thought of losing his nephew in the woods scared the shit out of him. He entered the forest, looking to the ground for any footprints or signs of activity.

A branch cracked up ahead, and he jerked the gun up, aiming the light in the area of the sound. A blurred movement shot past the periphery of his illumination, and he quickly flashed the light in its direction. The figure was low and out of sight. Maybe Sammy was army crawling through the snow to remain hidden? Or it could be his dog, sniffing out the kid. He took off toward it, feeling the snow fill the inside of his boots, instantly soaking his socks.

"Scooter!"

At the sound of his voice, the animal stopped running and turned back toward Ian. Only the outline of its body was visible, but it was approximately Scooter's size. Ian continued walking toward it while letting his eyes scan some of the larger trees as he went, hoping to find his nephew pressed up against one. He brought his attention back toward Scooter—but the dog was no longer there.

"God damn it, Scooter. Come!"

A soft jingling sound came from behind Ian, and he immediately recognized it as the dog collar. Confused, he whipped around and saw his dog sprinting through the footprints to catch up to him. He kneeled and petted Scooter, who was panting after struggling to reach his master.

"If you were back there..."

Ian turned around wielding his light, and there it was. The shape he previously assumed was his dog, still watching him from a distance. *What the hell?* While he couldn't see it clearly, he could feel the animal's eyes locked onto him. Scooter walked to his side and spotted the animal for the first time. Instead of chasing after it, Ian felt his dog shaking as he leaned his weight against Ian's leg. Scooter let out a low growl and bared his teeth.

The animal remained frozen in place, its growls matching the dog's. Suddenly, it took off in a sprint. In motion, Ian realized he wasn't looking at a dog, but a large black cat. But something in its eyes terrified him.

Scooter took off after the cat before Ian could tell him to stay.

"Scooter! No! *Scooter*!"

For a moment, he stood in silence, listening for his dog. The strong gusts of wind continued to prevent hearing anything with clarity. It felt like an eternity, but eventually Scooter came trotting back to him, wagging his tail. He was clearly proud of chasing away what he considered a threat.

"Good dog... Now, let's go find my nephew—"

Ian looked down, spotting a red dot in the center of his chest. Before he realized what it was, the electronic sound of a fake laser blasted out from behind one of the larger trees in the distance. He looked up, aiming his light toward the tree, and spotted Sammy peering around the side with a wide smile.

"Gotcha!" he yelled.

"Dude! You scared me to death... Why didn't you come when I called you?" Ian asked, slightly agitated.

Sammy came running up to him laughing.

"I told you I'd win! I couldn't blow my cover, Uncle Ian. You know that. Besides, I heard you say a bad word. I won't tell my mom though." He smiled again.

Ian rubbed the top of his head. "Thanks buddy, appreciate that. Listen, I didn't realize how cold it was out here. What do you say we hold off on this game until tomorrow when the storm's done?"

"Okay... I guess it is kinda hard to see in this."

"Hey, did you see that cat? Thing was creepy as hell," Ian said.

"Yeah, it came up and started rubbing on my leg. I thought it was going to give away my spot. I hope it finds its home in this bad weather."

"It'll be fine. Cats are pretty smart. I thought Scooter was going to tear the thing to pieces though. Let's go have some hot cocoa, what do you say?"

"That sounds awesome!"

Sammy followed him out of the woods, walking toward the house as snow continued to fall at a forty-five-degree angle into their faces. Ian scanned the area, looking for the cat as they went. It was nowhere to be seen. But that didn't stop him from feeling like they were being watched. He tried to shake the feeling as they went inside.

CHAPTER 19

Kosa sat at the dinner table, slurping up her soup in silence. If Mother knew about her breaking the rule of leaving the attic, she showed no indication. Mother seemed to be in good spirits, and while she wasn't in her best health, her current condition was a far cry from when Kosa was a little girl and thought the old lady was on the verge of dying. She looked forty years younger, her hair no longer thin and scraggly, but black and full of life. Her eyes—which had been absent of any white space while she was at her worst—were now a beautiful blue, reminding Kosa of the pictures of the ocean she'd seen in a magazine Mother had given her. And then there was her skin, which previously sagged from her bones as if it was on the verge of melting off. Now, it was so smooth, so soft. Kosa couldn't help herself and had to say something.

"You're so beautiful, Mother. I love seeing you like this..."

Mother looked up from her soup, staring into Kosa's eyes for an awkward moment before speaking. "Thanks, my dear. That's so kind of you to say." And then she put her focus back on her bowl and continued eating quietly. Kosa didn't dare say anything else until spoken to; that was usually one of the rules she had to follow. Had she not just complimented Mother, there was a good chance she'd be facing consequences after dinner. Even with the compliment, that was *still* a possibility. Kosa dunked her spoon in her bowl, then filled her mouth with a hearty piece of meat along with the broth that tasted of spice and salt. The soup was extra spicy tonight, and she savored the flavor after starving for much of the day.

"Dear... I know you think you're in trouble for leaving the attic while I was gone. I know you're scared. But I need you to remember why it's so important to stay in there all day while I'm gone, trying to provide for us," Mother said, her eyes remaining on her bowl.

An uneasy feeling marinated with the soup in her stomach as she waited for what was next. Mother appeared to be in a good mood, but that could change in seconds if something triggered her.

"What do you think would happen if someone discovered you while I was gone? A beautiful young woman like yourself, just sitting here all alone? Do you think they would leave you alone? No. They would find you defenseless, and do awful things to you, Kosa. There's a reason I protect you from the outside world, dear. It's full of awful people who would take advantage of you, rape you, and then dispose of you in a ditch like a piece of litter."

Kosa's eyes began to burn, tears glossing over her vision.

"And if they didn't do that, they'd wonder why a young girl was home alone and start to question it. We don't need anyone snooping out here in our business. I've worked hard to make sure we don't need them to survive. I'm protecting you, girl. And the magic inside you. Don't you see? If they knew about your abilities, they'd want to pick and prod you, run tests on you, and likely lock you in a cage like some lab rat."

"I'm sorry, Mother," Kosa mumbled, afraid to speak any louder, or say any more.

"Being sorry wouldn't save your life. I know it can be boring up there all day in the attic, but it's the safest place for you to be. I wish I didn't have to leave you so much, Kosa. But if I didn't, we would have no food, no vegetables to plant out back. There are certain things I need to get from those people, even if I don't want to. But I sacrifice that so that you don't have to. You're too important..."

"I don't do anything to try and upset you, Mother. I know sometimes I make choices that get me in trouble, but all I ever want is to please you and make you proud. I... I just get so lonely up there all day. And it's too dark to read books most of the time because I have to stay away from the window. I wish we could spend more time together," she said, now sobbing.

"Dear... So do I. I'll tell you what. Soon, when I have time, we will put more up there for you to keep you busy. Maybe I can give you a reading light, so it remains hidden from outside but would allow you to read your books."

Kosa was hoping for more, but she knew better than to push it. She forced a smile, thankful that Mother was actually being nice right now. Younger Mother was much happier than Older Mother. That thought snapped her back to reality, and what still needed to be done tonight. Marta's transition to her old self was already starting, as it did every night. She needed what Kosa provided her, and soon. Kosa instinctively slowed down her eating, wanting dinner to last a bit longer. The pain she would endure tonight would help keep Mother healthy; what were a few more minutes of waiting? Mother had other thoughts. She lifted her bowl and slurped the rest of the soup dry, then stood from the table and went to the sink. She wouldn't wash the dishes though, that was Kosa's job. After setting the bowl in the sink, she turned around to face Kosa.

"Let's get on with the evening, shall we?" Her beautiful smile showed a hint of sadistic glee as she walked to Kosa.

"Yes, Mother…"

Kosa didn't finish her soup, her appetite now all but vanished. She put her bowl in the sink and followed Mother to the sitting area near the fireplace, which was already consuming a few logs. The crackling of timber would soothe most, but to Kosa it reminded her of pain. Her hair stood on end at the base of her neck, as if it was trying to escape her body and avoid what was about to happen. She sat in her rocking chair as tears welled up in the corners of her eyes. She prepared to sing "Mary Had a Little Lamb" in her head, for after all these years it was still her safety blanket in this moment. Most nights the pain would end before the song was done. Not tonight. Mother's good mood at the table shifted as they prepared for the ritual.

"I never said you wouldn't be punished, girl. You know the rules… and you broke them. This will be more painful than you're used to, and I will take my time. You will never disobey me again; do you understand me?"

Kosa didn't dare make eye contact with her. Instead, she continued to stare into the fire as the warmth began to burn her cheeks. "Yes, Mother. It won't happen again…"

"I know it won't. Because if it did, you would wish to experience what's about to happen again, rather than what I would do. Now... sit still."

Closing her eyes, Kosa began to hum her song, taking her mind off the pain. She felt those bony fingers wrapping strands of her red hair and pulling it tight.

"*Da mi moc... izlijeci me...*" Mother whispered. Kosa never learned what it meant, though she'd heard it whispered every night.

With a sudden force that jerked Kosa's head back, Mother tore a patch of hair from her scalp. The sensation was like a hundred needles stabbing into her head, and sent jolts of pain all the way to her brain. There was much more force behind the pulling tonight, just as Mother promised. Mother repeated her phrase, then tore more hair free. That familiar sound, of her hair being shoved into Mother's mouth and chewed, filled Kosa's ears. It reminded her of when Tom came in with a mouthful of grass that he ate from the back lawn—he would sit and start chewing at the air as the grass wrapped around his dry tongue, forcing him to gag.

That was the worst part about this. Mother almost always gagged while she swallowed the hair, but Kosa never had the heart to look and make sure she was okay. She wasn't sure she could handle seeing the red strands getting sucked up like spaghetti, the roots covered in bloody marinara sauce.

The ritual continued with a viciousness unlike any Kosa had ever known. Normally, Marta was grateful to be healed, to keep herself young. Tonight, however, it was almost as if the infliction of pain was more satisfying than the actual healing itself. Kosa openly sobbed, but if Mother heard it, she showed no sympathy. The crown of Kosa's head throbbed. She just wanted it to be over. Finally, after what felt like a lifetime, the act was done. She sat there and breathed deeply, attempting to regain her composure.

"Very good. I think you know to never cross me again, Kosa. If you've learned your lesson, we can go read a book together now."

The last thing Kosa wanted was to read a book with her mother. What she *really* wanted was to go to her room and bury her face in her pillow and cry. She bit down hard on her lip, tasting the coppery flavor of blood, then turned to face Mother—who was staring out of the closest window into the night. Kosa spotted one of the cats running across the driveway toward the front door. Mother had a wide smile cemented on her face as she watched the cat get closer.

"Dear... story time is going to have to wait. Mother has some business to tend to."

CHAPTER 20

Ian awoke in an unfamiliar bed with his shirt sticking to his sweaty skin. The dream he'd just had was one of the scariest he could ever recall having. It was already fading away with every second he remained awake, but he knew it had something to do with that damn cat he saw in the woods. At the time, he didn't think much of its strange stare, other than feeling slightly creeped out, but in the dream, it was as if there was a person imprisoned behind those eyes, trapped in the cat's body and watching him. He'd never had a cat before, but he knew for sure their eyes didn't normally look like they belonged to a person.

He shook off the fear and sat up in bed, looking out the window as the snow continued to fall from the dark sky above. It was coming down much slower now, a sign the storm was likely coming to an end. The room had a terrible draft, which he hadn't noticed earlier when coming to bed. He reached out toward the window, trying to feel for frigid air leaking in, but the window was sealed tight. The mixture of cold air and his sweat-dampened shirt sent a chill through him.

Stretching his legs, he realized Scooter was no longer at the foot of the bed sleeping. That wasn't like his dog, who never left the bed until he knew it was time to go out and relieve a night's worth of built-up piss. Ian squinted, using what light filtered in from the moon to try and look around the room for his dog. He clicked his tongue in an attempt to call Scooter without making too much noise.

When his eyes adjusted enough to realize his dog wasn't there, nerves kicked in. Scooter was like a kid to him. If anything happened to his pup, it would destroy him. He kicked the blankets off and got out of bed, the cold wrapping around his bare skin like a straitjacket.

Why the hell is it so cold?

Ian opened his door, which was already ajar—he didn't recall leaving it that way when he came to bed. He tiptoed down the hall, listening for Scooter. The bedroom doors that lined the hall were all shut, so he continued past them into the main area of the hallway, which overlooked the first floor. The excessive number of windows lining the dining area helped illuminate the downstairs landing in a blue hue. But he still couldn't see his dog anywhere. He picked up his speed now that he was past the bedrooms and took the stairs two at a time.

"Scooter!" he whispered aggressively.

If he thought it was cold in his bedroom, it was even worse downstairs. *Maybe the central heating isn't working?* That wouldn't explain the draft swirling around inside the house. His bare feet hit the kitchen tiles, and he thought sticking them in a mound of snow might be warmer. He stopped once again to listen. A low whimper was coming from near the back door around the corner. With it, Ian heard scratching, like an animal was trying to dig its way through the floor to get out. If that was Scooter, Ian had never heard him so frantic.

"Pup?" he whispered.

He approached the hallway leading to the back door with apprehension. The whimpering transitioned to low growls, the sound of the digging picking up speed. As Ian got closer to the end of the hall, the cold air became arctic. He rounded the corner, now coming face-to-face with the back door.

Scooter sat with his back to Ian, digging at the floorboards. The backdoor was wide open, allowing not only the cool air in, but a trail of snow, which blew across the floor. The dog kept digging, like he didn't even realize there were flurries of snow sticking to his body. He was in a trance, oblivious to Ian approaching.

"Scooter! What are you doing, boy?"

Nothing made sense—the growling, the door wide open, the continuous digging—but Ian needed to do something. He reached down and rubbed Scooter's back carefully, immediately pulling his hand back. The dog was shaking so hard that his body was vibrating. Even upon being touched, he still didn't acknowledge his owner.

Ian attempted to step around him and shut the door, and that's when he noticed a few things that were out of place. First, it wasn't the floorboard that Scooter was digging at; it was a symbol drawn *into* the floorboard. Second, there were multiple sets of footprints leading from the back porch out to the lawn, and from what he could tell, they led to the woods.

Scooter wasn't himself. He continued to claw at the wood so aggressively that blood seeped out of his claws. Ian wanted to stop Scooter, to comfort him, but he was afraid to touch the traumatized dog.

He gave Scooter a wide berth, circling around him and kneeling in the doorway to get a better look. The dog continued to growl at the symbol, his white paws now stained red. His normally energetic eyes were zoned in on the floor, completely black. It was as if someone had poisoned him—or *something*. The sound of his nails scraping along the wood sent a shiver down Ian's back.

"Scooter! Sit!"

To his surprise, the command worked, though Scooter still focused on the floor, transfixed by whatever this symbol was. Even in the faint light, Ian noticed Scooter rapidly inhaling and exhaling, his ribs visible one second, gone the next. Ian risked reaching out to touch his dog again. Scooter remained frozen in place, looking down. His audible growls had ceased, but they still festered deep within, a bullet in the chamber waiting to be let off. When Ian's hand got within a few inches, Scooter lashed out and bit.

"Fuck!" Ian yanked his hand back, but he held no ill will; Scooter wasn't doing it to hurt him. The dog was doing it to keep Ian's hand away. Whether he was protecting the symbol, or protecting Ian *from* the symbol, Ian couldn't tell.

The sound of his master in pain snapped Scooter out of his trance; he looked up at Ian, meeting his eyes. He cowered and whimpered, knowing he'd caused harm to the man who cared for him. His eyes were back to normal, hidden behind a bushy, furrowed brow.

"What happened?" Ian was asking himself as much as the dog.

Another sharp breeze blew, reminding Ian he hadn't shut the door. He stood and gave one last look at the footprints leading to the woods, wondering what the hell was going on. While Scooter wasn't a big dog, all dogs thought of themselves as protectors, and it wasn't like him not to howl through the house like a defective alarm system if there was any sign of an intruder. Yet, he hadn't made as much as a peep, other than growling at the drawing on the floor.

Ian shut the door, sealing the house from the chill. Before he could take a minute to put the pieces together, a scream jolted him out of his thoughts.

"Sammy! Sammy!" Kristen yelled from upstairs.

Ian took off in a sprint through the dark house toward the stairs. He dreaded what he was about to see. Because in that moment, he'd realized something about the footprints he saw going towards the woods.

They belonged to Sammy.

"Yes, Officer Roberts... Okay... Please, help us find our baby. Yes. Goodbye." Kristen sobbed.

Ian hated not knowing what was being said on the other end. What he hated even more was knowing it was Chief Roberts she was speaking to. He was the cop that led the investigation into Chelsea's death, who gave up on looking for any and all possible outcomes. Ian didn't exactly have much faith in the chief's ability to solve a case, especially finding a missing child.

As expected, when he got upstairs, he'd walked into a child's bedroom to find no child. Kristen and Jack tore through the house looking for their son, checking every closet, room, and vehicle. Ian attempted—and failed—multiple times to tell them about the footprints outside. They were so caught up in the moment, understandably panicking the longer they went without finding Sammy, that they couldn't hear what he had to say. When Kristen called 911, the dispatcher said they'd send someone out, and then a few moments later the phone rang and the prick Roberts was on the other end, trying to calm Ian's sister the way he tried to calm Ian when his wife died.

"What did he say?" Ian asked.

Kristen choked on her tears as she attempted to compose herself long enough to respond.

"He... He said he'd be right here and to not go anywhere. He asked if Sammy has issues with sleepwalking..."

"Does he?" Ian asked.

"No. The closest he's ever come to doing anything in his sleep is talking about pizza while he was dreaming. This isn't something normal for him," Jack said.

"When you screamed, I was downstairs looking for Scooter. Once I got down there, I spotted the back door wide open. I could swear I saw footprints going to the woods. To me, it makes sense if we go look for him out there since we know he's not in here. Doesn't that make more sense than sitting here doing nothing?" Ian asked.

"Sammy's afraid of the dark, he'd never go out there in the middle of the night alone, especially with his jacket still here," Kristen said, nodding toward the bright orange jacket in the corner of the room.

"I still think we should check. If you want to wait here for the police, Jack and I can go out and look for him—as best we can at least. Scooter can help try and sniff him out or something... Christ, I don't know. I just want to help."

It was as if his uncertainty brought the seriousness of the situation back to Kristen. She collapsed on the twin-sized bed her son should have been sound asleep on, crying uncontrollably. Jack sat next to her and tried to calm his wife. None of it made any sense. If Sammy was really afraid of the dark, and he left his jacket, why was the back door wide open? And why were there footprints going towards the woods? Not to mention the creepy-ass symbol drawn on the floor that appeared to have kept his dog in some sort of daze like a hypnotist swinging a pendulum.

Ian and Jack threw on their jackets and boots. Ian grabbed his cellphone from the counter and headed to the door. He understood his sister was in shock right now, but if they didn't act fast, there was a chance her son could get lost out in the woods—or worse—die in the frigid temperature. Scooter ran to Ian's side, his paws still stained red but ready to follow Ian wherever he went.

"Let's go find Sammy, okay boy?" he said to the dog.

"Ian... Thanks for trying to think with a clear head right now. I'm a mess. I appreciate you taking charge," Jack said.

Ian nodded and stepped out into the arctic breeze, the cold air suffocating. He turned his phone light on and aimed it toward the ground, following what was left of the footprints that had already started filling in with the dwindling storm and snowdrifts blowing horizontally across the fresh powder.

"I'll check this way, if you want to follow that path?" Jack said.

"Okay, let's get out there, we've already wasted too much time," Ian said, then realized how harsh that sounded. "We'll find your boy, Jack."

Without another word, Jack took off in the opposite direction, leaving Ian and Scooter to start their search.

"Sammy! Buddy!" Ian hollered as he stepped underneath the canopy of the woods.

The wind howled in the darkness surrounding him. Ian remembered earlier in the night—hard to think it was the same night—when he'd nervously searched these exact woods for Sammy. He had a tiny ounce of hope that maybe the boy was out here playing tricks again. But he knew better. The kid wouldn't do this to his parents, especially in the middle of the night, when they wouldn't even notice if he was gone. There was also the second set of prints going toward the woods that ate at Ian's nerves. It was like someone snuck in and took Sammy from the house without anyone else waking.

He continued deeper into the woods, focused on the ground, hoping the prints would lead him to Sammy. His boots crunched through the snow. It was a struggle, but Ian forced himself to concentrate on any other sounds or signs of his nephew. But outside of Jack randomly shouting his son's name in the background, all he heard was the *lack* of other sounds. Including his dog, whose collar usually jingled like a Salvation Army bell every time he moved. Ian looked back toward the entrance of the forest. Scooter sat at the edge, watching him from a distance.

"Scooter! Come on boy!" Ian yelled over the whipping wind.

The dog didn't move. Instead, he began to whimper, afraid to come any farther. Ian whistled, but all that did was provoke a more desperate cry from Scooter. It wasn't like him at all to not obey. When Ian and Chelsea had taken him to puppy training, the instructor constantly praised Scooter for being a quick learner and highly obedient. The dog being too frightened to even step foot in the forest sent an involuntary shiver through Ian. He wasn't alone out here, and he knew it. It wasn't just Sammy; it was whoever was *with* Sammy. The silhouette of his dog sat motionless in the dark like a statue.

The whimpering ceased, and after a momentary silence, Scooter began to growl. Even with the distance between them, Ian saw him baring his teeth toward the trees over Ian's shoulder. He didn't have a chance to calm his dog before the snap of a branch behind him jolted him upright. Ian shot around, staring at the area the noise came from.

"Sammy? Is that you, buddy?"

He asked the question that he already knew the answer to. It wasn't Sammy. The energy had been sucked from the air, as if pure evil lurked just beyond his line of sight. Ian ran in the direction of the noise. If it was something malicious, odds were it was linked to his missing nephew. Scooter began to howl, and Ian couldn't help but feel it was his dog trying to warn him to turn back, to leave whatever it was alone and return to safety. But he couldn't do that—not until he knew for sure that Sammy was safe.

He picked up speed, the cold air burning in his lungs with each deep inhale. The beam of light coming from his phone flashed around as his arm swung back and forth while running. One second, it focused on the ground, the next it was aimed at the treetops, repeating this movement over and over, while the rest of the world around him remained lathered in darkness.

As the light rose once more, a set of eyes reflected off the beam, crouched low behind a fallen tree up ahead. Ian came to a stop, attempting to point the light where he knew the eyes were just seconds before.

They were gone.

"Sammy! *Saaaamy!*"

He swept the light left to right, looking for any sign of whoever was just staring back at him. There was no fucking way it was a trick of the light; nor was it just eyes, there had been a head peering over the fallen tree, hiding from him. It sure as hell didn't look like a little boy's.

Ian was deep enough in the woods now that he no longer had the hint of light behind him from the moon reflecting off the fresh snow. He took a few deep breaths, trying to regain his composure, when suddenly the forest was lit up with flashing red and blue lights. Ian realized it was the police, finally arriving at the house. He didn't want to leave until he found Sammy, but he had a feeling he'd need help searching the area.

Ian scanned the forest one last time with his light, then hesitantly turned around and walked back towards the house. Scooter remained frozen in place, whining, until he saw Ian approaching. The dog got to his feet and began wagging his tail, excited his master was okay. Against his better judgment, Ian headed back, ready to tell them what he'd just seen.

When Ian and Jack returned, Chief Roberts was already talking with Kristen and taking notes. What the fuck could he possibly be writing down? The kid was missing and they needed to find him, it was as simple as that. Instead, the cop continued writing a novel—in handwriting he probably couldn't even read. Ian tried to force down the hatred he felt toward Roberts, knowing there was no way it could help their current situation. But God damn, every time he saw the cop's face, he couldn't help but want to punch his clichéd mustache off it. He also couldn't help thinking of Chelsea when he saw Roberts.

The old officer put the notepad in his pocket, looking up to see Ian for the first time. A glint of annoyance behind those eyes told Ian all he needed; Roberts wanted nothing to do with him.

"Mr. Warner... I'm sorry to hear about your nephew. I think we should search the perimeter tonight. Normally, we'd wait to see if the boy comes back. But given the conditions out there, and his age, I feel it's best to get out in front of this." He wiped his grey mustache with his right hand before sticking it out for Ian to shake.

Ian didn't acknowledge the hand, though he forced himself to keep his thoughts about Roberts private. His hatred for the cop wasn't important at the moment.

"We just went out and searched the area. There were prints heading from the back porch to the woods... but Sammy's prints weren't the only ones. Someone's with him. We're wasting time here. I thought I saw something right before you got here, but it disappeared when I chased after it."

Robert's bushy eyebrows wrinkled, and Ian wasn't sure if it was because he didn't believe Ian's story, or he was concerned.

"Okay. With the four of us, hopefully we can spread out and find him. I really don't want to see this go unresolved into the morning. Supposed to get down below ten degrees tonight..." Roberts said.

The dark bags under Robert's eyes reminded Ian that the cop had just drove out here in the middle of the night to come help them search in close to sub-zero temperatures. He decided he should probably cut the guy some slack for now.

Kristen finished getting her winter gear on and approached the conversation.

"Let's go now." Jack said, his voice cracking as he tried to hold it together. "I can't stand to think of my boy out there alone in the cold. He must be terrified,"

"He's never sleep-walked, or tried to run away, nothing like that. This is so unlike him, Officer. Please... find our son," Kristen said, wiping tears away.

Roberts didn't say anything, but nodded, as if that would make them feel any better. They all marched outside and for the third time that night, Ian approached the forest. Whatever he saw out there moments ago still lingered in his imagination. The thought of someone or something watching him from some hidden location made him sick. What kind of fucking monster got their rocks off by kidnapping an innocent child and watching as the family helplessly searched for him?

"Ian, you go that way." Roberts nodded in a direction Ian had yet to search. "I'll head over here, and the boy's parents can spread out between us. Don't be afraid to shout his name, over and over if you have to. But be sure to give enough time to listen for any reply, okay? If he's already been out here for a while, with no jacket for that matter, his responses may be feeble at best."

They all spread out, far enough apart that it was nearly impossible to see one another without shining their lights. Ian trudged through the thickening blanket of snow, his breath visible in the chilly air. Once again, the forest was eerily silent outside of the gusts of wind whipping between the trees. The branches, weighed down from the day's heavy snowfall, cast disturbing shadows in the moonlight. Against all hope, he prayed they found Sammy safe and sound, but he knew the longer this went on, the less likely it would be that the night would end the way any of them wanted it to. Kristen and Jack yelled out Sammy's name from somewhere in the woods. Their words seemed to vanish into the darkness, unanswered. Their flashlight beams crisscrossed between the trees, like some cheap laser show, while the branches reached out for them.

"Sammy! Answer me, buddy!" Ian yelled.

He felt helpless, like the forest was taunting them. He forced himself to push forward, determination driving him despite an uneasy dread that continued to creep up his spine. He listened intently for any sign of movement, voices, anything. That's when he heard a muffled, distant cry. Ian followed the sound, running through the dense snow with his heart thumping in his ears.

"Sammy!"

It had to be him. There was no other option. Ian's phone light tried to give him a clear path as he sprinted through the uneven terrain, but the snow-laden branches did everything they could to keep the light from reaching more than a few feet. His lungs hurt. His feet were beginning to numb from the severely frigid temperature. But none of that would matter if he found his nephew. These woods had already taken the person who meant the most to him; he wasn't about to let them take another. The others continued shouting out Sammy's name in the distance, but Ian tuned them out, putting all his focus on the cries he heard.

He stopped to catch his breath, wincing at the pain burning in his chest—and spotted a small figure huddled against a tree, crouched low and shivering. Ian forced his legs to move once more, closing in on the tiny frame that he knew had to be Sammy. A flood of relief hit him as he approached the child. But as he got closer, that relief washed away. It *was* Sammy, but as the light shone upon the child, it became clear that he might already have been too late.

"Sammy... hey bud. Can you hear me?" Ian asked, crouching close by him.

Sammy stared at the ground, his body shaking as his teeth clattered together. Ian ripped his jacket off, the chill instantly searing his exposed skin. *This poor boy*, Ian thought as he wrapped the jacket around Sammy. He aimed the light at his nephew's face, taking in the purple lips and pasty white skin. But that wasn't the worst of it. When Sammy looked up at him, his eyes were completely black, like someone had replaced them with giant black marbles.

Ian fell back, gasping. He dropped his phone, sending the forest to darkness. He felt around for it, shots of pain running through his fingers as they penetrated the snow.

"She's still out here..." Sammy whispered.

Ian froze. He thought back to the second set of footprints leading to the woods. Panic rose in his chest, and he frantically plowed his hand through the snow, feeling around for the phone.

"Who's still out here, buddy? Who was with you?"

At first, Sammy didn't speak, instead only letting out a strange sound that was either a cry or laughter. Then everything went silent; Sammy's posture stiffened. Ian finally felt the rectangular shape of his phone and pulled it from the snow, hoping it wasn't broken. The light was off. Ian flipped the phone and the home screen lit up. With numb fingers, he fumbled around on the screen to turn the light back on, trying to keep Sammy talking while he did it.

"Sammy, we're going to get you warm, okay? But you need to tell me who was with you, and where she went..."

He opened the light app, prepared to turn it on, but before he did, Sammy spoke from the darkness.

"The lady... The lady with the black eyes..."

If gooseflesh wasn't already scattered across Ian's arms, they were now covered. His words reminded him of Sammy's eyes, as well as the way Scooter looked when he was scratching at the floor. Ian turned the light back on, lifting it to meet Sammy's gaze, fully expecting to see those black holes staring back at him. Instead, it was the beautiful eyes the boy had inherited from his mother. Ian took a deep breath, relieved to see his nephew looking normal—as normal as someone could look after being out in the freezing temperatures, possibly for hours.

"What lady, Sammy?"

Sammy stared back, confused.

"What? Uncle Ian, how did I get out here? I'm so c-c-cold..."

"Oh, bud. Let's get you back to the house. Can you walk?"

The boy hesitantly got to his feet, and Ian noticed he was barefoot. *Holy shit.*

"Let me carry you. We'll get the fire nice and warm," Ian said, then picked up Sammy and started walking back toward the clearing. He realized he hadn't let everyone else know he'd found him.

"I found him! Kristen! Jack! I got Sammy!"

Determined footsteps pounded through the forest, headed in their direction.

She's still out here...

It wasn't just the words: it was the robotic tone Sammy delivered them in. Ian continued toward the clearing as the others drew closer. As he reached the edge of the forest, he heard his sister and Jack panting nearby. The pair came into view, with clouds of breath blasting out of their mouths. Kristen ran to them, grabbing Sammy and hugging him tight. Jack was close behind. Roberts, while he should've been in better shape than any of them considering his occupation, trailed far behind as he tried to catch up with the desperate parents. With his hands now free, Ian turned back to face the forest.

She's still out here...

"Sammy, what happened to you? Are you okay? Did you get hurt?" Kristen asked one rapid fire question after another, and clearly Jack saw the fog floating around his son's brain.

"Hon... Give the kid a minute. Let's get him inside where it's warm."

The family walked back toward the house, but Ian hung behind, waiting for Chief Roberts to reach him. When he did, Roberts was huffing far worse than any of the others. Ian noticed sweat glistening down his forehead, pooling in his thick, salt and pepper mustache and freezing before it reached his mouth.

"Where... where was he?" Roberts panted.

"Listen: I found him far out in the woods by himself—but he wasn't normal. He was talking gibberish about some lady out there with him."

"Is he okay?"

"Yeah. But what are we going to do about... whoever was out there with him?" Ian scanned the area for any sign of the black-eyed woman, but the woods were desolate.

"First thing we need to do is get out of this shit cold weather. I can't think straight with my damn ears feeling like they're about to fall off the side of my head."

Ian wouldn't argue with that. His arms were so cold it felt as if someone had painted his exposed skin with acid. He wished he'd thought of wearing a sweatshirt under his jacket instead of a short-sleeved shirt. They walked toward the house. Ian knew he should be happier that he found his nephew alive, but with each step away from the forest, he kept hearing those words over and over in his head.

She's still out here...

CHAPTER 21

Chief Roberts spent the better part of an hour searching the house for any evidence of an intruder. He checked every window, every door, and, as Ian expected, he concluded that there had been no intruder at all. There had been no forced entry, for a start. Sammy wasn't helping the situation with his testimony. Whether it be from shock or the possibility of him sleepwalking as Roberts suggested, Ian didn't know.

Ian's mind kept going back to the strange design drawn on the floor, and the second set of footprints going to the woods. But it was more than that. Beyond the things he could see, the things he *couldn't* see were eating at him. Someone was watching him in the woods. He felt it—hell, he saw it—the first time he'd gone to look for Sammy. There were just too many coincidences lining up for everything to be some random episode of sleepwalking.

After they had gotten back to the house, Kristen and Jack removed Sammy's wet clothes and put him in a warm bath, careful to let his body warm slowly. The first few minutes were awful for Sammy. With the numbness slowly dissipating, the actual pain set in. The boy screamed, a blood-curdling howl, when the slight tingling transitioned to needle-like jabs continuously pulsating through the bottom of his heels up into his toes. The cries sounded so painful that Ian found himself crying at the thought of being unable to help the boy. Roberts examined Sammy's feet and said he'd somehow avoided frostbite, but Ian wasn't so sure about that. Most of Sammy's feet slowly returned to their normal color, but the bottoms remained a dark red, like someone had just finished scraping sandpaper along them.

Scooter curled up on the couch next to Sammy, nuzzling his wiry face into the warm blankets that draped the boy. Ian envied his nephew, who, after all the turmoil, somehow found a way to pass out on the couch while all the adults tried to hold their shit together. Jack had finally begun to calm down, but Kristen was a mess. Now that she knew her son was safe, she was picking apart all the things she'd allowed to happen under her roof. Ian sat in silence next to Sammy and Scooter by the fire while the boy's parents argued in the kitchen about which one had left the door unlocked, or who was to blame for not hearing their son get out of bed and walk by their bedroom, down the stairs, and out the door without anyone so much as stirring in their sheets. Kristen couldn't stand not having control of a situation, and when it involved her own son, forget about it. As much as Ian envied Sammy's ability to sleep through it all, he equally sympathized with Jack for having to deal with the anger consuming Kristen.

When Roberts saw the symbol on the floor, he concluded it was part of Sammy's sleepwalking episode, saying the boy must have drawn it without realizing what he was doing. It would explain why Scooter didn't bark, and why nobody else heard anything with his little feet sneaking through the house. It would also explain why he was still out in the woods alone. As Roberts pointed out: if someone made it *that far* into the woods with the boy, why would they just give up and take off without their prize? Even Ian found that hard to refute.

After one last sweep through the house, Roberts said his goodbyes and left. Ian didn't look at the officer as he walked by and wished him a goodnight. He'd been down this road with Roberts before. Always taking the easy way out, looking for the simple solution to the problem. Then again, the simple solution of sleepwalking made a hell of a lot more sense than someone sneaking in undetected and getting Sammy to leave the house without saying a word, *and* without alerting the dog. Scooter wasn't the type to just sit there and watch a stranger enter the house without putting up some sort of commotion. The damn mailman couldn't open the mailbox without Scooter howling out the window to alert the whole clan of neighborhood dogs that their sworn enemy had arrived.

The adults decided it was best to leave Sammy asleep on the couch and let him rest. Ian agreed to stay on the couch with him so he wouldn't be alone at Sammy's request. With his uncle saving him in the woods, Sammy didn't want Ian to leave his side once they got back to the house. After Kristen walked around checking every door and window once again, she hesitantly went up to bed with Jack, not wanting to leave her son, but conceding to his wishes. While everyone slept, Ian found it difficult to do the same. He sat, watching Sammy's eyes darting from side to side behind closed eyelids, wondering what the poor kid was dreaming about.

"What did you see out there, Sammy?" he whispered.

The fire crackled and popped, consuming logs long into the night. Finally, as the sun was close to coming up, Ian dozed off. The sleep felt like it was only for a few minutes when Sammy's shouts jolted him awake.

An immediate fear of someone trying to come and take Sammy hit Ian like a sack of bricks. Scooter jumped off the couch and started howling. Ian jumped up as well, prepared to stop the attacker—and saw Sammy standing over the stack of Christmas gifts, excited like any other child would be on Christmas morning.

"Uncle Ian! Can we go wake up Mom and Dad?" he asked, pulling on Ian's sleeve.

Ian laughed, looking up to the second floor and seeing Kristen and Jack shuffling down the hall in their pajamas, eyes still half shut.

"I don't think you need to worry about waking them up, buddy," Ian said, nodding to the balcony above.

Sammy spotted his parents and immediately grabbed the first gift.

"Hurry up, guys! It's time to open presents!"

They came down the stairs, and Ian smiled at Kristen. He didn't need to say anything, but both knew what the other was thinking. *Thank God he's okay...*

"Yeah, yeah. Let us make a pot of coffee first, got it? I think after what we've been through the last twelve hours we deserve some caffeine, don't you?" Kristen asked Sammy.

"*Fiiiine.* Can I at least open the gift Uncle Ian got me while you're doing that?"

"I guess so. But then you wait, got it?" Jack said.

"Got it!"

Sammy ran to the box Ian had wrapped and snatched it up, then ran back and jumped on the couch. Scooter climbed up next to him and sat, not sure why he was excited, but excited nonetheless.

"I think you'll like this, bud..."

"What is it?" Sammy asked excitedly.

"Open it and find out, ya goof!"

Sammy's eyes lit up and he tore into the wrapping paper, throwing it to the floor. He stared at the box, reading every little detail on the label before registering how great the gift actually was.

"Thanks, Uncle Ian! I've always wanted cool walkie-talkies! I wish you could take one and talk with me when we can't see each other..." He spoke without taking his eyes off the box.

"That's the best part, dude! These things can reach up to a thousand miles! *And,* they have built in GPS. So, we can always see where the other is when using them."

"That's so cool! Can we test them out?"

Ian thought back to the night before, wishing he'd given the damn gift to Sammy early. That sure as hell would have made finding him much easier. He didn't think his sister would exactly be keen on the idea of Sammy going back out to the woods only a few short hours after getting lost out there. Thankfully, the house was big enough that they could at least mess around with them inside.

"As long as we stay inside, okay? After last night, we don't need to be going out in those woods again anytime soon." As he said it, he saw a hint of something—fear, sadness, embarrassment—in Sammy and knew he needed to change the subject. "Remember how I said the gift I got you would annoy your parents?"

Sammy nodded.

"Watch this." Ian opened the box and grabbed one of the walkie-talkies. After getting the batteries out of their pain-in-the-ass wrapper, he put them in and turned both the walkie-talkies on. Looking to see if Sammy was ready, Ian pushed down on a button and held it, which led to the device bellowing out a long beeping noise. It was so loud and obnoxious; he couldn't help but smile as he pictured Kristen having to listen to that on a regular basis.

"Is that to warn others that you're around?"

"You can use it for whatever you want, but I think it's just there to annoy your mom and dad," Ian said with a smirk. "Test it out."

Sammy grabbed the second walkie-talkie and held the button down. A deafening beep blasted through the lake house. Ian plugged his ears and laughed. He knew Kristen would be pissed, but what were uncles for? A few seconds later, Jack and Kristen came back to the living room with full cups of coffee, both squinting at the irritating sound.

"You are so dead," Kristen said to Ian.

They sat next to their son on the couch and sipped their coffee while watching Sammy glow with excitement.

"Check these out! Uncle Ian said they can reach up to one thousand miles! And, they have GPS in them. How awesome is that?"

Kristen's eyes went wide. "And how much did Uncle Ian spend on these things?" she asked Sammy, but Ian knew the question was aimed at him in her passively aggressive way.

"Oh, sis. They weren't that much. And I thought it would be a cool way for Sammy and I to keep in touch. You know, when you're not stalking me and renting a house close by. Plus, he needs someone to complain about you to." Ian winked in Sammy's direction. This drew a laugh from the boy.

"Real nice, turning my kid against me, huh? You're lucky I love you."

"Can we test them out now, please?" Sammy asked impatiently.

"Hey, you got us out of bed to open presents, sonny boy. You can mess around with those things after," Jack said, his face still buried in his coffee mug.

For the next hour, they opened gifts, told jokes, and it was as if the previous night never happened. When they were done, Sammy didn't miss a beat, handing Ian one of the walkie-talkies and jumping from the floor. The pain was still visible in his expression when his feet hit the hardwood. They'd done everything they could to help ease the pain, including wrapping gauze around the feet. But there was no way the injuries would clear up anytime soon.

He took off and headed up the stairs with Scooter trailing him. One of the many things Ian loved about his dog was how great Scooter was with kids. He hadn't left Sammy's side the majority of the time they'd been here.

Ian turned up his device and waited for Sammy to speak first. Kristen and Jack decided to go out and clean off the vehicle now that the storm had passed, leaving the house silent outside of Scooter's jingle as he trotted around somewhere in the hallway above.

"*Testing, testing...*" Sammy's muffled voice bled through the speaker.

"Roger that. I hear you loud and clear... over," Ian replied.

"*So cool! Can you see me on the GPS?*"

Ian looked at the screen, spotting a red dot where the other device was located—although right now they appeared as if they were side by side because they were in the same house.

"I can! And I can see you are picking your nose right now... over."

He heard Sammy laugh from the bedroom before coming through the speaker.

"*It tastes good, leave me alone... over.*"

The kid had his mom's wittiness, Ian would give him that. He went to reply but Sammy beat him to it.

"*Wow, what's this? You gotta see this thing Uncle Ian!*"

Ian assumed it was just the kid's vivid imagination, pretending to find a lost treasure or some shit like that. So, he played along.

"I'll be right there; we'll need to search the area."

Ian walked up the stairs and into Sammy's room and reminded himself to stay in character. Sammy was holding something up in the sunlight unlike anything Ian had ever seen. A round, wooden design, like someone had magically bent a tree limb into a perfect circle and tied a design in its center.

"What do we have, sir?"

"Looks kinda like a dreamcatcher, doesn't it? Mom must have put it in my bed last night to stop my bad dreams."

Ian tried to hide his concern, but he knew he was failing miserably. *What the fuck is this thing? And why is it in his bed?*

"Can I see it?" Ian asked, holding out his hand as he broke character. Sammy handed it to him.

"I wonder if it was from the previous renters. Where'd you find it pal?"

"It was under my pillow! Almost like the Tooth Fairy leaving a dollar, right?"

"Yeah... could be," Ian said, turning the object over in his hand to check it out.

Whatever the hell it was, he doubted very much it was from Kristen or the previous renters. Having gone through all the weird shit since he'd been here, Ian found it difficult not to believe it was some sort of talisman. He realized Sammy was still watching him, waiting for him to speak. He faked a smile at the boy and continued holding onto the dreamcatcher, or whatever it was, much to Sammy's disapproval.

"Can I have it back now?"

"In a minute, okay? I just want to ask your parents about it first. You're not in trouble or anything, just wanna figure out what it is first."

"Okay, fine. As long as Mom lets me keep it."

Ian walked out of the room, still focused on the object. His gut was telling him to get rid of the thing as soon as possible, burn the damn thing to ashes.

Later, he would wish he had.

CHAPTER 22

Kosa awoke to find herself still in the attic. Confused, she looked around and realized it was daylight outside. Mother almost never left her up here all night unless she was being punished. To the best of her knowledge, she hadn't done anything to upset Mother last night. They were about to sit down for story time when Mother's mood shifted and she told Kosa to get back to the attic, that she had to tend to something. What could she have needed to do in the middle of the night? And why did she not come upstairs to let Kosa out when she got home?

Tom wasn't even in the attic with her, just her old toys, Lennie and Mary—both who had seen better days. She knew they weren't real, but they were a piece of her, and she found herself struggling to part with them. Plus, the friends Mother brought over always loved them. That was the excuse for still having them around, she kept telling herself. She left the toys in their designated spots and got up, stretching out the pain in her back after sleeping a whole night on the hard floor. She walked to the door, hesitant to open it in fear of upsetting Mother, but with Tom not in the room, she figured the least she could do was open the door and listen for any sign that Mother was home. Could she have finally fallen over and perished in the woods? The cold temperatures couldn't help her frail condition.

She pushed the door and cringed as it creaked open. After Mother made her aware she knew of Kosa leaving the attic while she wasn't home, Kosa figured Mother would install some type of lock on the outside to keep her in. Instead, it was as if Mother was reminding Kosa who held the power, daring her to try it again and see what happened.

As wonderful as it could be getting fresh air on the porch, Kosa had no intention of doing it again any time soon. Just thinking of what she went through during the ritual last night sent shots of pain through her scalp

The house was silent. That didn't mean Mother wasn't home, but Kosa found herself becoming more and more concerned for the health of the old woman. As concerned as she was, she still felt it was best to play it safe and announce her exit from the attic.

"Mother? Are you home? Are you okay?"

She waited for a response that never came. When it was evident that nobody was home, Kosa exited the attic onto the upstairs hallway and quietly walked to the top of the stairs. She crouched and attempted to see the lower level, and again all she saw was empty rooms.

"Mother?"

Nothing....

Kosa tip-toed down the stairs and looked around the second-floor hallway. She walked past her bedroom and glanced in as she passed by—nothing appeared out of the ordinary. As she passed Mother's bedroom, she heard a muffled sound coming from behind the door. Whatever the noise was, it didn't sound right. Was something wrong with Mother? Kosa started to reach for the doorknob, then stopped herself. What if there was nothing wrong? What if she opened the door to help, only to find Mother completely fine? Not only would she have broken a rule by leaving the attic, but to interrupt Mother behind closed doors wouldn't bode well for Kosa.

It sounded like someone moaning in pain, as if every breath taken was a laborious effort. Kosa put her hand on the doorknob again, her clammy palm shaking as she gripped it. If something really was wrong with Mother, Kosa would never be able to live with herself if she just stood outside the door and did nothing to help. Surely Mother would understand the effort to help was more important than breaking a rule? Kosa put her ear to the door and listened. It was definitely Mother on the other side, and she was in obvious pain.

"Mother?" Kosa whispered, almost hoping there was no response.

The moaning stopped, bringing the room to silence. For a moment, Kosa just stood in place, ear to the door, and listened for any sign of life. She swallowed hard and took a deep breath. Her mind was made up, she had no choice but to open the door at this point.

CRACK...

At first, only one crack amplified from the other side of the door like a whip. Then the moaning returned, and multiple cracks followed, like someone jumping on a pile of dead sticks. Kosa opened the door and burst in, no longer caring if she got in trouble. Mother sat on her bed with her back to the door. She was hunched over, nude. The room was dimly lit, but that did little to hide the horrible scene. Mother's black cloak sat on the floor at the foot of the bed. Her body began to convulse, her muscles tensing and spasming. Kosa watched in awe, the bones visibly cracking and snapping below the surface of Mother's skin. The joints popped with each movement. Sweat poured down Mother's back as she pushed through the excruciating pain.

"Mother?" Kosa whispered.

Marta turned her face slightly, her once smooth skin beginning to sag and wrinkle, the black hair turning gray and brittle. Kosa wanted to vomit. Mother's spine twisted, slowly and painfully curving to bring back the poor posture of an old lady. The youthful sparkle that had returned to her eyes just the previous night was now lost to the black holes Mother's soul escaped from every single time this transition occurred. Kosa had never actually witnessed it happen, only seeing Mother at each stage upon completion. Sure, she'd heard it happening when they performed the ritual, but up until now she'd always avoided seeing it. And she'd only heard the opposite transition, of Mother going from old to young again. Somehow that seemed far less severe, the pain not nearly as terrible. What concerned Kosa the most was that Marta usually transitioned to her younger self during the day; this was uncharted territory. Why was this happening to her?

The transformation continued, the once beautiful lips of young Mother now thinning and cracking, her gritted teeth yellowed and decayed. Her hands transformed into gnarled, bony sticks as they clenched the bed sheets. Then, as if it couldn't get any worse, a deep, hoarse growl worked its way up through the old woman's chest and blasted through her vocal cords like a firehose, so loud that Kosa had no choice but to cover her ears. Kosa wanted to run, get as far away from the room as possible, but something held her in place, glued to the horror.

Finally, the room returned to silence. Marta's exposed ribs pushed against her bruised skin with every deep intake of breath. Kosa knew she'd been seen, yet Mother continued to look straight ahead as if she was alone in the room. She stood from the bed, leading to more joints popping and snapping under her sagging skin; a trail of purple veins traveled through her entire body like a road map leading to death. Mother limped to the corner of her bed, stopping in front of her mirror and looking at herself. Kosa likewise couldn't take her eyes off the disgusting figure.

The reflection from the mirror displayed Mother's front side, her sagging breasts dangling over her withered torso. A patch of white pubic hair hid what Mother called the "special place." Kosa's face burned with embarrassment at seeing a part of the body she knew her eyes weren't meant to see.

Mother continued to stare at her aged body in the mirror, whispering something under her breath. Kosa didn't realize until her hand began to sting that she'd been squeezing the doorframe so hard her skin had gone pale from lack of blood flow. She took a step back, ready to leave the room, and stepped on a weak floorboard that groaned.

Mother's black eyes shifted from observing her own body and looked directly at Kosa's reflection in the doorway.

Kosa covered her mouth.

"Mother... I... I'm so sorry. Are you okay? It sounded like you were hurt..."

Marta turned to face her, not even attempting to cover her body. A scowl spread across the old woman's face, but before she could speak, her legs buckled, and she had to catch herself on the bed. A violent cough came next, and with it, a red spittle that sprayed across her sheets.

"Mother!"

Kosa forgot all about the horrific scene she'd just witnessed and ran to her side. She frantically looked around, trying to figure out what to do first. She grabbed the robe from the floor and draped it over Mother's nude body, and then helped her sit on the bed.

"Oh, no... Please tell me you're okay, Mother. I need you."

Marta, who sat hunched and focused on the blood splashed across her bed, looked up to meet Kosa's stare. The all-black eyes now had blood vessels branching out across them like crimson spiderwebs. She wiped the blood from her chin and continued her labored breathing.

"Dear... I think it's time you learned about my past. About what I need to survive, and why it's so important I stay young. I know you see it getting worse for me, I'm no fool. So—" Her words were interrupted by another bout of coughs, this time into her bulbous palm. It was as if all the blood had rushed to her extremities, swelling her hands and ankles.

Kosa panicked, just wanting to help her. Without thinking, she started ripping out her own hair, ignoring the pain she felt with each yank.

"Take this, I know it'll help..." she said, handing the clump of hair to Marta.

A sad smile formed on the old woman's face as she lifted her trembling arm with a weakness Kosa hadn't seen from her before. She grabbed the hair, shoving it into her mouth. Her eyes rolled, revealing the slightest hint of white under the darkness resting in her sockets. As much as Kosa didn't want to watch, she couldn't stop. At this point, she'd already seen more than she ever had in all her years, and she wasn't so sure it mattered anymore. Everything that had just happened had robbed Kosa of any dreams she'd be having anytime soon, replacing them with an endless loop of nightmare fuel.

Mother swallowed the hair so quickly that she began to cough it up. Seeing it happen was so much worse than hearing it and trying to sing a song through the ritual to distract herself. Marta's body hitched and spasmed, the frail muscles of her neck bulging as she tried to force the hair down her windpipe. She repeatedly opened and shut her mouth, as if chewing on invisible food. She snapped her teeth together, over and over. Finally, she swallowed hard, and Kosa watched as the clump of hair slid down her bulging throat like a python swallowing its prey whole.

For a moment, nothing happened. Kosa began to think maybe it would do no good, that Mother was past the point of healing. And then, a ripple swam under the old woman's skin. Her cheeks shifted, filling in the sunken space with a smoother surface—though not completely smooth like when Mother was fully transformed. The ugly trails of veins faded, as well as the blood pooling in each of her limbs. The hair helped but didn't fully heal her. Kosa knew it was a temporary solution.

"Thank you, dear. You know Mother well. But... Not as well as you think. Please, sit," she said, pointing to the bed next to her.

Kosa made sure to find a place on the sheet without any blood on it, and then sat by Marta's side.

"You see, there's a reason I must do what I do with you each night. I know I've told you that you possess what I need to grow strong. Many, many years ago, I was a beautiful young woman—"

"You still are, Mother, even when you're... *older*," Kosa interrupted.

"Thank you, Kosa. But don't interrupt me... I was part of a coven, over sixty years ago. I came here from the country of Croatia with nothing more than a suitcase. My family grew up in the region of Slavonia, where it was normal to have nothing, to live a life of poverty... My parents died when I was a girl not much younger than you are now, and I was left to fend for myself. I was desperate. When you're digging scraps from the garbage to survive, you'll do almost anything to make your life better. This is where things go wrong for me, Kosa."

Kosa had never seen this side of Mother. Her life was a mystery, and anytime Kosa asked about it, it usually led to punishment. Based on how bad her life was, Kosa was beginning to understand why Mother never wanted to talk about it. After another coughing fit, Marta continued.

"Before I came to this country, I met a man who said he could help me. He told me he'd be able to make me the most beautiful woman in the world, and that he'd make it last forever. It sounded too good to be true. All I had to do was agree to help him out in return. A deal with the Devil situation, you see?"

"What's that? What did he make you do?" Kosa asked, although she was starting to put the pieces together.

"He worshipped *Tamna Sila*, which means a dark force, one that possesses almost infinite powers. The thing is... to keep those powers, this force needs to feed. It feeds off many things, really, but what it wants most is to feed off children, their innocent souls. It's complicated if I'm being honest. Many years ago, the object that this man gave me, it held the *Tamna Sila* inside it. And that's where *you* come into the story, Kosa. Somehow, this force inhabited you. The object became useless, no longer giving me the power which I needed to live. That power moved to you, dear."

Kosa's eyes began to burn, tears welling up. She didn't know what to say. She knew there was something inside her that wasn't normal. Even without Mother needing to do the ritual, it was something she felt internally. Whenever she was around her friends, she was struck with a burning sensation in the pit of her stomach. It felt good. But it also felt hungry. She always assumed it was just excitement, but the blank stares that the boys and girls would give back to her made so much sense now. It was as if her body was pulling the energy from their life—or soul as Mother said. She wanted to throw up, knowing that she was possibly hurting her poor friends. But the thought was conflicting, as she knew it was necessary to keep Mother healthy. As long as she wasn't hurting them, she reasoned, it was okay.

"Mother... do you promise that the kids being around me doesn't hurt them?" The question was out before she could stop it.

"Oh, Kosa. Of course not. Being around you is the best part of their day. And yours. The energy feeds off their emotions. And when I take them away? It is what must be done. You now see why I say they are here to serve one purpose. It's what *Tamna Sila* needs. It's what *we* need."

Kosa thought about it, then nodded.

"Good. Now let me finish my story. So, when I came to America—before you were born—I didn't know what to do. For a few years, I wandered around with no plan in life. I saw how awful the world truly was. When I left Croatia, I thought I was getting away from it all, only to come here and see it was no better. I learned to despise people. You see, it can be very dangerous for a beautiful young woman that's alone with nobody to protect her. Everyone thought I was a freak. That was until I met a group here in New Hampshire. A coven. They welcomed me with open arms, teaching me their way. It was the first time I'd felt normal in all my life. They taught me how to use my powers, how to practice the craft of the Book. And then, there was an accident. Many, many deaths. We were forced to move on from one another, and I found myself alone again. Having to fend for myself."

The story was far better than any bedtime story Mother read to her. Kosa was enamored with all of it. She still didn't understand why, after all these years, Mother was finally telling her this.

"I moved into this home, thinking it was far enough away from everyone but close enough to reunite with the coven if we were ever able to do so. That never happened, so until you came along, I had nobody. If you're wondering why I'm telling you this now—which by the look in your eyes, you are—there's a reason. When I was younger, I used to be able to go much longer without needing the energy. As my body grows older, you see what happens to me if I wait too long. And if the *Tamna Sila* doesn't get what it needs, my powers also weaken. Which is what is happening right now, you see. It's why I need more children than I used to. I'm afraid if I don't find a solution soon, this can only go on so long."

"What can I do, Mother? How can I help? I need you..."

"You're doing everything you can, my dear. But I need you to be sure to follow my rules. Don't make things harder on me by forcing me to punish you. You are a woman now, and it's time I started treating you like one."

Kosa didn't know what to say. As much as she needed Mother to survive, she'd never shown this type of compassion toward Kosa. A sense of pride flowed through her at hearing Mother call her a woman. Even though she was getting older, she still viewed herself as a kid. The pride vanished when she was reminded of the grave condition Mother now found herself in. She needed to help her.

"Mother... I can give you all my hair. That would help, right?"

"No, dear. It would help short-term, but I'm afraid unless I find a way to please this force, my days are numbered."

"That's not fair! There must be something that can be done. Can't you let me go look for friends? So you can rest?"

"I'm afraid not. It's not as simple as that, Kosa. I will go out later, once I'm rested up, and I will bring a friend. And then I'll continue to study the Book, looking for a way to get rid of this once and for all. What I need from you is to fetch me a bowl of soup and bring it to my room. There's some left over in the fridge. Do you think you can handle that?"

"Yes, Mother. I'd do anything to help you."

Kosa left Marta's room, letting her rest. With each step away from the bedroom, she kept telling herself the same thing over and over. *I need to do more, or Mother is going to die...*

CHAPTER 23

Ian pulled into his driveway and killed the engine. The entire ride home, the feeling of doing something wrong continued to eat at him. His gut told him not to leave Sammy. It told him to stay until they left for home, to make sure they got out of that house without any issues. He even considered calling out of work on Monday so he could stay the extra night until Kristen and Jack had to leave the house. Instead, he'd listened to his sister, who insisted things would be okay. She said they would make sure Sammy didn't sleepwalk again and would make sure every door and window remained locked.

As soon as Ian walked into his house and tossed his travel bag down, he fed Scooter and then grabbed his walkie-talkie.

"Sammy, it's Uncle Ian. Can you hear me? Over."

Every second that passed without a response made Ian sick with worry. He was about to talk again when the walkie speaker produced a static sound.

"*I can hear you, loud and clear, sir. Over.*"

Ian was instantly flooded with relief, unable to stop the smile from spreading on his face. Scooter tilted his head to the side and observed the strange object in Ian's hand that the voice was coming from.

"It's Sammy, pup!"

Scooter replied with a low, friendly howl. Ian rubbed his head as the dog went back to his meal, then held the talk button on his walkie.

"Can you see me on your GPS, buddy? It should work. Over."

"*Yep! I see a red dot showing your street. This is so cool! Over.*"

"Nice! Tell your mom and dad I said thanks again for having me stay. It was great spending time with you guys. And buddy?"

"*Yeah?*"

"Be careful. I love you guys. Over."

"*Love you too, Uncle Ian. Thanks for this awesome gift. Over.*"

When Ian had presented the wooden symbol to Kristen, she shrugged it off. She said it must have been there from the previous renters. Ian wasn't ready to just pretend it was nothing. His sister already believed he overthought every situation, looking for bigger issues that didn't exist. So, he didn't tell her that he was planning to research symbols as soon as he got home. The problem was, he had no idea where to start. How the fuck do you narrow down a search for creepy wooden designs left in children's beds? It wasn't exactly a common occurrence.

He opened the fridge and grabbed a beer. After popping the top off, he scanned the shelf for anything worth eating and then remembered all he had was old Chinese take-out. Embarrassingly, he considered giving the leftovers a sniff test. He decided against it and shut the door, taking a swig of the ice-cold beer.

"Okay, Scoot. Time to figure out what the hell that thing was, whatcha say?"

Scooter continued crunching on his food, one piece at a time. Ian sat at the breakfast bar and grabbed his laptop. Once it powered up, he opened a web browser and stared at the blank search bar, thinking of how to explain what it was he'd found. He typed the words "cursed wooden symbols."

He scrolled through the images, mostly of fake Etsy creations for people who loved the witch aesthetic, and quickly realized he needed to be more specific. He thought back to what the symbol looked like, trying to remember specific design characteristics. Was there a star in its center? It was almost a pentagram-like design. He spent the next twenty minutes typing in different word combinations that he hoped would show a similar enough result to make him feel he wasn't wasting his time. Finally, he spotted one that looked similar and clicked on it. The image wasn't quite right, but one thing he kept seeing over and over was the mention of witches. Not TikTok witches: real-ones. Curses. The witch's mark. *What the fuck? What is this stuff?*

Ian skimmed the article which contained the closest looking symbol to what he found in the bed.

In some traditions of witchcraft, it was believed that witches could leave a mark on their victims as a sign of their pact with the Devil, or as a way of identifying them as witches' prey. These marks were often said to be given through a kiss or a prick with a sharp object, such as a needle or pin.

He envisioned the design again and remembered the sharp point at the top of the symbol, almost like a thorn glued to the wood. After rereading the few sentences, Ian's heart began to race. *Why the hell are you swallowing all this voodoo shit?* This was real life: the idea of marking a child or anyone with a curse was ridiculous.

And then he remembered Sammy finding the object in his bed. How had he found it if it was under the pillow? Was it possible the object punctured his skin?

Ian reached for the walkie-talkie again, but then thought better of it. No need to scare Sammy. Instead, he grabbed his cellphone and dialed Kristen. It went to voicemail.

"Fuck!"

He ended the call and dialed back. Again, it went to voicemail. This time, he left a message.

"Kristen… I know this will sound strange, but can you check with Sammy to see if he's got a cut on his finger? I'll explain more when you call back, but please let me know ASAP. Hope you guys are having a good day. Thanks again for having me; you were right. Love you, Sis."

He got up from the breakfast bar and paced around the kitchen for a few minutes, hoping his sister didn't wait too long before responding. The whole situation felt ridiculous, but he couldn't get those thoughts out of his head. Nobody else saw the extra footprints. Nobody else saw those eyes staring back from the darkness. And nobody else saw Scooter trying to rip apart the floorboards to get rid of that symbol. The worst part of it all was the look on Sammy's face when Ian found him curled up in the woods. Those eyes staring back at him were lost, off somewhere else, and while they were part of Sammy's face, they sure as hell weren't the eyes of an innocent child staring back at him.

Scooter drank the water from his dish until it was gone and then licked the remaining drips from his white dog beard. He walked to Ian and paced with him.

"What did we see out there, boy? Why the hell am I so scared right now?"

Scooter wagged his tail, and then went to the door and nudged the bell dangling from the handle. Chelsea had worked extra hard to not only potty train the dog, but to get him to nudge the bell every time he needed to go to the bathroom. Everything in the house reminded Ian of his deceased wife. As time passed, the pain only deepened, every creak in the floor, every object residing in its designated location, all reminding him of Chelsea.

He grabbed the leash and hitched it to Scooter's collar. They exited the house and Ian shut the door. Had he been paying attention, he would have realized he forgot his cellphone. He would have noticed that his phone was buzzing, a text message from Kristen flashing across the screen.

Kristen: Yeah, his finger got cut pretty good, but it's ok! We got it cleaned up and put a band-aid on it. Thanks for coming brother! Love ya...

CHAPTER 24

Chief Kevin Roberts sat at his desk with an uneasy stomach full of coffee and self-doubt. He knew part of it could simply be lack of sleep after being woken in the middle of the night to go searching for the missing boy, but that was at his request. The officers who reported to him knew anytime they received calls about something in those woods, he insisted on being the one to go out there, whether he was on duty or not. Nobody else knew the history of the area, or the information about the missing kids. Roberts was in his spot to make sure the town was safe, and he planned to do just that.

Ian Warner questioning how he did his job wasn't something he had the time to deal with. It was bad enough when Ian's wife passed that he had the nerve to undermine their investigation, but here the little shit was again, staring at him like he wasn't any good at his job. Roberts had had a gut feeling, as he drove to the lake house, about exactly what had happened to the boy, and the symbol on the floor all but confirmed his gut was right. When they found the kid in the woods alive, that blindsided him. Maybe they had found him before he was taken out in the woods far enough? Whatever the reason, Roberts wanted to nip it in the bud quickly. The town didn't need to worry about missing children again.

The problem was Ian Warner. He was a pesky one and wouldn't give up just because they found the kid. Same with his wife's death. Everything pointed to a suicide, especially once the discovery of her infertility issues popped up. Most spouses would have taken that information and understood that maybe there were deeper concerns than they knew about. But not Ian. No, he'd call the station a few times a week asking questions about the case: wondering if any new leads had been uncovered, any newfound evidence that might point to something besides suicide.

Dealing with such inquiries was hell, but a necessary one. That's likely why Roberts was still single. His wife left him years ago because she felt he was more married to the job than her, and that he cared more about protecting the citizens of Sunapee than he did about his own marriage. He couldn't blame her, but he also couldn't stop making his job the most important thing in his life. There were a few thousand people depending on him to make sure they were safe, and considering how important tourism was to the town's economy, he needed to make sure nothing hung around too long that would hurt that income source.

He had a feeling Ian would be back snooping around. It was hard to fault the guy for wanting to protect his family. Lord knew Roberts would do the same if the roles were reversed. Lord also knew part of the reason Roberts' wife left him was because of his obsession. There were no nights out on the town with the Roberts during their rocky marriage. No children to raise together and teach to become wonderful human beings. Again, he couldn't blame his wife for leaving him because of that, but after some of the gruesome murder scenes he'd seen over the years—many of them involving families—he couldn't bring himself to have kids, to bring them into this world knowing they could possibly end up like that.

Moving out of town wasn't an option, he had too many responsibilities to tend to, agreements to follow through.

Roberts had promised the family at the lake house he'd continue to make his rounds to check in on them until they left to go back home, so he would do just that. He'd make sure nobody else needed to get involved and that the holidays could be celebrated in peace.

Certain things, he'd keep to himself. Such as the fact that the symbol drawn on the floor had been at the scene of many of the local murder scenes over the years. And every single time they found the symbol, a missing kid always seemed to be the next chronological step in the story. That lake and the woods surrounding it were no place for kids to roam around. The locals knew that. But Roberts couldn't help it if tourists were stupid enough to let their kids play in the woods. With only a few cops on the Sunapee PD payroll, he couldn't exactly afford to have one keeping watch to make sure nobody went out there.

There was also the fact that he and Marta had come to an agreement years ago. Yet another reason his wife left him. She knew he turned a blind eye when tourists rented houses near the witch. He tried to explain to her it was to protect the town and her, but she would have none of it. She promised not to tell anyone, but it didn't stop her from leaving a stack of divorce papers on the kitchen counter one morning and leaving the house before he got home from an overnight shift.

Roberts stared at his computer screen, realizing he hadn't done a damn thing since coming to the office a few hours prior. He needed to get some work done, then he'd take a ride out by the lake and check on the family. The phone rang, startling him out of his daydream. It couldn't be anything important, likely a local with one of their typical small-town bullshit problems. He sighed and picked up the phone.

"Chief Roberts..."

Sure enough, it was Maggie Sale on the other end. Ever since she'd retired as the town librarian, she called the office at least once a week about suspicious activity in her garden, even in the winter when there was no damn garden to speak of. Roberts answered the old woman's questions on autopilot. His mind continued to drift back to the kid, and how the poor little bastard had no idea what he was getting himself into. If Marta knew that Roberts helped rescue the kid from the woods, he'd likely know about it by now. The witch had one simple rule for him if he wanted to be guaranteed the children of Sunapee would remain safe from her: make sure she had an ample supply during the tourist seasons so that she didn't need to seek them out elsewhere. It was the least he could do to protect his town.

He decided once Maggie shut up about her missing garden gnomes that he'd take a ride out by the lake house and see what was going on. Or whether he had another mess to cover up for the witch.

CHAPTER 25

Mother spent most of the day resting. Kosa occasionally checked on her and brought her food, but other than that Marta had asked to be left alone. All Kosa wanted to do was ask her more about her past but found herself too afraid to push it. She'd gone her entire life without knowing anything more than Mother's real name to all of a sudden learning about her rough childhood and upbringing; it was both fascinating and heartbreaking. No wonder Mother was so strict and cold toward Kosa. The poor lady had been shown no love her entire life; why would she magically know how to show it toward Kosa?

She always knew her life here was a bit different than the outside world, that she wasn't raised the same as the kids she often played with. Now she had answers as to why.

The only silver lining to Mother being bedridden was that it allowed Kosa to explore the house more than she ever had. Specifically, the Book Mother read from each night. Through the years, Kosa assumed Mother was reading a book like the ones she read Kosa before bed, except for grownups. She had no idea the Book was something that could obtain Marta's potential freedom from an evil dark force. Kosa was determined to search the Book and look for answers. In doing so, she'd be breaking another of Mother's rules—do NOT touch the *Book of Vjestica*.

Kosa sat in the rocking chair, the one in which she usually sat during the ritual. She scanned the area for any sign of Tom or the other cats, more out of habit than expecting them to be around. One thing she'd realized a few years ago was that when Mother was weak, so were the cats. Whereas she used to think Tom was nicer to her sometimes, it was more the case he was also weak, that Mother's hold over him wasn't as strong. The two nameless cats were nuzzled up in bed with Mother—another major reason why Kosa had no desire to go in the room unless asked.

She opened the Book and was immediately hit with the stale smell of old paper. Carefully, Kosa flipped through the first few pages, almost giving up before she even started reading. Much of the writing was either handwritten, so sloppy that she couldn't make out what it said, or in a different language altogether. Random images scattered throughout the pages helped guide her to at least know if what she was looking at had anything to do with the problem.

There were pages about cats transforming, but the images were so horrific that Kosa flipped through that section quickly, too afraid to see what it said. Next, she scanned through a chapter that talked about the powers of Mother's cloak. It included some ingredients or spells that gave the cloth the power to protect her.

That helped explain why Mother could go out during the day when she struggled with daylight. Apparently, the hood provided some sort of UV protection that blocked the sun from reaching Marta's eyes. It was all so fascinating, but again, offered no resolution to the current problem. Mother read from this Book every single day. Kosa realized the odds of her picking up the book for the first time and instantly finding something that could cure Mother had to be slim. *What kind of daughter would you be if you didn't at least try to help?* she asked herself.

Again, she skipped to another section of the book; every second that she held it felt like she was toying with her own fate. Recipes, talismans, translations for spells… The book was loaded with information that given more time, Kosa would've loved to devour. None of what she saw was helpful for Marta's condition. She flipped to a section including many symbols with explanations beneath each. Quickly examining them for anything that might help, she landed on a symbol that she couldn't take her eyes off. It was called "The Children's Lock." She swallowed down the fear and read the explanation.

Some of it was in a different language, likely the language Marta often spoke. She really wished Mother had taught her to speak Croatian. But some words were clear as day. Control. Erase their thoughts. Possess.

She slammed the book shut and set it on the table next to the chair. Everything came crashing down on her. It was one thing to know the children's fate, it was another to read step by step what Mother did to control them, the process she went through to prepare their bodies for feeding. All of a sudden, Kosa felt sick to her stomach. And for the first time she could recall, she had a small feeling of resentment for Marta.

Movement from upstairs brought her back to the moment. With trembling legs, Kosa jumped from the chair, looking for a place to go. She couldn't go back upstairs, for she'd have to pass Mother's room to get to her bedroom. There was no way she could do that without Marta discovering she'd disobeyed orders again. Thankfully, she'd thought to shut her bedroom door when she came downstairs. Now she just had to hope Mother didn't open the door to ask for something. The floorboards groaned overhead, moving in the direction of the stairs. Kosa scrambled down the hall, desperate to find a place to hide until Mother went back to bed. As weak as Mother was, Kosa assumed she would be safe until nightfall.

Kosa approached the kitchen area as the steps got louder. The scuffing of Marta's slippers on the old wooden floor scratched a dull warning of her location. If Kosa didn't hide somewhere quick, she could kiss her freedom goodbye. She opened the hallway closet and stepped inside, slowly shutting the door. Darkness consumed her, reminding her of her nights in the attic. Sure enough, Marta's footsteps descended to the ground floor. A tiny pinpoint of light shone in through the closet's keyhole, cutting the darkness in half. Kosa kneeled, squinting through the small hole, trying to see what Mother was doing.

The scuffing of the slippers got closer, dragging out longer with each step.

SCRRRRR....

Kosa held her breath, waiting for Marta to get close enough to see. A new sound joined the scuffing. It was Mother's forced, heavy breaths. Each step was a burden. Her hunched figure appeared in the hallway, using her walking stick to hold herself upright. The loud *TICK* of the stick slamming down on the floor joined the slippers and heavy breathing. A fleeting thought that Marta was only heading this way because she knew Kosa was behind the door crossed Kosa's mind, but before she could stew too much on the idea, Mother passed the tiny viewport and entered the kitchen.

Marta exited the small space that Kosa could see, Kosa's imagination taking over to provide a picture of what she was doing out of sight. The refrigerator door opened. There was a clanking of glass being moved to the side. The door slammed shut. More heavy breathing. And then, loud gulps, over and over, followed by a slurping sound.

What is she doing? Kosa wondered.

The slurping resumed but was cut short by the sound of liquid splashing off the countertop, and then an explosion of glass shattering on the floor. Kosa jolted back, slamming into the closet wall. *No, no, no....*

The house was silent, but inside Kosa's head it was anything but. Did Mother hear her? Was Mother okay out there? Should she risk getting in trouble to help her again? She reached for the doorknob, trying to will her shaking hand from trembling. Before she grabbed the knob, Mother spoke to herself in Croatian.

"*Sto mi se dogada....*"

Kosa had no idea what the words meant. She decided against opening the door, thinking if Marta felt well enough to speak, she was well enough to get herself back to bed. The old woman's footsteps returned, along with the clacking of her walking stick. Whatever mess Mother had made, she wasn't wasting what little energy she had left to clean it up. Kosa would surely be assigned that duty later on. The hunched figure of Marta appeared in the hallway again, but this time stopped halfway. Kosa couldn't see her face in the dark space, but it looked like Mother was staring in her direction.

Right at the closet.

Kosa slowly backed away from the keyhole and did her best to remain still.

The smacking of the walking stick almost forced a scream from Kosa, but she thankfully held it in. Whatever had stopped Mother didn't hold her attention and she was on the move back toward the stairs. Kosa let out a deep sigh, her body continuing to shake. She wiped a tear away and closed her eyes, taking more deep breaths. She opened her eyes and kneeled to look out through the hole again, just to be sure that Mother was gone.

Large soulless eyes stared back at her from the other side.

This time, Kosa did scream. The door whipped open as Mother hunched, staring into the closet.

"Naughty, naughty girl...."

Before Kosa could react, Marta pulled her out by the hair, something she'd usually avoid given the importance of it. Kosa yelled in pain as she was dragged from the dark closet. She looked up at Mother from her worm's eye view, staring into the sickly-looking face of the unhinged witch. Sweat rolled down Marta's face, finding its way into the ample wrinkles and cracks of her deteriorating skin.

"You've broken the rules for the last time, girl! You want to disobey me? Now you see what happens...."

"Mother! I was worried about you. I was trying to help, I promise!"

"Nonsense! You know to only leave your room if I call for you. I didn't need your help!"

Kosa didn't know what to say. The softness that Marta had shown her only a few hours earlier had vanished, now replaced by pure hatred. She had to assume it was due to her desperate state of health, that Mother would never treat her this poorly if things were good. At the moment, none of that mattered. She had no idea what would come next. The old lady snarled at her, then looked around as if she was trying to come up with a proper punishment. Her obsidian eyes met the closet again and her snarl turned upward into a sadistic smile.

"You want to hide in the closet? Very well. You can stay there all night. After all I do for you, all I teach you, this is what you make me do. I'm very disappointed in you, Kosa."

Marta again grabbed Kosa by the hair and her strength surprised Kosa. Marta looked even worse than she did earlier in the day, but she felt much stronger than her appearance indicated. Kosa knew better than to say anything, swallowing the pain down to avoid crying. A powerful force behind Mother's push sent Kosa flying into the wall, causing her head to smack off the shelf. Sparks fluttered across her vision, floating around even as she tried to blink them away. She curled into a fetal position and sobbed, only daring to look up at Marta after a moment of silence.

"I'm sorry, Mother. I know I was wrong…"

"I'm sorry too. Sorry I have to do this to you. If you behave, I'll let you out in the morning."

She started to slam the door shut, then paused, opening it fully again. She reached in, grabbing hold of Kosa's hair once more. For a moment, Kosa thought she was getting dragged back out. Instead, Mother ripped a handful of hair from her head, sending shooting pain through Kosa's scalp. The door slammed shut, sending the world back into darkness.

CHAPTER 26

Ian laid in bed, staring at his cellphone, reading the last text from Kristen over and over. He'd tossed and turned for the better part of the last four hours, trying to force himself to go to sleep, telling himself everything was okay. Unfortunately, no matter how many times he attempted to convince himself, it wasn't working. Kristen told him that Sammy had a cut. As embarrassing as it was believing in what he read online, the pieces sure were starting to match up. He considered sending another text, but realized that even if things were okay, the odds of Kristen responding in the middle of the night were slim. And if she did, she'd be pissed off. He also considered getting out of bed and driving out to the vacation home to check on them.

"Stop spooking yourself..." he whispered. Scooter lifted his head at the foot of the bed, curious why Ian was talking in the dark.

He checked to see how many calls and texts he'd made to Kristen since he got back from walking Scooter. Sixteen times. *Yikes*. And that didn't include the attempts he'd made over the walkie-talkie to Sammy. Ian was about to set his phone down and try sleeping again when three dots appeared in the conversation with Kristen. She was texting back. The dots appeared and disappeared a few times, dragging on the torture.

Kristen: We are ok. Thank you for checking in. Packed and ready to go in the morning.

Me: Thank god. You almost gave me a heart attack by not responding. Goodnight, sis

Kristen: Good night

Now relieved, Ian set his phone back on the nightstand. He felt so stupid for worrying about them. Of course, they were okay. They were just busy on vacation and avoiding their phones all day. What was wrong with that? He shook his head and rolled over to face the wall. His eyelids forced themselves shut, bringing on a light sleep in the process. He had one last thought as he passed out.

Kristen always ended her chats with him by calling him brother, just like he always ended with calling her sis. It was probably nothing, but it entered his mind and wouldn't escape. And then he slept until morning.

CHAPTER 27

Kosa awoke to a sharp pain in her neck. Somehow, she'd found a position that made it possible to sleep, but now she was paying for it. It was so dark in the closet that she had no idea how much time had passed since Mother left. She got to her feet and felt another pain shoot through her back. Ignoring it, she looked through the keyhole and noticed it was brighter than when she'd entered. That meant she had slept the entire night in the cramped space. Her stomach growled to remind her she didn't get dinner the night before.

She heard someone talking deeper in the house. It wasn't Mother, but a kid. They sounded young. The conversation was far enough away that she couldn't make out what they were saying, but the voice was getting closer. Before they got too close, however, Mother spoke.

"Not down that way, dear. Come with me and I'll fetch Kosa to play with you. I'll show you where she plays with friends."

"Okay..." The child spoke in the all too familiar tone Kosa had come to expect from them.

Kosa tensed up, knowing Mother was approaching.

The door opened, and Mother peered in with disgust.

"Not that you deserve it, but I've brought a friend for you to play with. Don't you dare say a word about this punishment. No need to scare the boy. Understood?"

"Yes, Mother."

"Very well, then. Come out and have some fun. I'll fix you something to eat."

Kosa hesitantly walked out of the closet, and the bright light immediately brought back the headache from when she'd smacked her head on the wall. She followed Mother down the hall, into the Big Room where she always played with the children. The boy was already sitting on the floor, observing his new surroundings. She noticed he was a few years younger than her. Marta pushed Kosa into the doorway, losing patience with her reluctance.

"Go on now. You have an hour."

The boy turned around at the sound of their conversation, and Kosa's heart broke. He was such a cute, innocent child—except for those black eyes. She knew she needed to pretend to have no idea about Mother's spells, so she approached the boy and forced a smile.

"Hello. I'm Kosa. What's your name?"

He gave a hollow smile back.

"Sammy. Nice to meet you, Kosa."

CHAPTER 28

When Ian awoke, Kristen's text was still burned into his brain. The more he thought about it, the less it sounded like her. Sure, maybe she was just overtired texting in the middle of the night. But it came across so robotically; it didn't sound like her at all. He waited until Kristen and Jack would be awake and checked out of the holiday home before calling again. Ian couldn't hold it in any longer. He grabbed his phone and dialed Kristen.

Voicemail...

He dialed Jack, who he almost never called, in hopes Jack would be a bit more understanding if he answered.

Voicemail...

"God damn it!"

Scooter whimpered in the corner at the anger in Ian's voice.

"Sorry, pup. What do you say we go for a ride?"

The dog's ears perked up and he immediately jumped to his feet and ran to the door. Before exiting, Ian grabbed the walkie-talkie in one last attempt to reach his family.

"Sammy, buddy. Are you there?"

Ian waited a minute and then tried again.

"Sammy. Did you guys make it home okay?"

Nothing came back. Ian checked the GPS on the walkie, and the red dot for Sammy still appeared to be in the vague area of the rental property. Panic set in. He grabbed his keys and attached the leash to Scooter.

"Let's go, boy."

Kosa jumped back at the noise in Sammy's pocket.

"What was that?" she asked, startled.

Sammy's black eyes changed in an instant, the darkness draining from them like a pen leaking ink, bringing back his regular color. He looked around, confused.

"What? What just happened?"

"Something was talking in your pocket. What was that?"

Sammy shook his head, then felt in his pocket, pulling out the walkie-talkie. Before he could speak, his legs wobbled, and he grabbed hold of the wall to stop himself from falling.

"I'm so confused. How did I get here? Who are you?"

Guilt prevented Kosa from speaking. She wanted to tell him everything, but that risked Mother finding out. And she was *always* listening. It surprised Kosa she hadn't come in yet to see what the sound was, but then she remembered Mother was going to grab her some food.

Footsteps approached from the kitchen area.

"Quick, give that to me! Please?"

"My walkie-talkie? No. Why would I give this to you? I don't even know who you are..."

"Please! She'll take it if she sees it. You need to hurry."

Sammy furrowed his brow in confusion but handed the walkie-talkie to Kosa. She shoved it into her pocket just as Marta pushed through the door with a tray holding two plates, covered in fruits and vegetables. As Sammy shifted attention to Marta, Kosa noticed his eyes again filled with the empty darkness. How did Kosa not see this before? Every time Mother was around them, the children went back into this trance. Most of the time, they remained trapped in this foggy state. But it was as if the device in Sammy's pocket had jolted him out of his daze. Mother told her that the force inside Kosa was what made the kids this way, putting the blame on her. After seeing Sammy's swift transition with Mother back in the room, Kosa wasn't so sure what to believe.

"Here you go, children. Enjoy. It's important to keep a healthy diet, right Kosa?" Marta set the tray down between Kosa and Sammy. She paused, looking back and forth between them. "Is something wrong?"

An imaginary burning sensation filled Kosa's pocket, a flashing light telling Marta to look and see what she was hiding.

"No, Mother, everything's fine. This food just looks so delicious."

"Very well. I will let you two play," she said, and then walked out of the room, shutting the door behind her.

"Listen to me. I don't know what she's doing to you, but I want to help," Kosa whispered.

"Huh? I thought we were playing?"

Kosa tried to come up with a plan. She wanted Mother to get better, but she didn't want it at the expense of harming kids anymore. It was tearing her apart inside. There had to be a way to make Marta better without this. She grabbed the walkie-talkie from her pocket and looked it over.

"What's that?" Sammy asked.

"It's yours, Sammy. Someone tried to talk to you on it. Do you know who it could be? I couldn't hear everything they said, but it was someone asking if you were okay."

Again, he just looked more confused, as if his brain was hurting at trying to think about anything beyond playing with her.

"I... I don't know. My parents know I came to play, the old lady told them."

Good. That's good, she thought.

"Okay. Well, I'm sorry. Are you feeling okay?"

"I feel great. I want to play now," Sammy responded.

"Okay, I'm sorry if I'm acting weird. Let's go play before you have to go home," Kosa said, and then put the talking device back in her pocket.

CHAPTER 29

Ian was relieved to see Kristen's vehicle gone when he pulled into the vacation home driveway. It didn't explain why nobody was answering his calls, but at least they had left. He decided to check the house out still, just to be sure. He got out of his car, allowing Scooter to jump out behind him before shutting the door. His feet crunched on the now frozen surface of the snow as he approached the house. Ian found the door locked. He didn't have the passcode to unlock the key box, so he moved to a porch window and peered through the glass into the living room. The house was empty, all belongings long gone. Everything pointed to the family leaving the home.

He was about to head back to his car, feeling stupid for being so worked up ever since he left them the day before, when a thought occurred to him. Now that it was daylight, maybe he could find those footprints he knew for sure he'd seen in the middle of the night. Maybe it would bring closure once and for all? Maybe he'd realize he was losing his damn mind, and needed to let things go. He stepped off the porch and circled the perimeter of the house toward the wooded area. The lake gave off an icy breeze that wrapped around Ian's exposed neck as he entered the backyard. *I can't wait for winter to end*, he thought.

As he crouched to inspect the disruption on the snow's surface, Scooter ran to the edge of the lawn, staring into the forest. He howled at the trees, his fur standing on end.

"What is it, boy?" Ian asked, then got up and followed his dog to the tree line.

Footprints of different sizes climbed over the snowdrifts leading to the woods. Ian followed them with his eyes until he couldn't see any deeper into the darkness created by the treetops. His gut told him to follow them in, see where they led. Before he could step into the mouth of the forest, the sound of tires crackling over the icy driveway stopped Ian in his tracks. He turned and walked back around the front of the house to find a police cruiser parked behind his car. The door opened, and Roberts stepped out, first spotting Ian's car, then seeing Ian coming toward him.

"What are you doing here, Mr. Warner?" Roberts asked, shutting the car door.

"I could ask you the same question. If you thought everything was fine, why are you out here checking up on my family?"

The agitation in Roberts' eyes was obvious. He bit the inside of his lip and then spoke.

"Well, it's my responsibility to look after this town, so I'd say I'm doing my damn job. I don't appreciate you questioning me. After what happened with the boy, I felt it best to make a drive out here and check on the place. Make sure everything was good."

"They aren't answering my calls, my texts, nothing. I'm worried. I know, everything is gone, and the rental company said Kristen called to check out. So why don't I feel any better right now?" Ian asked, more to himself than to Chief Roberts.

"Because you've been through a lot. Listen, I may come across like I don't give a fuck about what happened, but please believe me when I tell you that's far from the truth. Something didn't sit right with me the other night either. What were you looking for out back, anyway?"

Ian considered saying nothing, but what did he have to lose at this point? Roberts already thought he was a paranoid asshole.

"I thought maybe I could see those prints better in the daylight. I don't know…"

Roberts rubbed his hand over his mustache, fixing some of the stray whites poking up.

"Okay. The only problem with that is that we were all out there looking for him together. How exactly do you plan to differentiate our prints from the others? You don't exactly come across as a master tracker," Roberts said.

Ian couldn't tell if he was attempting a joke, or if he was being a sarcastic prick. Probably a bit of both. He hated himself for not even considering that part of it.

"Shit. I'm just worried, man. I'm not thinking straight. I don't know what the hell to do. They're all I have left after losing Chelsea."

The mention of her name acted as an invisible slap to Roberts. He winced, averting eye contact as he looked toward the woods in silence for a moment.

"I'm sorry, I really am. I've never been great at showing compassion. Sometimes a little coldness helps with the job, but other times—like with your case—it creates some enemies. And I'm too stubborn to try and fix my ways at this stage of my life. But you need to understand one thing: I'm a damn good cop. So, when someone questions how I do my job, I sure as hell take offense to it. That doesn't mean I was right to treat you the way I did though. So, for that, I'm sorry." When he finished talking, he finally took his eyes off the woods and looked back to Ian.

"I appreciate that. I probably could've handled things better on my end too. If you knew what it was like to lose the person you care about most, and then have to accept that she actually killed herself—I think anyone would react before thinking in that situation. That doesn't mean I think she did it, though, but with each passing day I realize I may have to accept that..."

Both men stood uncomfortably quiet for a minute, until a cold breeze broke the silence.

"What do we do if I don't hear from them? As annoying as my sister can be, I know she wouldn't go a day without getting back to me. The whole damn reason she rented this house was to make sure I was okay after everything that'd happened. The last thing she'd want to do is get me upset right now," Ian said.

"Honestly? We have to wait. They checked out. The house is clear. She texted you saying they were leaving. The only reason we are both here is because of how strange it all is. We have no hard evidence that there's anything wrong."

"How long do I have to wait?" Ian asked, wanting to say more but forcing himself to be reasonable.

"A few days. It's the holidays. We can't search for a family that's just on vacation. If you don't hear from them in a day or two, get back to me." Roberts said.

That at least brought some semblance of comfort to Ian, but he still felt uneasy. They said their goodbyes and left. Ian held his phone the entire ride, praying that Kristen would call him.

CHAPTER 30

Kosa watched as Mother walked out of the room with Sammy. Everything felt so different now that she had seen one of the kids in their normal state of mind. Marta told her they all acted the way they did because of what was inside Kosa, yet this entire time it had been her controlling them and forcing them to act that way. Why would she lie to Kosa?

She walked up the stairs and into the attic at Mother's behest, hoping that Sammy wouldn't have to suffer much before it was over. It remained dark as ever in the attic. Tom followed her in and walked over to his cat bed, making multiple laps before finally plopping down and training his eyes on Kosa. She walked to the window and looked out, thinking maybe she'd catch one last glimpse of Mother walking with Sammy. With all the friends she had played with over the years, none of them had ever come fully out of their mental paralysis induced by Marta. Yet Sammy acted as if he'd just awoken from a decade-long hibernation when the talking device buzzed.

That reminded Kosa that she still had the device in her own pocket now. She pulled it out, turning it over in her hands to get a better look at it. Sammy had called it a "walkie-talkie". He didn't tell her what it was for, but it appeared to be some sort of communication tool to the outside world. The idea both excited and terrified Kosa. If Mother found it, she wouldn't only destroy it, but Kosa would be in even more trouble than she had been the night before. Did Kosa really want to communicate with people out there? She'd been raised to believe everyone was horrible. That her playmates were the only outsiders who were worth talking to. One thing she knew for sure was that she needed to figure out how to turn it off for now, so she didn't risk Mother hearing it go off again.

She pushed down the biggest button and held it, and the device barked out an alarming squeal. She panicked, dropping the walkie to the floor. Tom lifted his head and stared intently, but quickly forgot about it and went back to his cat nap. Kosa leaned down and picked it up, hoping the fall didn't break the device. She didn't know why, but it felt like the device was important.

A knob on the top of the walkie-talkie turned side to side, so she turned it all the way in one direction. As she did, the humming coming from the speaker increased, and again she almost dropped it. She was about to turn the knob the other way when a voice spoke from inside the box.

"Sammy? Was that you? Are you okay?"

Kosa froze, afraid to do anything. After a moment passed, she aggressively turned the knob in the other direction until it clicked off. Her heart was pounding in her chest. She knew Mother couldn't find this, or it would be destroyed. She quickly ran to the corner of the room and knelt, finding a small opening in the wall: the hole that her old friend Jerry used to come out of searching for scraps of food. It had been years since she'd thought of the little mouse, and as she stuck her hand into the hole as far as she could reach, she had a passing thought of something far worse than Jerry waiting in the hole for someone stupid enough to put their hand in. She yanked her hand out, wiping away the cobwebs on her pants. This hiding spot would work.

Who was that trying to talk to Sammy? Kosa got to her feet and looked out the window, searching for Sammy in the muted dusk light. Sammy was nowhere in sight, but Marta was, exiting through the bulkhead in the basement. Whether it was the memory of her little mouse friend, or the sight of Mother, Kosa found herself thinking about the long-buried memory of discovering Marta's secret room down there when she was a little girl. She saw things no child should see. Heard sounds that still gave her nightmares.

Stop it. She raised you. Protected you. She's a good woman...

For the first time in her life, Kosa was beginning to doubt those thoughts.

CHAPTER 31

"Sammy! Was that you?" Ian yelled into the walkie-talkie again.

He looked at the screen and noticed the red dot indicating the GPS location of the other unit was no longer visible. Either Sammy had turned it off, or someone did it for him.

"Damn it!"

Ian grabbed his phone and dialed Chief Roberts.

"So, you heard..." Roberts said, his tone trying to force compassion.

"Heard what? What the fuck happened?"

"They found your sister's car a few miles down from the rental property. They... They crashed into a tree head on, Ian. They didn't survive. I'm so sorry..."

Ian dropped to his knees, his trembling hand dropping the phone. Everything inside him told him something was wrong, yet all he wanted was to be proven incorrect. Instead, Roberts delivered the worst news he could have possibly received. Ian heard Roberts' muffled voice coming from the phone on the floor and picked it up.

"He was just a boy... I fucking knew they were in danger! You told me it was under control, Roberts..."

"I'm sorry, Ian. There's something I need to tell you, even though it's still being investigated..."

"What? What else could you possibly need to tell me?" Ian said, now sobbing uncontrollably.

"The boy... He... he wasn't with them. They searched the surrounding area of the accident, and he was nowhere to be found. We are out searching right now. I'll keep you posted."

Ian hung up the call without responding.

Roberts didn't even give him time to mourn his sister before dropping that bombshell on him. Ian tried to regain some composure, knowing he needed to try and find Sammy. He was done putting any faith in the local police to accomplish anything. The fact that Sammy was missing from the car told Ian all he needed to know. That the accident was no "accident." Whoever had been trying to get Sammy before wasn't stopping until they finished the job.

The last location on the GPS was somewhere in the area of the rental home. The footprints he had been ready to follow could have led somewhere, and he was hating himself for not following through and going into the woods before Roberts showed up. He wasn't going to make that mistake again. He grabbed his jacket and threw it on, alerting Scooter of his intentions. The dog lifted his head from the couch, waiting for instructions.

"Not this time, buddy. I'm going on my own. Be a good pup," Ian said and tossed a treat to Scooter, who caught it midair in his mouth and wagged his tail.

Ian exited his house and got into his car, setting his walkie-talkie on the passenger seat along with a bag of supplies: snacks, water, and a flashlight. He screamed into the steering wheel, punching the horn over and over until his fist throbbed in pain. Swallowing down the emotional pain, he started the car and backed out of his driveway. It was getting dark and the last thing he wanted was to roam around in the woods again with nothing more than his phone light.

He sped down the desolate roads leading toward the lake, constantly looking over to see if his walkie-talkie showed the other being turned on again. Had he been thinking straight, Ian would've taken a picture of the screen with his phone, so he had some idea of which direction to head once he got to the woods. There was always the possibility that Sammy accidentally left the walkie-talkie at the vacation home, but Ian highly doubted that. He was far too excited to get the gift to just up and leave it behind—child or not.

The sky continued to darken, and Ian knew at best he had about an hour of full light before the early dusk turned to the evening that New England brought this time of year, a black sky with freezing temperatures. Even going well above the speed limit, he felt the ride was taking forever. As he ascended into the mountains, the sense of dread continued to amplify. His ears popped with the increased elevation, and he had a fleeting thought that it was his blood pressure getting so high that it was causing a brain hemorrhage.

Up ahead, the lake came into view over the side of the steep embankment. Patches of thickening ice had begun to form over the water's surface as winter continued to take hold of the area. Ian slowed to go around a sharp corner and spotted the driveway of the home his family had stayed in over the weekend. He pulled into the empty driveway—thankful that nobody else had rented it yet—and killed the engine. Wasting no time, he grabbed his bag and got out of the car, immediately heading for the woods. The prints were still there, frozen in time until the next storm came to erase their memory. He followed them into the woods, knowing full well they could be his own footprints from the search for Sammy a few nights prior. *At least following them will get me in the general area,* he thought.

The cold air burned his lungs, but Ian pushed himself forward. Twenty minutes into his trek, he stopped to grab a drink. As cold as it was, he still needed to remain hydrated—especially his out-of-shape ass. He cursed himself for letting his body go to shit after Chelsea died.

While resting, he scanned the area, trying to determine if anything looked familiar. He knew it was a lost cause, not just because it was nightfall when he was out here last, but also because he was terrible with directions. Chelsea used to pick on him, asking how he survived in the world in the days before GPS systems. He was just thankful he hadn't lost the trail of footprints going through the forest.

Darkness rapidly approached, and the thought of having to go back through the woods to get to his car wasn't at all appealing. But it would all be worth it if he got answers.

"No rest for the wicked," he mumbled to himself, forcing his legs to continue moving.

After a few more miles, with the daylight now a thing of the past, Ian spotted a clearing up ahead in the distance. Not only a clearing, but what looked like a museum or some old Victorian mansion in the opening. The sight of something besides endless trees gave him hope. He picked up the pace until he reached the edge of the forest, and then stopped. What if this was the person messing with them at the lake house? He came prepared to search for his family, not defend himself against someone evil enough to drag a child into the woods.

    The house was massive. It could use a bit of remodeling; given its size, he couldn't imagine the owner lacked enough money to fix the place up. And it wasn't abandoned: there were lights on inside. He reached into his bag and pulled out his walkie-talkie, giving one last look at it to see if Sammy had turned his back on. Unfortunately, the screen was still blank. Ian tossed it back into his bag and walked out onto the lawn.

CHAPTER 32

Kosa sat at the table, finishing her soup. Mother looked awful, lifting a trembling hand to her mouth in an attempt to eat the soup before it splashed out of the spoon. All that meant was that the ritual would be more painful tonight. Phantom pain pulsed through Kosa's temples at the thought of it. She didn't even want story time tonight, instead preferring to just go to bed and be done with this day. Hopefully a good night's sleep would get her out of this funk, where she felt anger every time she looked at Mother. She knew she was being ungrateful, that Mother was only doing what she needed to survive. But it was the way Sammy looked when he came out of his trance that bothered Kosa. He appeared sick. Or in pain. She couldn't put a finger on it, but it was clear he didn't like how it made him feel.

"Mother, Sammy was a nice boy. I hope you didn't make him suffer," Kosa said, waiting for Marta's reaction.

The old woman sighed deeply, then sipped another spoonful of soup.

"How many times must I say it, Kosa? That is none of your concern. You can't get attached to the source of your power."

Before Kosa could respond, there was a knock at the door. They both went still, listening for it again. Marta snarled and looked at Kosa.

"Go to the attic, girl."

Again, the knock came, this time much louder.

Without a word, Kosa got up and ran to the stairs, both excitement and fear swirling around in her stomach. She climbed them two at a time and headed toward the attic. And then curiosity got the better of her. Instead of going to the attic, she snuck into one of the spare bedrooms that overlooked the front yard. She saw the top of a man's head looking toward the front of the house. It was the first time she recalled ever seeing another person that wasn't a child. Kosa soaked him in, reveling in the fact that she was seeing someone closer to her age. She was so enamored by him that she didn't move away quickly enough when he stared up toward the window.

Ian prepared to knock a third time when two things happened. Movement from the window above grabbed his attention. When he looked up, the figure backed out of sight. Nightfall hid most of her features, but in the quick glimpse he saw her, she didn't look much older than a teenager. Then the front door opened slightly, revealing an old woman with a leathery face, her eyes mostly hidden by the darkness of the house. No, not hidden. They were black, blending with the shadows.

The woman with the black eyes...

Just looking at her gave him the chills.

"Hi, ma'am. I'm just searching the area for my nephew. I was wondering if you might have seen him? His parents were in an accident nearby, and well... his body wasn't in the car with them," Ian said, choking on his words. He pulled out his phone and opened a picture of Sammy, who was flashing a joyful smile—the photo had been taken the last time they had a sleepover together.

"I've seen no boy..." she said through thin lips, her accent thick, possibly Eastern European.

Ian couldn't tell if she was looking at him or not; there were no pupils in the center of her eyes. But he hadn't walked all this way just to get a four-word answer and turn back.

"Well can you at least look at the picture and see if it rings a bell?"

"I said... I've seen no *boy*. It doesn't matter what he looks like. If you don't mind, I'm getting ready for bed," she said, starting to shut the door in his face.

"Can I ask your daughter at least?"

The door stopped, then opened back up.

"I have no daughter. I live my life *alone* with my cats, just the way I prefer it. Alone. Now please leave..."

"I... Okay. Can you please keep an eye out? I think he came through these woods and may have gotten lost; the accident was a few miles down the road." He'd initially planned to question her about the presence of the girl in the window, but realized this woman wasn't going to help him.

"Nobody comes out here. If he's lost in those woods, he's probably dead. Now please leave," she snapped, and slammed the door in his face.

"Bitch," he whispered.

He walked down the steps and turned back to glance up at the window once more. He could've sworn he spotted movement again. While it was too dark to see her face, he saw fiery, red hair that brightened the area around it. He scanned the other windows as he backed away from the porch, noticing a black cat sitting in one, watching him like a guard dog. A terrible feeling festered inside, and it only escalated at the sight of those black eyes. Roberts had mentioned multiple children going missing over the years: could the girl he saw in the window be one of them? Ian had no idea what to do. He couldn't go to Roberts, who would just play it off. He wasn't about to sit around and wait on him. An internal clock told Ian he was running out of time, but he needed to try and find more information about the missing persons cases—anything that could possibly help him find his nephew.

CHAPTER 33

Sammy opened his eyes and found himself in an abyss of darkness, chained to the wall. Vague memories flashed through his mind: of the woman luring him into the woods, of her talking with his parents, telling them to leave the house and their son behind. Why did they listen to her? He didn't remember why he wanted to go with the woman, just that in the moment, nothing sounded better than following her. He looked down at his hands, seeing his wrists tightly constrained by rusted chains. It was impossible to tell the size of the room in the darkness, but he tried to force his eyes to adjust. His throat felt as if it had been filled with thumbtacks, each swallow bringing a sharp pain. He risked trying to get to his feet, immediately regretting it as his legs buckled beneath him.

An earthy aroma filled the space, and as he dug his feet in place to prevent himself from falling, he realized the floor was made of compacted dirt, and that his shoes had been removed. Was he in a basement?

"Hello?" he asked the darkness, reinvigorating the needle-like pain in his throat.

Now that his eyes had been open for a moment, he was beginning to make out the outline of the room. No specific details stood out, but the approximate dimensions were now coming into focus. It was a small room, not much bigger than his closet at home. So, while it appeared to be part of the basement, it was clearly a separate room branching off from the main area.

All he wanted right now was his mother. It wasn't what he could see, it was what he *couldn't* see that scared him most. The corners were completely shrouded in darkness. He wanted to yell out again, scream at the top of his lungs for someone to help him. But he knew in his gut nobody would hear him down here.

Sammy forced himself to think again about the events leading up to this. Not just coming to this house, but before that. He remembered waking to find the old woman standing over his bed, her black cloak camouflaged by the shadows. Her cats had jumped up on the foot of the bed, staring at Sammy with their strange eyes. Then she spoke, chanting something he couldn't understand. The next thing he remembered was getting out of bed and following her into his parents' room, where she again chanted something foreign before his mom and dad agreed to whatever she asked. He remembered that he still had his walkie-talkie in his pocket, that he slept with it so he wouldn't miss Uncle Ian saying anything. *The walkie-talkie*!

He felt around in his pocket as best he could with both hands chained together, and quickly realized it was no longer there. The young girl—Kosa—she had taken it from him. Sammy needed to find a way to communicate with her. She seemed nice, and not in the fake way the old woman, Marta, acted.

Whatever the lady did to him was wearing off, which brought on a stronger bout of nausea. He leaned against the wall and closed his eyes, attempting to calm himself and get rid of the stomachache.

Something moved in the corner of the room, and Sammy's eyes shot open, looking around frantically for the source of the noise.

"Is somebody there?" he whispered, his voice trembling with fear.

Something shifted in the darkness. He didn't dare say another word but continued watching the corner, waiting for the movement again. It was as if a darker shade of black moved over a lighter shade. Maybe he was seeing things. But he knew he also heard movement.

"Who's there? I can see you..." he said, trying to sound tough.

He stood still again and listened. His chains rattled, startling him out of his silence. Then he realized he hadn't moved; it wasn't *his* chains clinking. It was someone else's.

"She'll come for us... she takes us one at a time and then we never come back," the voice of a little girl said.

"Who's there?" Sammy asked again.

"My name's Angela. I'm sorry you're here..."

The admission of defeat in her voice made any hope of getting out alive sink in the pit of Sammy's stomach.

"Why did she take us?" he asked.

"We don't know, just that once she comes for you, you'll never come back from here."

"There's more than just you here?"

"There was... The old lady took my other friend a few days ago," she said, and Sammy could hear her choking on tears as she spoke.

"How long have you been down here?"

"I don't know. I think a few weeks. She brings us bread and water twice a day. At first, I counted the meals, but then I gave up. I told her my mommy and daddy would come looking for me, but she... she said they were dead."

Sammy thought back to his parents agreeing with Marta. Did something happen to them? The thought of losing them was too much to handle. He needed to get out of the dark room and find the girl. She could give back the walkie-talkie. Uncle Ian would call the cops and save them.

"Is it always the old lady who comes to give us food? Or does the girl come too?" he asked.

"I've only seen the witch. But I only remember things once I got in here. Before this, the last thing I remember is being in the yard at our vacation home, building a snowman. I heard someone shouting for help in the woods, so I ran to the edge of the lawn to see who it was. And then she was there, and everything went fuzzy..."

Even though Sammy couldn't see her, he heard her struggling to talk without getting sad. She said her parents were dead, that she had been here for a while, and only eaten bread and water. He hadn't even been here long enough for a meal to arrive; the thought of spending weeks in a dark box terrified him.

"We need to get out of here. Can you think of anything that would help us? Any weapons? Tools? *Anything*?"

For a moment, the room was silent. A soft, sobbing noise broke it.

"If I had something, I woulda tried to get out already. She doesn't even give me toilet paper. Or my stuffy. All I want is my bear and my blanket. To sleep in my own bed and see my family again. The last time I saw my parents, they were fighting. That's why I went out by myself to play, so I didn't have to listen anymore. It was about me, and now they are dead. It's all my fault…"

Sammy's heart broke for her. But he couldn't spend much time feeling sorry for someone he didn't know. There was a real chance his parents were also dead at the hands of this lady. Angela had just called her a witch, and it seemed fitting.

"I'm going to get us out of here, I promise. We need to talk to Kosa somehow," he said, realizing he sounded far more grownup than his age dictated. He thought his parents would be proud of how he was handling the situation. Then he remembered how serious this was, and that not only could they be dead, but he might also not have much longer if the mean lady came for him. Suddenly, the weight of the situation hit him, and he dropped to the floor, hugging his knees. He stomped his feet and screamed, letting all the emotions come to the surface. He slammed his fists into the dirt floor repeatedly, until pain shot up his arms. When he was done, he took deep breaths, trying to calm himself. He rubbed the dirt floor with his palms, squeezing handfuls of dirt into his chained hands, massaging the pain away.

"I'm sorry, Sammy… I think, if it's okay with you, I'd like to go back to sleep now. I'm tired, and sleeping helps me forget about this," Angela said.

Sammy half-heartedly acknowledged her, but his mind was elsewhere. He had an idea, one that he felt could possibly save his life. A thin line of light burned through the darkness on the floor in front of him, and he realized it was where the door was located. Angela was already snoring, fast asleep thanks to the exhaustion and food deprivation. Sammy wouldn't sleep. Instead, he watched the light at the bottom of the door, waiting for possibly the only chance he'd get to save himself.

PART IV
TO TAKE A SOUL

CHAPTER 34

Ian sat on his couch with Scooter nuzzled in his lap sleeping, scrolling through articles about all of the missing children and bizarre cases in the surrounding area over the last few decades. How had this not been a bigger deal? Sunapee wasn't exactly a big town; these types of stories should have been huge news. Yet, he didn't recall ever seeing as much as a quick headline on the evening news about them. He wasn't sure what he was looking for. All he knew was there had to be a connection, somewhere, and he would find it. He'd spent the last few hours scouring articles and blogs. The biggest problem was that there appeared to be no sign of any survivors. Either the entire families were found slaughtered, with one of them being blamed for a murder-suicide crime, or they'd all up and vanished.

And then he came across a case from nearly ten years ago. The Larson family had rented a house near the lake, a mother and her two sons. The husband had stayed home with the flu and didn't travel with the family. The youngest son, a boy named Bryce, was never found. Timothy Larson was the only surviving member of the family. Apparently, he was questioned initially, until his alibi checked out when they saw how sick he truly was.

Scrolling through the article, Ian stopped on an image of the vacation home. It was the exact same one his family stayed at.

Ian searched for the husband and found an address. He lived out of state, much too far to drive. Maybe he could find a phone number and reach out? What would he even ask him if he did get in touch? Who knew the state of mind a guy who'd lost his entire family, and in such gruesome fashion, would be in. Hell, Ian had lost Chelsea to suicide—he found himself starting to give in to that fact—and he felt like he had nothing to live for. Now his sister and Jack were also gone. If he also lost Sammy, he wasn't sure he could go on living.

After scanning through some reverse phone search sites, he found a phone number that supposedly belonged to Timothy. He took a deep breath and hit dial.

After the third ring, the line picked up.

"Hello?" an agitated voice asked. Ian could hear the pain in his voice.

The words were hard to bring out, as if he subconsciously hadn't expected anyone to answer.

"Hi... My name's Ian Warner. I'm calling you because... because I'm desperate. I know you lost your family, and I've lost mine as well, at the same house." He paused, waiting to see if this guy would just hang up on some looney calling him out of the blue.

"I'm sorry to hear that. Can't say it gets any easier as time goes by. My Bryce woulda been in college right now, probably starting in center field... What is it exactly that you think I can do for you?"

"I don't know. I thought maybe if I talked with someone about this house, or what happens there, maybe it could help me find my nephew..."

"The boy's parents are gone, I take it?"

Ian choked down a sob, fighting to finish the conversation.

"Yeah. I got a call earlier today. They found them... found em' in their car off the side of the road. The car was wrapped around a tree. But my nephew, Sammy, he wasn't in the vehicle."

"And let me guess, you don't think that was no accident, do you?"

"I don't know what to think. I had this weird feeling ever since I left the house after spending the holidays with them. My nephew—he had an episode the night before I left. Scared the shit out of us all. I found him huddled in the middle of the woods, wearing his pajamas. He was talking about the lady with the black eyes, bringing him out to the woods. Next thing I know, he's back to himself and didn't remember anything."

Silence on the other end led Ian to think the man had heard enough and dropped the call. Then, he finally spoke.

"So, I'll ask again, and please don't take this the wrong way, but why the hell are you calling me about this?"

"Let me ask you: do you think the story the police gave you is what really happened with your family?"

"No," Timothy said, and even though it was through the phone, Ian could sense him grinding his teeth as he said it.

"And have you ever looked into the other occurrences that took place in that area? Maybe wonder what the fuck goes on in those woods?"

"Of course. Heather would've never done that on her own to our kids. I even went out there myself trying to find answers. But it got me nowhere. My suggestion? Accept it as it is. Something out there does this to families and the local authorities don't give a shit. Something about that cop in charge I didn't trust. I'm sorry I couldn't be of more help..."

"I think you've helped me more than you know. And I'm sorry to call you and stir up this stuff again. The thing is, I could never just accept it. Not without knowing if Sammy is alive or not. *Especially* now that his parents are gone. Thank you for taking the time to talk today, Tim."

"I don't think you'll find anything; Lord knows I did everything *I* could. But I wish you the best, just the same. Good luck."

The phone line disconnected before Ian could respond. While Timothy hadn't said anything specifically that would help Ian find Sammy, the conversation helped solidify that Sammy was still out there, that someone took him, and this wasn't just some car wreck due to black ice. It also brought back the hate for Roberts that he'd felt for months. Roberts had to know more than he was letting on, but wouldn't admit it, nor do anything about it.

Images of the red-haired girl in the window came back to Ian, and it gave him an idea. He opened his laptop up again and searched for missing children in the area going back about sixteen years. While the window's reflection made it difficult to see her, she had the build of a teenage girl. Again, he spent close to twenty minutes skimming links and looking for anything that seemed useful. He was about to give up when he clicked on an article about the Brock family. Alan and Bridgett Brock had been found with their throats ripped out, both lying face down in their bed. Their newborn baby was nowhere to be found. It wasn't the story that made him stop, it was the images of the husband and wife in the article. The mother had long, red hair, and olive skin. Obviously red hair wasn't a rare trait, it could be anyone. But the timeline matched up.

Ian printed the article with the image of the parents and folded it up, stuffing it into his jeans pocket. If this old lady—this witch—had kept a girl alive for sixteen years, that meant there was still a chance Sammy was alive. He called Roberts' cell one more time, again getting his voicemail. This time, he decided to leave a message.

"Roberts... I know everything that's happened between us in the past would lead you to think I'm overreacting, but I think there's a chance I can save Sammy. If you get this, meet me at the lake house. There's a trail going through the woods that leads to a large house where an old lady lives. I... I think she's behind all of these missing children," he said, and ended the call.

He wasn't sure he could trust Roberts, but maybe if he brought him directly to the source of the crime, the cop would have no choice but to help him.

Scooter ran to the door, as if he could read Ian's mind. Ian quickly packed a bag, threw his walkie-talkie in, then looked to his dog.

"Okay, boy. Let's go save Sammy."

CHAPTER 35

Kosa ate her soup, like she did every night, but it now brought on a taste that made her want to gag. All these years, Mother had convinced her that eating the remains of her friends was what had to be done, that these kids were part of the problem in the world and were here only to serve one purpose.

Until Sammy, Kosa never thought much about it. Marta had been forced to tell Kosa the truth about her friends after Kosa discovered the little boy, Bryce, being cooked alive in the basement ten years ago. It took time to adjust to the truth, but over the years Mother had helped her realize it was a necessity for the *Tamna Sila*.

But then Sammy came out of his trance. For the first time, she saw a real person staring back at her. The poor boy just wanted his parents, he was confused. Mother told Kosa that these kids knew their fate and had accepted it, and that she should never talk about it with them while they played. If she did, she wouldn't be able to have fun before they were sent off to their demise.

She chewed on a piece of meat, wondering which friend it had come from. Each child typically lasted a few months, but Mother needed more of them now—either that or the dark force needed more to provide Mother with the power she needed to survive.

"Eat up, dear. Mother is in a great deal of pain tonight. I need to satisfy the *Tamna Sila*..." she said, almost sounding desperate.

Kosa held her breath as she swallowed down the meat, quickly washing it down with a gulp of water. Marta noticed the change in Kosa's eating habits and paused her own meal, watching Kosa chew. Kosa knew her cheeks were burning red as Mother's eyes bored into hers.

"Girl... what's floating in that brain of yours? Why are you acting so strangely tonight?"

"I... I'm just not that hungry, Mother. I know I need to eat though. To help you."

"Good, good. You know, that was a man looking for his missing nephew today. I'm slipping in my ways. There should have been no trail to us. I need you more than ever to listen to me when I give you instructions. Do you understand?"

"Yes, Mother."

"Very good. I'm all done with my meal. I need to go tend to the children before the ritual. Clean the dishes while I'm gone," Marta said, then got up from the table and limped away from the kitchen.

Every step appeared agonizing for her, but she continued to defy her age. The term "tend to the children" set an uneasy feeling in the pit of Kosa's stomach. She knew that meant Mother was about to take one of them, preparing them for meals. For the first time in her life, she wanted to stop it.

CHAPTER 36

Sammy's wrists were starting to turn raw. He'd spent the last few hours struggling to free his hands from the tight restraints that bound him in the cold, damp confines of the basement. *The witch's basement*, he thought. *Like something from a story.*

Finally, his hands slipped through the chains as blood trickled down his wrists. He couldn't help cracking a smile, even in the dire conditions.

"What are you doing?" Angela asked.

"I'm trying to get out of here. She's going to come back soon and I wanna get out when she does," he said.

With his eyes now adjusted to the darkness, he saw desperation and fear etched across Angela's face. She didn't say a word, instead just continued watching him. Summoning his courage, Sammy took a deep breath and felt good enough about his plan to tell her.

"When she comes, I'm going to throw dirt in her eyes. If the door's still open, we can make a run for it and get out of here. Think you can do that?"

A single tear slid down her dirt-crusted face, creating a trail of mud on her cheek.

"I... I don't know. It hurts to even stand."

Sammy got to his feet and ran to her side, ignoring her self-doubt. He worked at the constraints around her wrists, and she cried out as the metal rubbed against her bruised skin.

"I'm sorry. It might hurt, but it's the only way to get you out."

Angela's hands were beginning to slide through the chains when approaching footsteps echoed on the other side of the door. Angela quickly yanked her hands free, biting down on her shirt to block out the pain.

"Just wait, go back to your spot," she whispered.

Sammy ran to his corner and sat on the floor, grabbing a handful of dirt. He held his hands in place to give the illusion of still being restrained. The sound of his racing heartbeat consumed his senses, but he forced himself to focus on the door, waiting for his opportunity. A set of keys jingled, muffled by the metal sheets that had been screwed to each side of the wooden door. Sammy assumed it was to add to the security of the structure, keep the children in at all costs.

The handle jiggled. Metal scraped along the dirt floor as the door was swung open to a rusty groan.

The old woman stood, hunched over, as if even the simple act of opening a door had taken the energy from her. *Good, maybe she's weak*, Sammy thought. The newfound light leaking in from the room behind her was dull, yet after hours of darkness it felt like he was staring directly into the sun. Sammy squinted, almost lifting his hand to shade his eyes before remembering he had to pretend to still be tied up. The witch's black cloak gave her a menacing look, the hood hiding much of her face. For a moment, she just stood, staring at them without speaking. Sammy looked at her hands, and noticed she wasn't holding the keys. They must've been in the door still. He also noticed she didn't have any food. She wasn't here to feed them. That could only mean she had other intentions with them.

He squeezed the dirt tightly, digging his nails into his palms.

"You know, I don't enjoy this part. It's part of the agreement, and therefore I must follow through. So, which one of you would like to come first?"

Angela backed even further into the corner, as if that would protect her from whatever the old lady had planned.

"Why are you doing this to us? My family will come looking for me!" Sammy yelled, trying to distract her.

She let out a cackling laugh, exposing her jagged teeth and all their rot.

"Boy, your parents aren't looking for anybody. Don't fight the inevitable," she said as she approached him. "I think you made my decision easy... I don't appreciate being talked to that way."

The witch leaned to grab hold of him, and Sammy saw his opportunity. He hurled the dirt, aiming for the witch's eyes. The dirt connected with its target, causing the witch to shriek in pain and confusion. Blinded temporarily, she stumbled, grasping at the air. Sammy seized his opportunity and jumped to his feet.

"Let's go! Come on!" he yelled to Angela.

She remained frozen in place, too scared to move past the witch. The old woman dropped to her knee and forced out a violent cough—apparently some of the dirt had gone into her mouth as well.

"Patit ces zbog toga, ti kretence!" the woman bellowed.

Angela finally got to her feet and clung to the wall, trying to stay out of reach from the witch's flailing hands. Sammy fled the cramped room, a newfound adrenaline coursing through him. He darted through the dark hallway, his small frame weaving through the labyrinth of corridors. Shadows danced around him, as if conspiring with the witch to stop him before he escaped. He looked over his shoulder and saw Angela behind him, but she wasn't moving nearly as fast. Her body was too weak, she couldn't maintain any level of speed before slowing down.

Movement behind Angela in the hallway caught Sammy's attention, and he screamed at the sight of the witch stumbling out of the makeshift dungeon toward them. Her black eyes followed them, her rage melting every ounce of confidence he'd earned from escaping the prison.

"Hurry! She's behind you!" Sammy shouted.

He couldn't wait for Angela; his life was on the line, and he needed to get out of this house. Sammy rounded a dark corner and spotted three doors. One of them had to go up the basement stairs into the main part of the house. He tried the first door, opening to find a room with shelves lined on each side of the wall. An orange glow emitted from a hole in the wall, and he realized it was a fireplace. Flames devoured a bundle of firewood, giving him enough light to take in the room. Different sized bones littered the shelves, jars full of strange liquids and seasonings. When he registered that the fire was fresh, that the witch must've recently started it, it sent a chill down his spine. He glanced back to the bones, then once more to the fire, seeing a large pot dangling above it.

Those bones belonged to kids, he thought.

Sammy left the room, moving to the second door. The distant wails of the injured witch were getting closer, so he entered the second room, desperate for a place to hide. This room looked more like a home office straight out of a haunted house movie. Angela screamed from the hallway. Sammy heard her enter the room he had just left, her cries muffled through the thin wall. He searched for a place to hide; this room was much darker as there was no fire to guide him. He spotted a heavy oak desk in the darkest corner of the room. Climbing underneath it, he curled into a small ball, his breath coming in ragged gasps. The silence enveloped him, broken only by the witch shouting in her foreign language.

In the darkness, he clung to hope, knowing he'd at least given himself a chance by getting this far. His parents would be proud of the fight he put up. The thought of them brought him to tears, but he realized he didn't have time to feel sorry for himself right now. That could happen later when he was free from this nightmare. With each passing second, he whispered a silent prayer, hoping the witch's sight wouldn't return, and that he'd find a way to escape this malevolent horror once and for all.

Sammy realized the witch wasn't talking anymore, and that the entire basement had gone completely silent outside of the pipes moaning overhead. He closed his eyes, trying his hardest to hold his breath, keep his composure long enough for the witch to search another area of the house and get past him. The silence that followed was terrifying. What was the witch doing? As if she could read his mind, he found out exactly what she was doing.

Angela screamed from the next room, jolting the calmness from Sammy's body that he'd worked so hard to maintain. He curled up tighter, begging whoever was in his thoughts for help. The screams got louder, followed by thumping around. A glass shattered. The witch yelled. Angela's cries were cut short. And then the sound of a body being dragged across the dirt floor entered the hallway. The first thought that invaded Sammy's mind was that the witch had killed Angela and was dragging her dead body to prep for her feeding. But then he heard Angela whimpering, a low, painful cry. As the sound got further away, Sammy realized he had to act now. He hesitantly got out of his hiding spot and snuck to the door, peering his head around the corner.

The image he saw would be drilled into his memories for the rest of his life—however long that might be. Angela appeared mostly unconscious, her eyes fluttering open and closed. A trail of blood lined the dirt floor as her arms dragged behind her. The witch had her back to Sammy, dragging Angela by the feet back toward the dungeon. She muttered something under her breath. Sammy snapped himself out of his trance, remembering he had one final door to check, which *had* to be the one leading to the upper level of the house. He ran out of the room toward the unopened door, a tickling sensation working its way up his back at the anticipation of the witch turning to see his attempted escape, a nest of spiders crawling up his spine.

He hoped the old lady hadn't thought to lock the door before coming to them. As he reached for the handle, a sudden thump sounded behind him of something smacking on the dirt floor. He turned to see that the witch had dropped Angela's feet.

She was staring at Sammy.

He turned the knob and ripped the door open, relieved that it opened so easily, and that he was now facing a set of ascending stairs going up to another door—to the main level of the home. Sammy took the stairs as quickly as his little legs allowed, making his way up the dark enclosed hallway toward the next door. The metal door to the room he'd just escaped slammed shut, no doubt locking Angela back in to face her pending death at a later time. He reached the next door and opened—and was hit with a brightness that almost made him fall backwards down the stairs. Once his eyes adjusted, he realized it was just the normal lighting of the home, but he'd been locked in the dark so long that even the dim glow of low wattage bulbs hurt to look at.

The size of the house took Sammy by surprise after being confined to the cramped space for hours. Only brief flashes of his time with Kosa stuck with him; the rest was a blur, so he had no idea which direction to head in. Basement stairs cried under the weight of the witch's feet, letting Sammy know he had to make a decision. He turned, realizing he hadn't shut the basement door behind him to buy more time. She was already halfway up the stairs, limping along.

"Look at me, *boy*! You will suffer a terrible death for this!"

Sammy realized something in that moment. She wanted him to look at her because it was her eyes that controlled him. Staring into those large, obsidian spheres somehow took over his mind and made him do whatever she asked of him. He avoided eye contact, then slammed the door shut. A last second thought to lock the door came to him, and he turned the latch. As he started to sprint down the hall, the basement door rattled, followed by another scream of rage from the witch. He picked a direction and took off, running down the hall as fast as possible, no longer concerned about making any noise. The lady had been slowed down, but he knew she would get out, especially if one of her keys opened that door.

Sammy came to the big room that he had played in with Kosa. The sight of the open floor plan again brought back flashes of earlier that night. All he had to do was get through this room and he would be out to the main hallway leading to the front of the house. He had never wanted to touch snow so badly. Where would he go once he escaped? Who would he turn to? He'd need to get to Uncle Ian, who would do anything to protect him.

As he got closer to the room's exit, the sound of the basement door slamming against the wall as it was opened startled him. The witch was out and limping down the hallway toward the big room. He pushed the door open and walked into the dark hallway. A wave of guilt hit him at the idea of Angela trapped back in the dark room, all by herself. The defeat in her eyes when Sammy told her he would get them out stuck with him. After everything he had gone through to get out, she was right back where she started the night. He liked to think that he'd send help to save her, but deep down he knew it was probably too late. The witch had already hurt the little girl a great deal.

Sammy took off in a sprint, oblivious to his bare feet slapping on the hardwood. When he reached the end of the hall, he stopped dead in his tracks. Three cats paced in the entryway, eyeing his every move. At first glance, one might think they were just normal black cats. But as he looked closer at them, he saw their eyes. He couldn't explain what it was, but the way they stared at him froze him in place. Their black fur looked as if someone had dipped them in wet tar. They were growling, more like tigers than household cats. He looked around, spotting a window overlooking the front yard. He ran to it, trying to lift the frame, but it was locked. The animals stalked toward him, taking their time, as if they knew his attempt at escaping was pointless. Feeling around for the lock, Sammy realized it was nailed shut. There was nowhere to go.

The cats closed in, forcing him to back up. Behind him, the witch entered the big room, her heavy breathing turning his legs to rubber.

He was trapped.

"Tom! Stop it!" A voice yelled from up ahead.

Kosa walked around the corner. Her face lit up with shock when she saw Sammy standing in the hallway.

"Help me!" he yelled.

"I... What are you doing up here?"

"Please, I need to get back to my family. She's trying to kill me!"

Kosa hesitated, then approached Sammy. The cats moved out of her way, but he noticed she was as afraid of them as he was. Two of the cats looked sick, their fur disheveled. She reached out to Sammy.

"Come with me..."

He grabbed her hand and followed her between the cats, who swiped at him as if he was running through a gauntlet. One of their paws connected with his leg, sending a soaring pain through his calf. He glanced down and saw his pants had ripped, blood already soaking through the material.

Sammy and Kosa reached the main entrance where the front door sat in front of them, a beacon of hope. But then, Kosa stopped, squeezing his arm.

"What are you doing?" Sammy asked.

"Mother will be so mad at me. I'll get punished..."

"*Please*... come with me," he whispered in desperation.

Something had changed in her eyes. Sammy realized she was battling within, trying to figure out what to do.

"You don't understand. She needs me, or she'll die. She needs *you*..."

"What do you mean? We have to hurry, she's getting closer!"

It was as if mentioning her made her appear, like some sinister genie; the witch now approached from the hall.

"Kosa! Stop him, now!"

Kosa looked to the front door, then back to Sammy. Tears streamed down her face. Her brow furrowed in sorrow as she stared into his eyes.

"I'm... I'm so sorry, Sammy. She needs you."

"No... No, no, no!" he yelled.

He attempted to run around her, but she grabbed hold of his wrist again, holding him tight. Slapping at her arm with his free hand did no good, she was older and far too strong for him. He felt her body trembling as she cried. It was clear she didn't want to do this, but that didn't make Sammy feel any better.

"Let go of me!"

"I can't..."

Sammy tried once more to rip free, but then noticed Kosa looking over his shoulder. At the same time, rancid breath tickled his neck. He looked up, seeing the witch standing over him with an angry glare.

"Good girl, Kosa. You, boy, not so much!"

The witch grabbed him by the hair, but he squeezed his eyes shut to avoid eye contact. He had to prevent her from taking control of him again, or he knew he'd die. The old lady twisted his hair, sending needle-like pain into the top of his scalp.

"Look at me, boy!"

"No!"

The warmth of urine spread down his pants as he could no longer hold in the fear. He sensed something getting closer to his face, but before he had time to prepare for it, the witch's gnarled fingers pinched his eyelid, prying it open. Sammy screamed, squinting so tightly that his head hurt. His eyeball began to water as she squeezed harder, pulling on his eyelashes to force it open.

"Open, you little brat!"

And then, the pain outweighed the desire to fight it. He opened his eyes, still trying to stare off to the side. He witnessed Kosa standing in the corner, watching as she hugged herself and cried. The cats stood guard, baring their fangs with pure hatred towards him. The witch grabbed hold of his jaw, her curled nails threatening to poke through the skin, and she yanked his face in her direction.

"Sada si pod mojom kontrolom, djecace!" she spat.

It was as if a magnet forced his eyes to hers, locking on the deep pools of darkness in her sockets. She continued to chant something as Sammy lost the strength to fight. His vision faded, blurring so that *she* was the only thing left for him to focus on. The last thing he saw before everything went dark was her contorted smile.

CHAPTER 37

Kosa went to the attic at Mother's behest. Not that she wanted to see what happened next anyway. If stopping Sammy from escaping was the right thing to do, why did it feel so wrong? She knew Mother needed his soul, but he was such a good kid. In all her years, nobody had ever escaped and forced her to make that decision. It had been hard enough to push it aside, knowing the true outcome of each kid, but after seeing the fear in Sammy's eyes, and hearing the desperation in his voice, she found herself tempted to let him go. She even came close to letting it happen, until Mother appeared, insisting she stop Sammy.

At this point, it was all irrelevant anyway. Mother had dragged him back to the basement to do whatever she did when preparing the children. Kosa remembered when she was a little girl, Mother typically only took one child at a time, which lasted them months. But over the last few years, she needed more, which meant the dark force wanted more in order to provide her with the energy she needed.

She tried to keep herself busy, hoping to take her mind off what was happening downstairs, but it felt like a lost cause. To know that *she* was the reason Sammy didn't escape and get to live another day continued to eat at her. She sat in her regular corner, on the blankets that made up her sitting area for a good part of her life. Every time she tried to convince herself to stop Marta from taking the children, it always came back to one thing: she needed them to live. Could Kosa bear losing Mother if it meant no more children being harmed? Could she survive on her own if Marta was to perish and leave her nothing but a large house and cats that wanted to kill her? She didn't think so. This house was all she knew. Mother was the only person who understood her. Who loved her. Who *needed* her. But then there was the way Sammy made her feel when he snapped out of his hypnosis. Kosa'd had lingering questions floating around in her mind for years, more so after discovering the pages of the Book, but it wasn't until she saw those eyes transition back to normal that she considered what was happening to a living person. That interaction made him *real*, not just some abstract soul to help keep Marta alive. That's exactly what she had been raised to believe: that all of these kids were nothing more than fuel, and that they served no other purpose than to give *Tamna Sila* what it needed.

It also wasn't Mother's fault that she had to do this. After hearing the story of her life, the struggles she'd endured, the hardship she went through just to survive, she had been tricked into making a deal with the darkness. If all this was true, why did she still feel so awful about it? Kosa wanted to scream. She buried her face in her blanket, the stale scent of the humid attic thick on the fabric. She cried, letting her scattered thoughts rest. It was becoming clearer and clearer that she couldn't continue to live her life knowing what was happening. She also had no intention of letting Mother die for it.

A thump outside the window brought Kosa back to the attic. She jumped to her feet and ran to the window, peeking out into the dark driveway. A car with lights on the roof sat in front of the house, and a large man stood beside the car with his hands on his hips, staring up at the house. Was he looking at her? She dropped to the floor out of sight. After going her entire life without seeing another adult besides Marta, she'd now seen her second within a day. She got the feeling things would never be the same.

CHAPTER 38

Ian exited the woods within a minute of Roberts pulling into the old woman's driveway. *Thank God, he got my call after all*, Ian thought. He approached Roberts, who stood by his car observing the house. Apparently, the chief was so focused on the house that he didn't hear Ian coming from the woods. Ian's feet crunched on the ice-crusted driveway, and Roberts whirled around. Ian was sure the cop was about to draw his gun.

"Christ, you scared me. What the hell are you doing coming from the woods like that?"

Scooter ran to his side, ready to defend his human if Roberts did anything.

"It's the only way I knew to find the place. I know she took Sammy, and I know she's responsible for all the missing children. We have to search the house for Sammy before it's too late," Ian pleaded.

"Hey, I'm here, aren't I? But listen: I can't search the house without a warrant. And I can't go on your 'hunch' to obtain said warrant. I suggest you stay back and let me do the talking, got it?"

Ian didn't want to agree, but he also didn't want to waste any more time. He nodded, and then trailed behind Roberts as he walked up the front steps. Ian stopped before climbing the first step, afraid he would just piss Roberts off if he came up on the porch. Roberts knocked on the door, looking around the porch as if he was expecting something to come out of the darkness. When nobody answered, he knocked again.

The front door opened a few inches, but it was enough for Ian to see the old woman looking out at the officer standing on her porch. She scowled at the sight of him and said something in a different language that Ian couldn't make out.

"I'm sorry to bother you, Marta. But this man here has reason to believe that you're holding his nephew against his will. That true?"

She looked toward Ian, sending shivers down his spine. She glared at him with a piercing intensity, as if her black eyes were staring into the deepest corners of his soul, unraveling his darkest secrets. Feeding off his fears.

Scooter growled at her, backing away, as if his primal instinct was to retreat, knowing the very essence of evil had fixed its eyes on them.

Ian had been so distracted by the woman's threatening stare that it took him a second to realize Roberts had identified her by name. Did he know her? Why was he asking her about Sammy so nonchalantly?

The woman—Marta according to Roberts—stared at Scooter, flashing her rotting teeth at him. Scooter whimpered, then backtracked even more and sat underneath Ian for protection. His trembling body rattled against the inside of Ian's legs.

"I know this. This man comes to my house once already, and now you both have the nerve to show up here when I'm getting ready for bed, accusing me of such acts? You should be ashamed..." she said, turning her attention back to Ian. "And you... I told you I had seen no boy. I *told* you to go away, yet here you are disturbing my peace again."

Ian went to respond, but Roberts held up his hand before he could.

"Listen, I'm sorry to come out here like this unannounced, but—"

"Are you fucking serious? *Unannounced*? Are you supposed to give some child abductor a warning before casually coming over for a cup of tea?" Ian snapped.

Roberts turned to him, and Ian spotted a glint of fear behind his official mask. Why was he scared of this lady? Ian hadn't brought up his hunch about her being involved in witchcraft to Roberts. But it was as if the cop already knew about her and what she was. Roberts quickly shook off the fear and glared at Ian.

"I said let me do the talking, didn't I?"

When he turned back to Marta, her black eyes were somehow even darker, staring right through Roberts. An awkward silence followed, and then the lady said something that completely took Ian by surprise.

"Fine. If you don't believe me, come look for yourself. You will see how ridiculous you are. I'm just an old lady…"

She backed out of the opening, making way for them to come inside. As Roberts started to go, Ian ran up the steps and grabbed hold of his uniform, stopping him from entering.

"Don't listen to her, something's wrong. We can't trust her," he whispered.

Roberts turned to face him, and Ian expected an angry stare. Instead, the eyes of the cop looked like they had been glossed over with shiny black paint. It was the same stare Sammy had given him out in the woods.

"We do what she says, and everything will be okay."

Ian didn't want to follow, but he felt he had no choice. He stepped into the house as Scooter still lingered on the walkway, whimpering. Ian turned to call his dog, but Marta slammed the door shut.

"The dog cannot come in. He will bother my cats."

Her tone told him there was no arguing the point. Scooter could handle himself outside, but Ian hoped his dog could deal with the especially low temperatures.

Roberts stood as stiff as a mannequin sitting in the window of a Macy's, acting as if someone had frozen him in time. It reminded Ian of a game he used to play with Sammy, where the boy would pretend to have magical powers and freeze Ian in place, then take Ian's finger and make him stick it up his own nose before pretending to unfreeze him; Ian would act confused as to how he was picking his own nose. Sammy would laugh so hard that tears would leak out, every single time. The memory brought him back to Sammy, and what thoughts could possibly be going through the poor kid's head—assuming he was still alive to have those thoughts.

Stop it, you can't think that way.

Marta walked ahead of them, limping along as though arthritis was tearing apart her joints with each step. She was clearly in a great deal of pain, but that didn't make Ian feel any safer. Roberts followed her down a dim hallway, looking straight ahead as he did. The whole thing felt wrong. Why did Marta all of a sudden have a change of heart and tell them to come in when she was so pissed off at them for showing up in the first place? Ian's instincts were screaming for him to turn and run and get the hell out of the house. But he had to do this for Sammy. If there was any chance he was really here, which every fiber in Ian's body told him he was, Ian had to see this through. Even if it meant putting his own life on the line.

They walked past the kitchen, the aroma of spices filling the air. All that did was turn Ian's stomach into knots even more. After passing a few closed doors in the hallway, they entered a larger room with an open floor plan. Marta stopped in the center of the room and turned to face them, the wrinkles in her face giving her a constant grimace. She began to whisper something under her breath, and the faint whistle between her words tightened an invisible grip on Ian's throat. What was she whispering? Why were they in this room?

Marta began to back away, never taking her eyes off them as she got closer to the far side of the room, still chanting something under her breath. Roberts remained silent. Something moved behind them, in the entryway they had just entered. Ian whipped around to find three mangy-looking cats stalking toward them.

"Roberts! Look out!"

Ian turned back to Marta, but she was gone. It was a trap, all to lure them in here and let her animals attack. And then, as if things couldn't get any worse, the lights went out, plunging the room in suffocating darkness.

CHAPTER 39

Every second that passed since Kosa had helped Mother stop Sammy from escaping was torture. And, to see how much the adult man cared for Sammy by looking for him really hit home. If these kids only served the purpose of feeding Marta's power, how could they be so loved by others? Mother said eating these wicked children was no different than people eating animals; wasn't lamb simply the supple and soft meat of a sheep's child? It had been imbedded in Kosa's mind from the first time she discovered little Bryce hanging above the fire as his skin charred to a crisp. The sound of the rope swaying back and forth, his little body thumping off the brick wall within the chimney. It haunted Kosa most nights.

The thought of the man who came looking for Sammy reminded her of the device he had tried to communicate through. Kosa got up from the corner of the attic and walked to the hole in the wall where the device remained hidden. She pulled it out, and just holding it again, knowing there was communication to the outside world, filled her with nervous energy.

Tom wasn't in here to watch her; he remained with Mother while she took care of business in the basement. This was Kosa's chance to tinker with the device. What if someone spoke back to her? Would she answer? She turned the knob on top, hearing a click as she rotated it. Hesitantly, she pushed and held down the button on the side. At first, she just stood in the corner, waiting for something to happen. Then, like a teen awkwardly leaning in for their first kiss, she lowered her face to the walkie-talkie.

"Hello?"

Ian almost jumped out of his shoes, the sound coming from his backpack would have been shocking enough, but he had been focused on the glint of multiple sets of eyes closing in on him in the darkness. He backpedaled, unsure of where he was going, but getting further away from these cats was all he could think of right now. Roberts lumbered around like a dementia patient trying to figure out how to get home, and Ian bumped into him.

"Roberts! Snap out of it, man. We need to get out of here!"

"We are here to serve the *Tamna Sila*. It's what she wants..."

"What the fuck are you talking about?" Ian asked. He shoved the cop to the side, hoping it would snap him out of his delusional state.

"*Hello? Can anyone hear me?*"

The voice was muffled by his bag, but he still knew it wasn't Sammy. It wasn't the old lady, Marta, either. So, who the hell was trying to communicate?

He quickly unzipped the bag, keeping his eyes locked on the corner the cats were approaching from. He found the walkie and pulled it out.

The cats remained fixed upon their prey.

Silently, their sleek forms moved with a predatory grace, their bodies blending seamlessly into the darkness that occupied the room. Their near-invisible presence sent shivers down Ian's spine. Each step they took appeared calculated and deliberate. He fumbled around on the walkie-talkie and found the talk button.

Eyes still glued on the stalking cats, he said, "Who's this? Where's Sammy?"

When he didn't get a response, he was sure he'd missed his window of opportunity to communicate with someone that could help him. But then a loud static disturbed the silence.

"*I'm sorry for what happened to him... He was a good kid. Mother needed him though, it's not her fault...*"

The urge to vomit all over the fucking evil cats came quickly, but Ian forced the feeling down as he continued slowly backing up.

"What... What do you mean? What did she do to him?" Ian yelled.

As he waited for the girl to speak again, it was Roberts who spoke next.

"Ian... We need to get out of here. It's too late for the boy. She'll kill us next if we don't go now." His voice was now back to normal—as normal as it could be given the circumstances.

The cats advanced, their movements synchronized, their eyes never wavering from their target. These weren't normal cats, that was obvious. Their eyes were devoid of any mammalian warmth. Instead, they held a malevolence that shook Ian to his core. With each step he took, they mirrored his movements, matching his pace. Their claws, already unsheathed and ready to attack, clicked softly against the cold, wooden floor, creating an eerie music in the dark.

"What the hell is happening, Roberts? You *knew* about this lady?" Ian asked.

"I... I do. I mean, it's not like she left me any choice. She's a powerful woman, Ian. One you don't want to cross, and now I'm afraid you've done just that. I came here to try and stop you, but it was clear that you weren't going to stop until you confronted her. Whatever you do, don't look into her eyes. She'll make you do things that'll haunt you the rest of your life, believe me."

"What the fuck are you talking about? What's she made you do? What did she do to Sammy?"

The walkie buzzed once more.

"*You need to get out of here, or she'll kill you too...*"

Suddenly, Ian felt dizzy, suffering from what he knew were the early stages of a panic attack. He'd been struggling with them ever since Chelsea died, often brought on without warning. The room felt like it was shrinking, the walls closing in as the cats drew nearer. His heart raced. The uncomfortable sensation of his chest tightening to the point he thought it might burst open. He realized he'd be of no use to Sammy if he got himself killed. Before he could do anything else, he needed to escape. And where was the witch? She didn't exit through the main door, which meant she had to be deeper in the house—in the direction Ian and Roberts were forced to move toward.

"I'm not leaving until I know what happened to Sammy. You can piss off for all I care, but I'm getting out of here and searching for him."

One of the cats pounced, but Roberts swatted it away, sending it scurrying back to the others as they methodically waited for their chance to attack. It was as if they were toying with their meal before going for the kill.

"I've avoided confronting this bitch since I moved to this town. Shit, it's why my wife left me. She knew the deal I had in place with Marta, and she just couldn't live with it anymore..." Roberts panted, backing up farther.

"Deal? You *worked* with this monster?"

"I wouldn't expect you to understand..." Roberts said, his tone all but defeated.

Ian expected Roberts to elaborate, but instead he pulled his gun, aiming it toward the cats.

"Won't shooting her beloved cats piss her off even more?" Ian said, not without a little wryness.

"I won't shoot unless they attack again. We need to find another way through this house. Follow me," Roberts said.

As the cats continued to close the gap, strategically approaching as if they knew his every move before he made it, Ian got a surge of adrenaline, lunging toward the door in the corner that Roberts had just exited through.

Just as he reached the opening, one of the cats leaped, its fangs bared, claws slashing through the air.

Something tore through Ian's pant leg: a set of teeth or claws, he wasn't sure. All he knew was the pain was excruciating, forcing him to scream as he tumbled into the next room. Roberts turned. Although this new room was brighter than the last, with the moon able to shine through the windows, it was still dark. Roberts ran to Ian, kicking at the cat with his steel-toe boot. The cat let out a combination of a hiss and unnatural squeal as it tumbled backward into the previous room.

Roberts slammed the door shut, blocking out the cats, but also blocking their only known exit.

"You realize she headed in this same direction, right?" Ian asked.

"Yeah, but we really don't have much of a choice, do we? We need to find a way out of here—"

"Are you fucking kidding me? I came to look for Sammy, and now more than ever I'm confident this lady has him. Dead or alive, I need to find him. No matter what it takes..."

"I know you want to do this, Ian. But what good does it do if you're dead too? I don't think you understand the power of this woman... Please remember what I said about her eyes. Don't look into them. If you do, you might as well slit your own throat," Roberts said. Regret immediately filled his face. "I'm... I'm sorry. I didn't mean to say that after how your wife died. I'm an idiot..."

Ian expected a statement like that to send him off the deep end, but instead, he oddly felt sorry for Roberts. It was clear he felt bad about the death of Chelsea.

"Don't sweat it. But you said don't look in her eyes. I know for sure I made eye contact with her more than once: why didn't she do to me whatever the hell she did to you and to Sammy?" "I'm not sure. Maybe she can only control one person at a time? Maybe she didn't see you as a threat yet? The thing is, now you *are* a threat. And she knows that."

"Well, whatever you decide to do, count me out of it. I'm staying here and finding out what happened to my nephew," Ian insisted.

"God damn it," Roberts muttered. "I'm not leaving you alone. But this is a death trap. Don't say I didn't warn you."

"Can't you call in backup? They could help us," Ian said.

"I can't. If they knew I helped protect this lady all these years, that I was somehow apart of it, I'd be done for."

"How exactly did you protect—"

Something slammed against the door they had shut behind them.

SLAM! SLAM! SLAM!

"We need to move, they're going to break this damn door down," Roberts said, ignoring Ian's question.

They moved further into the house, passing many closed doors. Ian realized Sammy could be behind any one of them and decided to check each in turn, even though it cost him time. The sounds on the other side of the barred door continued to intensify; they sure as shit didn't sound like noises a normal cat could make.

Ian walked up to one of the doors and opened it, revealing a simple coat closet. He moved to the next one, and found it locked. He turned and kicked the wall on the opposite side, trying to take out some of his frustration. The wall shifted. At first, he thought he'd kicked it so hard that he cracked a piece of the sheetrock straight down the center. Then he realized it was a secret door within the wall. He looked at Roberts, who stared back at him with wide eyes that plainly said, *Don't go in there*. Ian ignored the warning stare and stepped inside the dark room.

CHAPTER 40

Kosa stared at the walkie-talkie, debating what to say next. She went to the attic like she was told, but she needed to know what was going on downstairs. There was a lot of commotion, and she continued to hear slamming around, as though someone were trying to break down a door. The man with the car and the guy who came to the house before were together, and it sounded like Mother had let them in the house. She didn't know why, but she felt the desire to communicate with them. She felt guilty about what happened to the man's kid, like it was somehow her fault. When she turned on the walkie-talkie, she had no idea what she planned to say, and still didn't really know if she should say anything. She thought maybe if she warned them, it would make her feel better about letting Sammy get brought back to the basement.

Against her better judgment, she decided to go downstairs and intervene. She put the walkie-talkie in her pocket and exited the room, listening in the darkness. The men were either dead or hiding, because the cats wouldn't just give up their hunt that easy. She crept down the stairs, avoiding the usual spots that groaned the best she could. There was no sign of anyone on the second floor, so she continued downstairs to the first floor and looked around. The house was completely dark, just the way Mother liked to keep it. Even the fireplace was dead, full of smothered charcoal after being neglected too long.

She made her way down the hallway past the Big Room, and stopped dead when she spotted the door going to the next hallway toward the basement. Claw marks had gouged the wooden frame, but well above where any cat had the right to reach. The marks were eye-level with her and had almost completely broken through to the other side. The wood splintered around the doorknob, and she realized that while the door appeared shut, she could push it open without turning the handle—the lock was now bent in and warped. Kosa pushed the door open slowly, now seeing the hallway possessed a faint glow, the windows lining the wall all the way down to the end of the hall admitting moonlight. It didn't make her feel any better, only adding a strange hue to everything. She forced herself to continue, knowing time was running out. The closet door was open, but there was nothing inside. As she continued on, a sound on the inside of the wall to her right startled her. She stopped and listened and heard the muffled sound of someone whispering inside the wall. She leaned in close and put her ear to the wall, and again heard some type of movement behind it. Kosa reached out and swept her hand along the surface, then pushed in, not sure what to expect.

The wall parted, a door forming in front of her and opening inward. It was dark inside, but the faint light from the hall gave her enough illumination to see the two men standing in a room. The one with the hair on his face was aiming something at her.

"Get in here and shut the door," the younger man whispered.

Kosa hesitated, until she heard the cats walking around deeper in the house, hunting the men. She stepped inside and shut the door behind her.

Seeing her up close gave Ian all the confirmation he needed—this girl was the daughter of the dead parents from sixteen years ago. He didn't know what to say at first, but then realized Roberts was still aiming his gun toward the poor girl.

"Put the gun down, for Christ's sake, man. She's just a girl," Ian said.

"Who the hell is she?"

"I'm... My name's Kosa. I live here," the girl answered quietly.

"I don't understand, Marta doesn't have any kids. How long have you been here?" Roberts asked.

Her eyes began to water, and Ian realized she was terrified of Roberts and his pushy antics.

"It's okay. We aren't going to hurt you. I'm just here looking for my nephew, Sammy. I assume that was you talking on the walkie-talkie with us?"

She nodded.

"Has Marta done something to him? Can you take me to him?"

"I've been here my whole life. Mother needs the children; it's how she stays alive. It's just like people using animals to survive," she said, like it was a fact, something that was normal. Then she looked at Ian. "She took him to the basement. I really liked him. We played and had fun at first. It's what we always do before... before she takes them away."

Those invisible hands of anxiety wrapped tightly around Ian's neck again. The thought of that old bag harming an innocent child, let alone his nephew, both infuriated him and terrified him at the same time.

"Takes them away to where? What did she do with him?"

"Mother says they are here to serve Tamna Sila. Their souls give us what we need..." Kosa trailed off, perhaps seeing the absolute panic spreading across Ian's face.

"I don't mean to interrupt, but why are you here? If Marta does something to all the kids, why are you still alive?" Roberts asked.

"Mother needs me... I'm part of the ritual—that makes her better."

"Ritual?" Ian asked, more confused than before.

"Yes... Every night, Mother performs the ritual. She needs my hair. *Tamna Sila* is inside me. My hair gives Mother what she needs to survive."

Ian realized that this was all Kosa knew. To her, it was as simple as getting dressed for the day or doing her makeup. If she was going to help bring him to Sammy, Ian needed to make her realize the truth. He needed to erase a lifetime of lies that had been planted in this poor girl's head.

"She's not your mother," Ian said.

He pulled a folded-up piece of paper out of his backpack and handed it to her. He watched her eyes as she unfolded it and took in the article and images on the other side.

"What's this?" she asked.

"Those are your real parents, Kosa. Marta killed them and took you when you were a baby."

The paper began to tremble in her hands, she didn't say anything, just continued staring at the sheet and sobbed.

"How do you know they're my parents?" she asked, but it was clear she knew he was telling the truth. How the hell could she *not* know he was? The mother was a mirror image of her. "Mother taught me everything I know. She taught me her rules. She raised me..."

"I'm sorry. I felt you should know, because whatever she's warped your mind with, it's all for her own use. She's evil," Ian said.

"Elizabeth... My name's Elizabeth," she whispered to herself as tears pooled in her eyes. "She never told me. She never said she did anything to the parents."

Kosa dropped to her knees, the cries coming so hard now she could no longer stand. They let her cry for a few moments, but then Roberts looked at Ian and nodded his head toward the door.

"Kosa, we need to go find Sammy. Can you help us? Will you help us get out of here?" Ian asked.

She raised her face, as if she'd forgotten where she was for a moment, the shock of seeing her parents for the first time too much to handle. To Ian's surprise, her expression hardened, and she got to her feet.

"She locks them in the basement. It's where she prepares them."

Ian's heart lurched in his chest as fear clenched his every nerve. *Where she prepares them?* Kosa talked about it like it was a fucking deli in the supermarket, like it was just normal everyday life. She truly viewed these kids as a disposable food source.

"Ian, I'm telling you, Marta is too powerful to cross. We don't even know her weaknesses, or even remotely have an idea of how to stop her," Roberts said.

With a shake of the head, Kosa wiped away the tears.

"You don't know how to stop her, but I do."

CHAPTER 41

After Kosa told them her plan, they all exited the secret room cautiously, looking for any sign of the cats or Marta. Even with the regrets Kosa had about everything Mother was doing, she never thought she could feel hate for the old lady. It hurt so much. Waves of anguish crashed against her spirit, each one leaving raw, searing pain. For her entire life, she'd been led to believe that Mother's rules were the way of life, that everyone outside of her domain was someone beneath them. Kosa had real parents, and Marta killed them.

When Kosa was a little girl, Marta told her a story about how she came to look after her. She explained that Kosa's parents weren't fit for a child, that they left her for dead and went on to live their selfish lives. She said she saved Kosa after finding her wrapped in a blanket deep in the forest, and that her curse had somehow transferred into Kosa's body, linking the two together for life and creating a bond closer than any deadbeat parents could have. By the time Kosa was old enough to understand the impact of parents abandoning their kid, she grew to despise her real parents. It helped fuel her hate for the people outside the house. Now, all of Mother's rules—no, not Mother. *Marta*—were a farce. Kosa had lived her entire life following false beliefs. She couldn't even bring herself to think about all the kids who died thanks to these fake rules.

"If you see her, remember don't—"

"Don't look in her eyes. I got it. You two keep saying it so much I won't be able to help but look directly into them,' Ian said.

They approached the basement door, with still no sign of the cats or Marta. There was no way Marta had just left them to roam free in the house. Sure, she set the cats on them initially, but where did she go?

"She might be down here, so be careful," Kosa whispered.

Kosa opened the door, and they were presented with a mouth of blackness. Roberts took the flashlight off his police belt and turned it on, lighting up the stairs. It had been ten years since Kosa stepped foot down there, and she couldn't believe she was about to do it again. Thoughts of Bryce swaying above the fire tormented her imagination. Even the imaginary smell of cooked meat came back to her as they walked down the stairs.

By the time they got to the bottom step, Kosa realized the smell wasn't just her imagination. Something *was* cooking. *Someone* was being cooked. She stopped moving, blocking the others from continuing.

"What are you doing, let's go," Ian said.

"I... I don't think you want to go in there."

Roberts's light threw Ian's facial expression into clarity, and Kosa saw his jaw clenching.

"Let's go," he said again, firmly.

Kosa closed her eyes and sighed before walking to the door she knew to be the cooking room. Ian pushed past her, unable to wait any longer. He opened the door and walked in, the aroma of a hot summer barbeque taking over their senses. Kosa homed in on the fireplace, and what likely hung above the fireplace, just out of sight. Ian slowly approached the fire, the flames licking at something.

"No, no, no..." he cried.

Roberts aimed his flashlight toward the fireplace wall, the light rattling around in his trembling grip. Kosa didn't know what to say. She wanted to comfort Ian. She wanted to tell him not to look in the chimney. She wanted to convince them to leave the basement, but instead she found herself unable to talk. It was as if someone had reached down her throat and ripped out her vocal cords.

Ian dropped to his knees, preparing himself to look into the hole. Against everything inside him telling him to stop, he peered up into the chimney. Kosa couldn't see what he was looking at from her spot, but she knew what he'd find. The image returned of Bryce, hanging upside down, body crisped to the point that you couldn't even identify him anymore. She knew that was exactly what Ian was looking at, except it was his nephew.

An unnatural sound forced its way from within Ian's chest, cries more full of pain than anything Kosa had ever heard in her life. She wanted to reach out and comfort him but knew nothing would help right now.

A loud crack erupted from the doorway.

The beam of light guiding them through the room suddenly fell to the floor, spinning in a circle until it came to a stop, facing the shelf in the corner and revealing a macabre display of skull and bones.

Kosa and Ian turned to see Roberts staring back at them confused, his eyes fluttering, blood sliding down his forehead. And then his knees buckled as he collapsed to the dirt floor.

Behind him, Marta stood in the doorway, a thick walking stick in hand.

"Your boy is almost ready to eat. Care to stay for dinner?" A smile spread across her face, not matching her cold and calculated eyes, devoid of any warmth or compassion.

CHAPTER 42

Ian jumped to his feet, prepared to do whatever he needed to stop this crazy bitch. Even in a moment of pure rage, he reminded himself to avoid eye contact with her, instead focusing on the stone wall, where the flames created dancing shadows.

"Mother... You lied to me. All these years: your rules, your lessons, it was all for nothing!" Kosa sobbed.

"Dear, every rule and lesson I taught you is true. Regardless of how you feel right now, everything I taught you about the outside world is a reality."

"You killed my parents! You told me you *saved* me! That you found me in the woods. How could you?"

"We do what must be done to survive, Kosa. You want truth? Your parents stole the *Tanna Sila* from me. I tried to get it back, and instead it somehow ended up inside *you*. They stuck their nose where it didn't belong, and they paid the price. And believe me, if I could have killed you and ended your sorry life with theirs, it would've been very poetic. Unfortunately, I needed you, and you needed me. Without me, you would've grown up without the proper care for someone with your condition. Don't you realize that your body needs their souls as much as mine does? That you get weak when we go too long without feeding? Now, be a good girl and help me," Marta snarled.

"*Ughhh, Marta... you...*" Roberts moaned, trying to push himself up.

Marta stared down at him. Ian almost made a move but decided against it.

"You make yourself at home down there, scum. My use for you has come and gone!" Marta shouted. "Why don't I tell this fool before me how you really helped me?"

Ian had to hold back everything inside of him that wanted to attack her. He was afraid to make eye contact, but rage was beginning to fog any logic.

"I don't care what you tell me he did, this is between you and me now. You..." Ian stopped, looking back toward the chimney. "You took everything from me! From so many families. All so you could, what, stay young? He was just a kid!" Ian shouted.

Tears welled in his eyes, threatening to spill over, the anguish growing unbearable.

"I wouldn't expect you to understand the ways of the *Tamna Sila*. As for fat man here, I think you might want to know what he's been up to all these years. You see, I try to do most of the work myself. It's the way I was raised. But my body can't handle too much travel on foot these days. I needed someone to inform me when families were staying close by with children, someone to make sure there were no loose ends and could clean up the mess. In steps Officer Roberts..." Roberts began to stir but was clearly too concussed to do much.

If what she was saying was true, it meant Roberts tipped her off about his sister renting the house and on Sammy being there, all so she could take him to fulfill her sadistic desires.

"Greed is a powerful thing. It's what got me into this spot, and it's what got Mr. Roberts into this spot. All it took was me threatening to take his power and his family, and he agreed to help." She began to laugh. "And then, his wife left him anyway! How ironic. But you see, it wasn't just children he helped me dispose of. One day, as I traveled through the woods, seeking out a young child to get Kosa and I through the autumn months, someone decided to try to play hero and stop me. Any guesses?"

A gut punch of dread filled Ian. He didn't want her to continue. Yet, he needed to hear it. Marta didn't wait for him to answer before continuing.

"No? You're no fun, Mr. Warner. Your wife was a brave woman: it was a shame what I had to do to her. What are the odds? Billions of people in the world, and it's you who stumbles on my doorstep. If it weren't for Roberts, I wouldn't have known you were her husband. Such a small world!"

"I'm going to kill you!" Ian shouted, spit flying from his mouth.

"I'm... I'm sorry, Ian. She left me no choice," Roberts cried from the floor.

Ian glared at Roberts, then looked at the policeman's hand as he slowly removed the gun from his holster. As old as Marta appeared, her hearing must have been impeccable. She snapped her attention to Roberts as he raised the gun.

With one, swift motion, she drove the end of her walking stick into his eye, producing a squishy splat as a thick sludge leaked out of his socket. His body began to quiver, his hands instinctively going to the stick protruding from his eye, dropping the gun in the process.

With Marta's attention on Roberts, Ian saw his chance. He charged at the witch with his heart pounding against his ribs. But she sensed him coming, turning with her weathered hand, fingers curled into claws, swiping across his face. A set of gashes sliced across his cheek, sending him stumbling back.

Kosa trembled in the corner, watching it all transpire.

Marta advanced towards Ian with an unsettling smile playing on her cracked lips. Her eyes gleamed with a sinister light as she relished the fear in Ian's expression. She had him right where she wanted him—trapped, vulnerable, and at her mercy.

Ian's eyes flitted around the room, searching for anything that could help. An escape route, weapon, anything that might take her down. The gun was beyond reach, next to Roberts' dead body. Her lair seemed designed specifically to keep victims at her mercy. The heavy wooden door behind Marta was the only viable exit.

As Marta closed in, desperation took hold of Ian. His back hit the wall, the heat of the fireplace warming his neck. Marta grabbed him by the shoulders, attempting to force him to lock eyes with her. They grappled. In an effort to keep his eyes off Marta, Ian looked over her shoulder, and spotted Kosa kneeling near Roberts' dead body.

"Mother!" Kosa yelled.

The witch didn't loosen her grip on Ian, but she turned to face Kosa. Kosa held the powerful flashlight of Chief Roberts, the beam creating a trail across the grimy floor leading to Marta. All Ian could think was: *grab the fucking gun, not the light, you stupid girl*! But the light appeared to scare Marta more than the gun.

"Put that down, you brat!" Marta shouted.

Kosa ran toward her, lifting the light as she did. She aimed it right into the witch's obsidian eyes, causing Marta to scream out in pain. She let go of Ian, which he wasn't prepared for. He stumbled and knocked into the massive cauldron hanging above the fire.

Mere feet from where his nephew continued to burn.

The pot tipped, coming undone and falling into the flames, sending scorching wood down to the floor near Ian's feet. The room erupted in chaos as the spilled contents caught fire, flames racing up the wooden beams above. Ian stood at the crackling heart of a growing inferno.

He broke free from the witch's grasp, scrambling towards the door. Marta screamed as the pain continued to blind her. Ian looked over toward Kosa, but the smoke had already thickened to the point that he couldn't find her.

"Kosa! You need to come, now!" he yelled, hoping she could hear him over the roaring flames.

"My eyes! Kosa, you little bitch!" Marta screamed.

Kosa appeared through the smog, coughing on the thick smoke filling the tight space. Ian grabbed her hand and pulled, hoping he was heading in the right direction of the exit. His eyes burned, and he threw his shirt up over his nose as if that would stop him inhaling clouds of smoke. He crouched down, half-crawling towards the door. The gun lay at his feet, so he snatched it up. Marta flailed around, reaching for something to hold her up. Ian couldn't believe how quickly the room went up in flames. The smoke hid everything except her shape, but Ian heard her violently coughing.

They made it out of the door. He turned, expecting to see Marta reaching her distorted hands toward him, but instead the only thing visible were the dancing flames and black clouds that attempted to spread out the door behind him.

Ian's trembling hands fumbled with the latch, but he was determined to seal her in. He forced the lock in place, a triumphant click echoing through the basement. He stumbled backwards; his breathing labored.

"We have to get out of here, this whole place is going to go up fast," he said in a raspy voice.

Kosa looked toward the door, and Ian thought she might be second-guessing the decision to lock Marta inside. *What did this poor girl get put through?* he wondered.

Marta's cries of rage and desperation mingled with the crackling flames, creating a horrifying combination. A mix of relief and terror washed over Ian as he stumbled toward the stairs heading out of the basement. He opened the door heading up to the main level, and that's when he heard a thumping sound coming from behind another door in the basement. He looked to Kosa, who stared back at the door dumbfounded.

"What's that? Is there someone in there?" Ian asked.

"I... I thought she killed both of them. There was a girl too."

Ian didn't even think, he ran to the door and heard a muffled cry behind it. The smoke was quickly floating down the hallway, finding any crack and opening it could, filling up every space. Smoke had now entered the room with the girl behind the door. The flames weren't far behind.

He tried the door handle, and it didn't budge. *Shit*!

"I need to break it down! Is there anything heavy nearby?"

"Um, maybe one of those huge boards? Would that work?" Kosa asked, pointing to a stack of lumber that had to be at least 6x6.

Ian wasn't sure he could even lift one of them, but he had to try.

His lungs continued to struggle with the acrid, thick air, the fire now working its way up to the ceiling in the hall. He rushed to the pile of wood and found one that had been cut in half—still heavy, but much more manageable to swing toward the door. He lifted it, running to the door.

"Grab the other end and help me ram it in the center of the door! We need to break through!"

Kosa grabbed the back end of it, easing some of the strain Ian felt holding it by himself. Together, they slammed the end into the door frame like a battering ram, producing a thin crack that splintered the top half of the door. They did it again, and again. On the fourth strike, the center of the door shattered, creating a hole. Ian couldn't see in the other room, but he heard the child crying out. The warmth of the fire continued to get closer, hotter. With one final strike, the lock snapped off, sending the door flying inward and smacking off the stone wall. They dropped the wood.

Ian knew there was little time to waste and immediately hurried into the room. Kosa turned on the flashlight, attempting to give them any semblance of sight, but the blanket of soot and particles completely hindered their range. Ian crouched low, hoping to get below the smoke and find the source of the cries.

There was movement in the corner.

"Hurry, we have to go!" Kosa yelled from the doorway.

He fought through the heat, making it to the child who appeared to be motionless, facing the wall. Hoping he wasn't too late, he reached down, feeling for a pulse. He waved away at the smoke, then turned the child over.

His knees weakened. It took everything he had to stop himself from collapsing. It wasn't a little girl he was holding.

It was Sammy.

CHAPTER 43

The relief that filled Ian diminished quickly as Kosa yelled from the doorway. Still, even with the urgency of the situation, his mind tried to solve the puzzle of how Sammy could be alive. He saw the burning body. The witch told him it was Sammy. Accepting Sammy's death wasn't something he ever thought he could do, but his mind had at least started to force that fact on him. To see the boy now changed everything. It gave him hope. The smoke filling Sammy's lungs had taken its toll, however. He was struggling to stay conscious, and Ian wasn't sure if that was from smoke intake or whatever Marta had been doing to him.

"Ian! We need to go, now! It's spreading too fast!" Kosa yelled.

He picked Sammy up, trying to stay low beneath the smoke. The task seemed impossible while holding the dead weight of a child. Sammy lethargically buried his face into Ian's chest as they exited the small room. The flames were now above their head. Sweat poured into Ian's eyes as they approached the stairs. The heat was unbearable. Kosa ran up the stairs first, and Ian started to follow, but decided to turn back just to be sure Marta wasn't following them. Her screams had been drowned out by the scorching flames eating away at the structure of the home.

Ian gently sat Sammy on the floor when they made it upstairs, then turned and slammed the basement door shut, hoping it would help slow down the smoke from reaching the main level. They needed to get out of the house, but before he could do that, Ian needed to catch his breath.

"Sammy, can you hear me, pal?"

Sammy squinted, opening his eyes for the first time since being trapped in the dark for who knew how long. He raised his hand to shade his eyes from the light. Even though it was hardly a dull illumination, it was causing the boy visible pain.

"Uncle Ian... did you save Angela?"

He could only assume Angela was the little girl. Lying to his nephew wasn't something he'd become accustomed to, so he decided to change the subject instead.

"Buddy, we need to get out of this house now, it's coming down. Can you stand?"

Sammy didn't respond, instead attempting to get to his feet. Ian noticed he had no shoes on, meaning he'd have to carry him all the way through the woods. Unless Kosa had something that could cover his feet.

"Kosa, do you have any shoes, slippers, anything he can wear to protect his feet?"

She stared blankly at the basement door, watching as the smoke began to seep out through the small gap on the bottom of the doorframe. Ian felt awful for her, couldn't imagine what was going through her mind right now, but they needed to go. He put his hand on her shoulder and gave a gentle shake, and she turned to face him.

"I... Yes, I can grab a pair of slippers from upstairs."

"Thank you. I'll get him ready, then we need to go. Kosa? Everything will be okay, I promise," Ian said, not sure why he was making promises to her that he couldn't keep.

She nodded and ran upstairs, allowing Ian to focus on Sammy once more.

"Did she do anything to you?"

"She did something to my head, made me follow her here. The other girl in there with me, she said the lady killed her parents... Are... are Mom and Dad dead?"

Ian pulled Sammy into a hug and squeezed.

"I'm so sorry, Sammy."

Kosa came running down the stairs with a pair of pink fuzzy slippers and handed them to Ian. The look on Sammy's face when he saw them was proof that even in the face of his life crumbling, Sammy still had a little boy in him. He frowned and grabbed the slippers like they had been infected by a plague. As silly as it seemed, just that simple act of him being a normal kid gave Ian hope that everything would be okay. He'd take care of Sammy and raise him to know how good his parents really were.

"Thanks," he mumbled and reluctantly slid the slippers over his feet.

The flames now not only forced their way under the door, but through it, the smell of burning wood wafting upstairs. Given how old this house was, it was no wonder it caught so quickly. Ian just assumed its size would give them time to get situated before rushing out into the freezing cold.

They moved through the house, heading toward the front door, when another sound interrupted the crackling and popping of the wooden structure. Ian at first thought it was the flames getting louder. But this sound was different, like a low growling noise. He turned back toward the hall, leading Kosa and Sammy to look with him.

Through the dark gray cloud, something moved just out of sight. Multiple somethings.

"It's the cats! We need to get out of here, now!" Kosa yelled.

The shape he saw was far too large to be a cat. The head appeared to be eye level with him. As he turned to run to the door, he got a quick glimpse of exactly why things weren't adding up. This wasn't a normal cat. In front of the larger beast, two normal-sized cats leaped through the smoke, then stopped in the hallway only a few feet from Ian.

Those God damn eyes, he thought.

While the large monster trailed behind, taking its time getting to them, the other two cats hissed. Then they began to convulse, their forms contorting in unnatural ways. Their once graceful feline figures twisted and bulged, bones snapped and shifted beneath their black fur. Ian watched in horror as one of their spines arched so much that he saw it cracking beneath the flesh. Their limbs stretched and elongated, the black fur falling out and revealing greyish skin. Their already sharp teeth grew, the points extending beyond their open maw. The nails at the end of their paws stretched, turning into long, clawed fingers.

It was the most disturbing thing Ian had ever seen. The horrifying transformation defied all laws of nature.

With a blood-curdling scream that blasted through the house, their bodies contorted one last time, man-like figures emerging from what had once been cats. The creatures were some grotesque hybrids, part man, part beast. Their bodies were covered in mottled, patchy fur, with tufts of hair sprouting in random places. Elongated limbs, ending in sharp claws, dripped with a viscous, dark liquid. Their heads remained mostly cat like, but their eyes glowed with feral hunger, their mouths filled with rows of razor-sharp teeth.

Ian was so focused on the horror in front of him that he didn't even realize the animals were getting closer until Sammy screamed. The creatures snarled and lunged forward, moving with unnatural speed and agility. It was as if their transformation unleashed a primal, obsessive hunger within. They darted through the smoke and flames. Ian turned and ran, pushing Sammy and Kosa toward the exit.

Apparently, the cats' transformation wasn't complete, because as he ran, Ian heard their bodies continuing to shift, shrieks of bestial agony. Bones cracked and snapped, their forms writhing and pulsating with an energy that could only be supernatural. Guttural growls and snarls were mixed with human-like cries of pain.

Kosa opened the front door and pulled Sammy with her by the hand, exiting onto the front porch. Ian followed them out, trying to shut the front door, but one of the creatures reached out, grabbing hold of his forearm and digging its claws into him. He screamed as a trail of blood shot out of the newly open wound. Moonlight illuminated the scene; the true horror of the cats' transformation was revealed. The creature's flesh seemed to peel and split, revealing raw, pulsating muscle underneath. Blood oozed from its wounds, mixing with the rancid fluid that dripped from its claws and teeth.

The monster's human-like eyes sent a chill down Ian's spine. Its claws continued to dig into his arm for purchase, intent on making sure he didn't escape. The other two cat-man creatures paced in the background, waiting for their fellow beast to pull him back in. Ian wasn't about to let that happen. Not after everything they had been through to get free. He continued to pull on the door, putting pressure on the beast's forearm. With all the force he could muster, he yanked back, and the door gave way, snapping the cat's arm. The beast withdrew its grip and retreated back into the house, giving Ian the space he needed to slam the door shut.

He jumped off the porch, reaching Sammy and Kosa, who stood back at a safe distance from the home which was now being engulfed in flames. Looking down at his arm, Ian realized just how bad the wound was. He'd be lucky if the fucker had missed an artery.

A loud moan escaped the home. He couldn't tell whether it was the cries of the beasts being burned alive or the house starting to collapse in on itself.

Roberts' police cruiser sat in the driveway, but Ian's brief hope that they could take the car to avoid trekking back through the woods was quickly squashed when he noticed the keys weren't in the ignition.

"Damn it!"

The forest was alive with all too familiar howls. With everything they'd gone through, Ian had completely forgotten about his dog. He looked to the woods and saw Scooter sprinting out of the darkness toward him, tail wagging. Ian dropped to his knees, crying at the sight of him, and opened his arms. Scooter jumped through the snow and didn't slow when he made it to Ian, leaping onto his chest and sending Ian over backwards. He licked Ian's face as his poor body trembled from being locked out in the cold for what must have been hours.

"Hi boy!" he said, scratching behind Scooter's ear where he liked it.

Scooter's leg kicked in the snow, the involuntary twitch that everyone seemed to think was about the cutest fucking thing they had ever seen. Ian couldn't believe he'd forgotten about Scooter. He was lucky the dog hadn't frozen to death by now. He needed to get him somewhere warm—all of them somewhere warm, and fast. Sammy knelt and rubbed Scooter's head, and it was good to see the boy smile. He would be traumatized, have issues for years to come, of that Ian had no doubt. But Ian would do whatever he needed to protect Sammy. He looked at Kosa, who stared at the dog, fascinated by the animal. Ian realized she had never seen a dog. Hell, the only animal she'd ever seen were the cats, those mutant bastards.

"You want to pet him? He loves people," Ian said.

She hesitantly walked over and reached her hand out in a clumsy way that would have made Ian laugh had he not just been through hell. As she reached out to pet Scooter, a window shattered, likely the flames blowing out the sealed escape in order for the fire to continue its relentless expansion. Kosa took her eyes off Scooter and looked back at the house.

She gasped, her mouth forming a silent scream, while her eyes darted from one side of the house to the other.

"Ian? Ian!" she shouted, pointing to the house.

He jumped to his feet and turned, just in time to see the cat creatures attempting to break through the windows. They screamed in agony, their bodies wrapped in flames while they fought to get out. Ian only spotted two of the creatures, and wondered where the third was. Another window exploded, but on the side of the house he couldn't see, followed by a thump. He had no plan to wait for the third cat to see them before taking off.

"Go! Into the woods, we need to get back to my car!" Ian shouted.

Scooter's fur stood on end. He barked aggressively toward the side of the house, standing his ground.

"Let's go, boy! Come!" Ian ordered.

They all ran for the woods, the night sky glowing orange as the fire spread to the roof of the house. A dark cloud of smoke hung overhead, bringing with it the smell of a campfire. As they reached the end of the lawn, Ian turned back one last time before entering the forest. The large cat creature was hurt, but it had spotted them, its eyes narrowing. The monster screamed, a mixture of a cat's hiss and a man screaming.

The beast crouched, got down on all fours, and sprinted toward them.

CHAPTER 44

They hurried under the moonlit canopy of emaciated trees. Kosa ran. The cold winter air cut through her lungs with each gasping breath, and her heart pounded in her chest like a primal drum. Branches clawed at her sleeves, tearing at the fabric as if they were trying to keep her prisoner. She had never been out of the perimeter surrounding Marta's house, and she wished that her first experience wasn't such a terrifying one.

Ian and the dog ran ahead of her, regularly looking back to make sure she and Sammy were okay.

"We're getting close!" Ian said.

A thin layer of frost crunched beneath Kosa's slippers with each step as she pushed herself forward. Her wide eyes darted around, scanning the darkness behind her for any sign of the cat. She knew it was Tom. After everything they had been through together, Marta was still his master. He would do anything to stop them from escaping. While she couldn't see him, she could *hear* him—the rhythmic thudding of heavy footsteps, drawing closer with every passing second. The sound echoed through the silent forest, amplifying her fear.

The forest looked so beautiful from the attic window, but out here, it was terrifying. Every branch looked like a skeletal hand, reaching out for her with gnarled fingers. The frozen earth beneath her feet became treacherous, a mix of potholes and fallen limbs that threatened to trip her with each step.

Clouds of vapor escaped Kosa's mouth, mingling with the frigid air. Every sound was magnified by her sharpened senses—a rustling in the underbrush, a distant howl of wind, and the haunting echo of her own racing heartbeat. She realized her thoughts were a jumbled mess, and that she hadn't even had time to process the fact that Marta had betrayed her all these years. She'd had a family, one that would love and care for her, and Marta took that away before Kosa had even been home for an entire day with her parents.

She held Sammy's hand, hoping the boy could keep up with her. If anything, he seemed to be taking it better than she was, probably because he was more used to exercise, playing with other kids and running around. Kosa had spent her entire life in a home where running was against the rules, even while playing. Her cardio was poor, even for a child who should be in the prime of their athletic youth. With every stride, she fought against the fatigue threatening to overtake her drained limbs. Her muscles burned, but she refused to give in to the exhaustion.

In the distance, a flicker of light pierced through the trees—a large lake house providing a beacon of hope amidst the desolate woods. Kosa picked up speed as Ian stopped to wait for them.

"It's up here, let's go," he said through panting breaths.

They exited the woods, and relief struck her at the sight of what she assumed was Ian's car. With the adrenaline slowly leaving her body, she realized her slippers were torn, and that her feet were bleeding. Each step she took toward the car was excruciating.

Ian fumbled around in his pocket for his keys, looking back toward the forest as he did.

The woods fell into an eerie silence. The pursuit had ceased, the once thunderous footsteps now replaced by an unsettling stillness. Still, it didn't make Kosa feel any safer. Tom was likely just trying to find the best approach to them, just like he did with Jerry when she was a little girl. She didn't want to end up as shredded meat like her little mouse friend.

Something wasn't right. She knew Tom wouldn't just give up. He'd been right behind them most of the way through the woods. Where did he go? Why did he stop pursuing them?

And then, she got her answer.

From the mouth of the forest, Marta walked out with Tom by her side. Her cloak had been severely burned, but from this distance, Kosa couldn't tell if Marta herself had suffered any damage. Kosa knew the cloak protected Marta, and she should have realized that likely meant it protected her from the fire as well. She'd been so stupid to not think of that.

"Ian! She's coming!"

Ian had already seen Marta, reaching for Roberts' gun, which he'd stuffed into his belt. Marta had her walking stick, and those black eyes somehow glistened in the moonlight, like they were in their desired element. She muttered something to her familiar, and Tom took off toward them. Scooter let out a series of barks toward the cat, trying to scare it off, to no avail. Tom continued to charge and was closing in quick.

"Get in the car, Sammy! And lock the damn doors!" Ian said.

Sammy reluctantly listened, hopping in the passenger door and locking it behind him. Kosa considered getting in with him, but she needed to help Ian. He had done everything to save her, even after learning that Marta had killed his wife and fed Kosa dead children. As scared as she was, she knew Tom wouldn't kill her, nor would Marta. They needed her. She needed to use that to her advantage. But then her hope sank into the pit of her stomach. Marta stalked toward them at her own pace, somehow looking much younger. *How did she do that without me?* Kosa wondered. The thought terrified her—if Marta didn't need her anymore, her plan would completely backfire.

———————

Ian fired his gun in the direction of the charging beast. The first shot missed, so he fired again. The second bullet connected, sending Tom toppling over in the snow, but the beast barrel rolled and landed back on his feet, hardly missing a beat.

The beast was now within fifteen feet of Ian, so he tried to get one more shot off before he was attacked. The gun clicked. Ian threw it to the ground and ran away from the car, away from the kids. He was trying to get Tom away from Sammy and Kosa, trying to save them. He only made it a few feet before Tom pounced, darting through the air like a boulder launched from a slingshot. The cat monster landed on Ian's back, dropping him to the hardpacked snow.

"Tom, no!" Kosa yelled.

Tom ignored her, raised his clawed hand, and prepared to end Ian's life.

Scooter ran to Ian's side, biting the monster's elongated leg. He sunk his teeth into the ankle and clamped down. The beast roared, and instinctively backhanded Scooter, sending the dog skidding across the icy surface. Scooter yelped in pain, but he had done what he set out to do. It gave Ian enough time to kick the cat in the gut, sending the monster flying backward off him. He got to his feet, prepared to strike the animal again, when Marta spoke, this time much closer.

"Get the boy! I'll handle this fool," she said with a snarl.

While her appearance was much younger, her teeth were still rotting.

Tom shifted his attention to the car. The animal stood on two feet and stalked toward the vehicle; all Ian could do was watch. Marta began to chant something in Croatian, pointing toward Ian. At first, he just thought she was cursing him in another language. And then, it was as if a vacuum was sucking out his insides. It was the most painful feeling he'd ever experienced. He dropped to his knees, clutching his stomach. Marta continued to chant. *What the fuck is she doing to me?* he thought.

Marta raised her hands in the air, her tarnished cloak producing a smokey scent that only added to Ian's nausea. She screamed, a demented war cry. She was framed by the fire which had spread from her house through the woods, black clouds tinted with orange rising behind her like dark spirits. Ian felt something pop in his head, then a liquid started seeping out of his ears. He took one hand from his stomach and touched his ear, seeing blood across his palm.

She was killing him without even laying a finger on him.

Stars floated across his vision, and he thought his brain was about to explode like a firecracker with a short fuse.

"Mother! It's me you need. What good is any of this if I'm dead?" Kosa said, standing close to the lake's edge.

Marta stopped chanting and looked over to Kosa, who was making her way out to the ice. Ian immediately felt the pain in his stomach ease. The witch stared down at him, then swung her walking stick in a downward motion across the top of his head. Everything went black.

CHAPTER 45

Sammy climbed over to the driver's seat and curled up in a ball. His heavy breathing began to fog the windows, but he could still see the giant cat monster approaching the car. He double checked to make sure the locks were down. The creature knew he was there, so hiding was pointless, but Sammy still found himself trying to become one with the seat, pressing firmly against the fabric. From his location, he couldn't see out the window anymore. He wasn't sure he wanted to. The commotion escalated—shouts, footsteps, and screaming—but Sammy forced himself to stay low, out of sight.

The pointy ears of the beast appeared at the driver's-side window, mostly blocked by the fog covered glass. Sammy's eyes were glued to the window, and he held his breath, trying to remain still. The cat monster pressed its face to the glass, its nostrils expanding as if it was sniffing the car. Did the thing know he was in here? Its human-like eye came closer to the window, flitting from the front seat to the back of the car. Sammy could've sworn the beast locked eyes with him, but when he expected the thing to smash through the window, it dropped to all fours, out of sight.

It appeared the witch's familiar had given up and moved on to search elsewhere. Still, Sammy maintained his position, too afraid to move and draw attention to the car. He hoped Uncle Ian and Kosa were okay, that they could all get out of this nightmare once and for all.

The car shifted slightly. Again, something bumped into the side. Was the monster trying to tip the car? Find another way in? Sammy closed his eyes and took deep breaths, just like his mom taught him when he was stressed. His mom. He would never see her or his dad again. The thought broke his heart. They taught him everything he knew, helped him feel safe when he was scared, loved him when he was down on himself. He was struck with a wave of guilt at the thought this was all his fault. Had Marta not wanted him, his family would never have been targeted by her.

Once again, the car shifted, only this time it was much more aggressive. Sammy opened his eyes and screamed at what stood in front of him.

The cat beast was on the hood, crouched low and staring directly at him through the windshield. It opened its mouth wide, baring its spike-infested mouth, then let out a hiss that was far too low of an octave for any normal cat. The monster lifted his clawed hands and drove them down into the windshield like a sledgehammer, creating a spiderweb of cracked glass. It repeated the effort, over and over, leaving multiple indents on the glass. A mixture of blood and a black substance smeared the windshield, filling in the webbed cracks like a kaleidoscope from Hell.

The windshield was now almost impossible to see through, but Sammy saw movement on the hood, and then the roof of Ian's car sank a few inches. The creature had climbed onto the roof, slamming its claws into the metal. Sammy forced himself into the space below the steering wheel, the gas pedal poking into his back.

THUMP! THUMP! THUMP!

The roof began to fold in, and then as if it couldn't get any worse, a set of massive claws cut through the metal, fabric, and everything else in between, creating three long openings facing the night sky. The beast peered down at him through the holes and hissed. Sammy realized if he stayed in the car, he was likely going to die. Uncle Ian was hurt, Kosa was dealing with the witch. He had to make a decision himself. The beast continued to drive its claws into the roof, widening the holes. Jagged metal shards folded inward, like giant teeth trying to bite him to shreds.

The monster leaned toward the biggest hole, reaching his arm through the opening toward Sammy. The black substance leaking from its wounds dripped down onto Sammy's face, burning his skin. Like acid. He cried, trying to wipe it away, but the liquid continued to trickle out of the large gashes on the cat's unnaturally long arm. The claws were within inches of his face, but the beast could not quite reach him from his current location.

Sammy looked around frantically, spotting his uncle's window scraper on the passenger floor. It was plastic, but there was nothing else within reach that he could defend himself with. He grabbed the scraper, gripping it tightly. The beast retracted its arm, then Sammy's heart sank when he realized what the thing was about to do. The clawed hands gripped each side of the rend and tore it wider.

The monster crouched, starting to climb through the hole headfirst toward Sammy. Sammy screamed and attempted to open the door, but the beast would have none of that. It swiped Sammy's hand, snapping his wrist. Sammy cried out in pain. Its face was now only a foot from Sammy's, its breath smelled of blood and rotten meat. Sammy drove the window scraper into its mouth with his good hand, the sharp plastic end snapping as it lodged into the cat's windpipe. The animal jumped back through the hole, holding its throat. The sound escaping from its mouth ironically sounded like a cat trying to cough up a hairball.

Sammy wasn't sure where to go; all he knew was that he needed to get out of the car and get somewhere safe. Maybe he could lock himself in the lake house they had rented over the weekend. He opened the car door with his good hand and got out. Kosa was crossing the ice-covered lake, maybe she knew of an escape route. Sammy took off in her direction, hearing the giant cat fresh on his trail.

CHAPTER 46

Ian opened his eyes to a throbbing pain pulsating through his skull. He tried to sit up but was immediately reminded of the nausea building in his stomach. He leaned over and vomited in the snow, then pushed himself up on all fours, scanning the area to see where everyone went. The first thing he noticed was his car had been torn to shit. Then he remembered telling Sammy to hide in there. His brow furrowed with deep concern as he jumped to his feet, ignoring the queasiness. He looked in through the crushed windshield, but the car appeared empty. It didn't take long for him to get his answer.

Sammy screamed from somewhere to Ian's left. He turned in the direction of the sound, looking out on the lake. The moon shone down upon the glistening surface, highlighting multiple figures on the ice. There was no way in hell the ice was thick enough this early in winter to safely hold all their weight. Marta was face-to-face with Kosa, and they were screaming at each other. The giant cat—if that's what he could even call it—was chasing down Sammy. Sammy slipped on the ice, his feet flying out from under him, and landed hard on his lower back. The beast closed in. Scooter followed in pursuit as fast as his old body would allow.

Ian quickly opened his trunk, grabbing his crowbar. Then he stepped out on the ice, immediately sensing it shift beneath his weight. He didn't like it one bit. He'd be lucky if he made it to Sammy, and sure as hell didn't think he could move at a swift pace. But he had no choice. There was no way he had come this far just to stand back and watch the horror show. He took a deep breath and headed toward them.

"I'm done helping you, Marta," Kosa yelled. "You tricked me my entire life to believe your rules. I'm not letting you kill another kid!"

"I suggest you call me 'Mother', young girl. You will do what I tell you to do, and you will like it! You need them as much as I do! Without the souls, you will die as well. Your body needs them, don't you get that?" Marta said.

Kosa didn't care about any of that right now. All she cared about was Sammy getting out of here alive, and Ian and Scooter leaving this place and not having to worry about Marta ruining their lives.

"I'd rather die than help you anymore. Besides, *Mother*. I know your rules. *All* of them."

Marta lifted her upper lip in angry confusion, unsure of what Kosa was referring to. Kosa realized her distraction was working. She had wanted to yell to Sammy not to follow her out, that she had a plan, but she had to be careful Marta didn't realize what she was doing. Ian made his way onto the ice behind them, and Kosa did everything she could do not to scream at them and say they were messing it all up.

"Kosa... You listen to me now, girl. It's time you help me. Remember what your role is!"

Marta's eyes burned into Kosa; the anger was beginning to take its hold over the old woman.

Sammy tried to fight away the tears, but the pain in his lower back was intense. He didn't have time to cry about it though, because the beast was on him, clawing his face. Sammy held up his arm to block the incoming attack and was quickly reminded of the damage to his wrist when the cat batted his arm away. It took all the attention off the pain in his back but it also left him completely vulnerable.

The creature went to strike once more, but then roared and jumped off Sammy. At first, he didn't know why. Then he saw Scooter tearing at its ankle, puncturing the skin with his gnarly old teeth. The monster tried to swat at the dog but couldn't reach him. The monster turned, black clumps of fur now soaked with blood and black fluid. Sammy backpedaled away, watching in horror as the cat thing reached down and grabbed Scooter by the throat.

Scooter yipped, keeping his teeth locked in.

The clawed hand of the beast tightened its grip, digging its claws into Scooter's neck. Scooter's teeth slid along the skin of the cat's ankle, tearing it apart, but he lost his grip. The cat now held Scooter up in the moonlight by the neck, the dog's little feet flailing around.

"No!" Sammy yelled.

Sammy closed his eyes, unable to watch what happened next. Scooter had saved his life, and in return was about to lose his own. Closing his eyes could only help so much, as he heard every whimper the poor dog let out, desperate to survive. And then he heard another sound.

Uncle Ian yelling.

He opened his eyes in time to see Ian swinging a crowbar, striking the cat's head. A sickening crunch reverberated as skull and metal claw connected. Part of the cat's head caved inward, its human-like legs wobbling. The beast dropped to one knee. Ian yanked the claw out and struck again. And again. He hit the monster over and over, until its head was unrecognizable. The ice was painted crimson, a pool of bodily fluids spreading beneath the beast. And then, like a lone tree falling in the forest, the beast dropped. Its body twitched, letting out a horrific cry, and then went still.

"Are you okay?" Ian asked Sammy.

"I think I broke my arm," Sammy grimaced. "Uncle Ian, is Scooter okay?"

A look of panic spread across Ian's face, he ran to his dog, who lay on the ice, panting heavily.

"No, no. Please No," Ian whispered.

Sammy noticed the dog was still breathing. That had to be a good sign, right? Scooter couldn't die like this. It was hard enough losing his parents. Now the thing responsible for saving his life might soon join his mom and dad.

The ice shifted with an echoing crack. A line traveled from beneath the dead beast, spreading between Ian and Sammy. Sammy looked toward Ian with wide eyes, unsure of what to do as the ice beneath him continued to break apart. Water flooded up over the top, soaking the pink slippers on his feet. Ian started toward Sammy when the ice beneath his nephew separated, pulling Sammy out of reach as he clung to the remaining chunk of frozen lake beneath him.

CHAPTER 47

Kosa continued to back up as Marta stormed toward her. While she had never been on ice before, Kosa had seen puddles freeze on the porch, as she would often step on them and make them break beneath her feet, watching the water rise above. This ice looked much thicker, but it was already starting to crack and split in numerous places.

"Girl, you think you know what is best for you. *I* know what's best for you. You are nothing without me, Kosa. Nothing!" Marta screamed.

Kosa didn't respond, only backed further onto the lake, now near its center.

Kosa set her eyes on the amulet hanging from Marta's neck. A radiant green. As Kosa had skimmed through the witch's Book a few nights prior, one of the pages she came across displayed the very amulet that Marta wore every day. Kosa felt so stupid for not putting the pieces together earlier, not that she had any reason to question the witch before. Seeing the pages reminded her of one of the earliest rules she'd learned. She was just a little girl, no more than five, when she attempted to grab hold of the necklace, drawn to its mystique. Marta punished her by putting her in the attic with no food, no light, and left her there for an entire day.

Never touch my amulet...

She now realized what she needed was to get the jewel off Marta, take away her power.

"I spent my entire life in an attic, Mother. Do you know how awful that was? I went to bed terrified every single night. And now I realize it wasn't to protect me, but to keep me hidden. You didn't want anyone to know I was there because I wasn't yours."

"You are right on one thing, Kosa. You are not mine. Nothing so pathetic would ever come out of my womb. You are not mine, but you are *Tamna Sila's*. And whether I want you or not, *It* does. Now, get over here you little bitch!"

Marta leapt toward Kosa.

Kosa didn't have time to react, Marta's speed catching her off guard. The witch wrapped her bony hand in Kosa's hair and ripped in one swift motion, pulling away a handful of red locks. She shoved the hair into her mouth. Kosa watched in disgust.

Marta's black eyes rolled in her head; her body quivered in delight. The wrinkles in her skin spread apart, creating a smooth surface. She sucked the nutrients out of the hair, then chewed it. As she swallowed, Kosa watched Marta's neck expand, the hair sliding down into her stomach. The witch's necklace glowed beneath the cloak, and while Kosa feared what was happening, it further proved her theory that the necklace powered Marta.

"It's... *so*... good," Marta moaned.

As Marta's body continued to grow younger and younger, Kosa saw her chance. She reached for the amulet while Marta's eyes were still full of ecstasy.

As if she was prepared for it, Marta caught Kosa's wrist before it reached her neck. She dug her piercing nails into Kosa's flesh and squeezed tightly.

"You have been very naughty lately, Kosa. What do you think you're doing?"

The pain in her wrist was unbearable, dropping Kosa to her knees as Marta twisted her arm. Kosa's knees pressed against the frozen lake, sinking slightly below the surface as the ice cracked. The arctic water sent a shock through her body, reminding her of another of Mother's rules: Mother didn't allow her to use warm water when bathing, saying the cold water brought out the strength in Kosa's hair, and that baths weren't for pleasure but for preparing for the ritual.

Marta took her free hand and smacked Kosa across the face. It wasn't the first time in her life that had happened, but the pain was as shocking as ever, forcing a scream from Kosa as she dropped face-first to the ice, splashing in the chilled water working its way over the surface.

Ian couldn't get to Sammy without falling through the ice, but if Sammy could remain still, he'd be safe for now.

"Buddy, I need you to try your hardest to stay calm, okay? The more you move, the bigger chance of you falling through the ice."

Sammy nodded reluctantly but didn't say a word.

Ian checked his dog, who was still lying down, but breathing. He shifted his attention to Kosa, watching as Marta lifted her off the ice and smacked her again. He needed to save the girl. Carefully, he stepped around the dead cat monster and grabbed his bloodied crowbar. Marta was so focused on abusing Kosa that she didn't see Ian approaching. As he got closer, he realized she looked completely different, like a younger version of herself, beautiful even. She picked up her walking stick, prepared to strike Kosa just like she had Ian earlier.

He didn't give her the chance. Ian swung the crowbar, lodging it into her ribs. Marta gasped, but only flinched slightly. He pulled it free and prepared to strike again. She turned to Ian, and her beautiful face was somehow more frightening than the older woman he'd seen before. She radiated evil. And with all the commotion, he'd forgotten to avoid eye contact with her. Her eyes, like pools of darkness, fixed on his with her piercing gaze. She drew him into their depths, an unsettling energy crackling between them. Ian felt an inexplicable pull, as if an invisible force were tugging at his soul. He struggled to break free from her captivating stare, but her eyes held him in a trance, rendering him powerless.

"Now, now. Did you think you could outthink me? Outpower me? Stupid man. Look into my eyes... You will do everything I tell you to. Let go of the crowbar..."

Ian dropped it without a thought.

"Now, I want you to go to that hole in the ice behind you, and drop below, never to rise again. Do it for Sammy."

Ian began to walk toward the cracked ice. The hole had widened, now big enough to fit him. He stood at the opening, prepared to do what the witch demanded. Her cackling behind him found its way into his subconscious, and while he would do whatever she asked of him, he still knew he hated her, that this wasn't what was supposed to happen. But he had no control.

His left foot reached the edge, producing another crack beneath his weight.

"Ian, no!" Kosa yelled.

He turned, still dazed, the light of the moon somehow hurting his eyes now. He watched Kosa get up from the ground and jump on Marta's back.

"You brat!" Marta yelled.

Ian wanted to help Kosa. All he needed to do was move a few feet and he could grab the witch. But his body wouldn't let him. He began to shift his attention back to the hole in the ice. It was calling him. Before he turned, Kosa ripped something off Marta's neck, and Ian's vision was blasted by dizzying lights.

Kosa had the jewel in her hand. The power radiating from it was unworldly. A strange sensation formed in the pit of her stomach, as if whatever was inside her was reaching for the jewel. She hopped off Marta's back and sidestepped, expecting to see Marta's body rotting from the inside out. Without her magic, her true age should have been sucking all the life force she had left. But Marta snapped her head to Kosa, and the rage behind those black pools on her face said she was far from done. Marta grabbed Kosa by the throat, squeezing her windpipe beneath her grip. Kosa couldn't breathe, and then she felt a strange sensation of nothing below her feet. Marta had lifted her in the air with one hand. *How is she so strong?* Kosa thought.

Kosa kicked at the air, hoping to connect with Marta and break free, but the witch was far too powerful.

"My home is gone... My familiars are gone... It appears I'll be starting anew again, nothing I haven't done before, you little wench. That means, you are disposable to me now!"

Kosa's eyes filled up with tears.

Ian came up behind Marta, striking her with the curved side of the crowbar across the back of the head. Kosa watched in awe as the huge black eyes filled with crimson, fluttering as she staggered. Then Marta dropped Kosa to the ice.

The impact shattered the ice, forming several small isles that began to drift from one another. Marta spun around, almost falling into the open water, but catching her balance. The look in Ian's eyes wasn't one Kosa wanted to see. They told her that he was going to do whatever he needed, his mind made up. Two feet of water now separated Ian from Marta as the slabs of ice grew further apart.

"What do you think you can do to me, fool?" she said as her eyes turned to tiny slits.

And then Kosa noticed Marta's hair, slowly turning from the black of her youth back to the thinning white of her elder years. Her spine slowly curved, popping and snapping, bringing Marta back to her hunched posture.

Ian dove at Marta, colliding with the old woman. They both landed hard on the edge of the ice, mere inches from the frigid lake below. Ian had landed on top, but quickly spun off and got to his knees. Marta roared in anger, starting to climb to her feet. She made it to one knee before he pushed all of his weight into her, sending them both over the side, plunging beneath the surface of the waters.

"Uncle Ian!" Sammy shouted from a distance.

Kosa spotted Sammy on another chunk of ice, clinging to it. She looked back to the hole Ian and Marta had just fallen through, but it was too dark to see them underwater. For a moment, all was silent. Then, ten feet from where she stood, something thumped against the bottom of the ice, trapped below. She ran to the spot, careful not to fall in any of the openings now forming. She dropped to her knees, seeing a figure below the ice. It was too blurry to make the body out clearly, but then a hand scratched against the ice. The jagged nails and boney fingers could only belong to Marta, trying to come up for air. Water splashed around the rough edges of the ice as she flailed around below. Below Marta, another figure came into view, getting closer to the icy surface.

Ian's face floated into view, locking eyes with Kosa. She needed to save him. Ian's metal bar was close by. She ran to it and picked it up, returning to where the struggle continued. Kosa raised the weapon, ready to strike the ice. Ian shook his head, and while he couldn't talk with her, she knew what he wanted. He held onto Marta below, dragging her deeper into the lake.

"Save him, Kosa! Break the ice!" Sammy yelled.

Kosa cried, wanting nothing more than to try and save Ian. She waited for him to come closer to the surface, but the water went still again as the shadows sank. Light splashes continued to come up over the surface of the ice, sending bolts of pain through her feet. She looked down to the green necklace, realizing that the color had drained from its center. The glow was no more. Marta was no more.

CHAPTER 48

Kosa carried Scooter back to solid ground, careful not to touch his numerous cuts. Sammy trailed behind her, numb to the cold, continuously looking back in hopes that his uncle would come up alive. He knew that wasn't possible, that even if he hadn't drowned, the water was so cold it would likely kill him within minutes. But he couldn't help it.

Sammy collapsed next to Scooter, putting his face in the dog's fur. Tears flowed, nearly freezing before hitting the ground. He looked over the dog, hoping the poor thing would survive: Scooter was the last bit of family he had left. Uncle Ian had died saving them both.

Scooter lifted his head slightly and licked Sammy's hand, as if he was trying to say: *it will be okay, we will be okay.*

"Sammy... I'm so sorry," Kosa said. "But she's gone now and won't ever be able to do this again to anyone. We have to get somewhere warm. Can you move?"

He ignored her, keeping his focus on Scooter, continuing to pet the dog gently. His feet throbbed; his wrist was likely broken. But none of that compared to the pain he felt inside. His heart was shattered.

Kosa knelt and sat next to him, putting her head on his shoulder. She'd spent her entire life under the control of Marta, led to believe the only reality was her rules. They sat in silence for a few minutes, watching the dense cloud of smoke rising above the forest and blocking out the moonlight as the fire raged on. She wondered what was left of her childhood home. Of her memories. Kosa knew she was better off without Marta in her life, but that didn't stop the feeling of loss from taking over her thoughts.

She looked toward Ian's car, spotting his backpack on the ground. He must have dropped it during the scuffle with Marta. Without a word, she got to her feet and walked over to it, picking it up. She brought it back with her and sat with Sammy again. Her hope was to find something inside to warm them up. A shirt, hat, anything. Instead, she pulled out his cellphone, though she didn't know that was what it was called. It reminded her of the walkie-talkie, however, so she thought it might be a communication device.

"Sammy, do you know how to use this thing?"

He looked at the phone, wiped away a tear and nodded. Kosa handed it to him and watched as he pushed three buttons on the front of the device and hit a fourth before holding it up to his ear.

Kosa sat in the back of the vehicle with the flashing lights as a nice lady bandaged her feet up and made sure she was okay. Another worked on Sammy in the vehicle next to her. Scooter had been carefully placed in the back of the vehicle and slept as peacefully as his battered body could. One of the workers hollered to the lady taking care of Kosa.

"I'll be right back. Are you sure you're okay, hon?"

Kosa nodded.

"What's your name?"

"Elizabeth..."

"What a lovely name. Okay, I'll be right back, hon," she said again, then cut the bandage and set the scissors down on the bumper before walking to her coworker.

Kosa looked at the scissors and got an idea. She picked them up and tried to imitate what she saw the lady doing with them to cut the bandage. Then, she grabbed her hair with the other hand and held it out. She proceeded to cut strands of the fiery locks from her head, throwing them to the ground. She did this until she could no longer get anymore hair with the scissors. Her scalp felt patchy to the touch, but the chilled air sent a shock of energy through her body.

It was the hair that bound her to Marta. To *Tamna Sila*. For the first time in her life, she was free of them. She no longer had to follow their rules. It was time for Elizabeth to make her own rules.

THE END

Printed by
Libri Plureos GmbH · Friedensallee 273
22763 Hamburg · Germany